The Soul's Hope

Beverly Knauer

Wise Words Press

For information, address the publisher at:
wisewordspress.com

This is a work of fiction. All the characters, organizations, and events portrayed in this novel are either products of the author's imagination or are used fictitiously.

Printed in the United States of America
wisewordspress.com

Wise Words Press
1611-A S. Melrose Drive #265
Vista, CA 92081

First Printing, 2017

ISBN
Paperback
ISBN: 978-0-9977303-2-6

To my beloved goddaughter, Samantha Rosenthal, a very wise old soul.

Chapter 1

October 7, 2021

Being normal is overrated. Aria Cohen repeated the phrase in her mind several times as she glanced out the kitchen window into the backyard of her Los Angeles home, watching her daughter, Sammi, at play. She only wished she believed it.

A singular bead of sweat traveled from her forehead, crossed her tear duct—causing a stinging sensation—and flowed down the side of her nose, finally resting on her upper lip. She wiped it with the back of her hand. It was an autumn day and, in spite of soaring Southern California temperatures in the high eighties, she'd decided to spend her first day off of work in three weeks baking and enjoying the company of her daughter. She stood, hands on hips, in their newly renovated kitchen, admiring the bamboo parquet kitchen counters, new copper-infused stainless steel side-by-side refrigerator (with HDTV built right into the door), and dark walnut hardwood floors. They'd even decided to splurge on a special feature—a built-in baking station—that she was trying out for the first time.

Aria inhaled a deep breath. She couldn't remember the last time she'd smelled something as delicious and comforting as the sour cherry pies baking in the oven. The fragrance wafted through the air, filling her nostrils, enticing her to breathe in the marriage of nutmeg, butter, and sugar combined into a sensual scent. She'd discovered long ago that baking pies was her antianxiety therapy; almost magically, it instantly transported her back in time to pleasant memories of her own childhood, cooking with her mother and her nonna in Italy.

Drifting in the menagerie of past memories, she was jolted back to reality when she noticed how, just now, the television—playing softly in the background—seemed to turn itself off, followed by her cell phone turning itself on, playing a heavy metal tune. She grabbed her phone to silence it. *This is the fourth time this has happened. What's going on?* She had no explanation for the strange occurrence. But every time something peculiar like that took place, she felt nervous. *Interesting. It seems to happen whenever Sammi plays on the swing set.* It made her feel queasy, and her stomach quivered like gelatin. Mysterious events seemed to be happening more and more frequently.

The oven timer went off, and Aria grabbed a potholder for each hand and pulled the golden-brown pies out of the oven, set them on the cooling rack, and glanced out the kitchen window into the backyard again to check on Sammi. She noticed that some of the flowers she'd planted during the summer still lingered, dotting the yard with colorful yellow and red hues—gardening was her labor of love. Making a mental note to herself, she decided to pick a bouquet of her best blooms and take those along with a cherry pie for their trip to see her in-laws, Lizzie and Mark Hobbs, in San Diego.

The sun, blazing through the kitchen window, felt hot, and she brushed at the damp hair matted on her forehead, hoping to wipe away the contradictory feelings she had along with the sweat on her brow. She realized some things in life could be simultaneously mesmerizing and disturbing, but she hadn't expected one of those things would be her daughter. Maybe *disturbing* wasn't the correct word to describe it; maybe a better word would be *confusing*. That's how people often are about the unknown.

After pulling on her rubber gloves, she washed the baking bowls and utensils in the sink, gazing into her backyard as Sammi played on the swing set.

Aria smiled as she watched her. It was hard to believe she was five already, and Aria found herself amazed at how quickly a child could develop her own very distinctive personality. Sammi's facial features were delicate like her mother's—almost appearing angelic. She looked adorable with her upturned nose, long brunette hair, golden-brown eyes, and heart-shaped lips. From the day she was born, Sammi was a girly girl. Dresses, particularly pink ones, were always her fashion choice, and she refused to wear jeans or slacks. Her current favorite outfit was a sundress with polka-dot suspenders and pink cowboy boots, so worn down from constant wear there was a hole in the sole of the right boot.

It was natural for little girls to love pink things, but since Sammi's birth, Aria had noticed quite a few idiosyncrasies about her daughter that she wouldn't exactly call normal. At first, she'd just attributed the strange things to being a child. But she wondered—what was normal anyway? Was anyone normal? She figured that Sammi had probably just inherited some unusual traits from her father, Jonathan, who also seemed to have his own unconventional or uncanny abilities. Through him, Aria had learned about the nonphysical world of spirits and otherworldly things. Maybe it was her conventional upbringing, but sometimes it felt, well ... a bit spooky. So she didn't mention her concerns about Sammi to Jonathan or anyone else. Maybe a better word for Sammi was *unique*. She did seem wise beyond her years, like an old soul. The neighbors always invited her over to chat when they saw her because, they'd reported to Aria, they felt peaceful and at ease after an interaction with her.

Sometimes Aria would just sit and observe Sammi at play to see what she could figure out. *When you don't speak something out loud, you don't have to deal with it.* She worried it might be an unnatural thing to think her daughter was a bit strange, and she didn't want to seem unmotherly. Her goal in raising her daughter was to be the best mother she could possibly be.

But as Aria watched, she could see Sammi was engaged in her unusual play again. She'd often sit out in her sandbox giggling and laughing as though her best friend were next to her; yet no one was there. She certainly looked like she was having fun swinging, pumping hard with her sturdy legs, wavy hair flowing behind her, laughing and talking to the invisible person on the swing next to her. In fact, Aria had to look several times to be sure there really *wasn't* someone sitting next to her.

Just the day before, Aria had seen Sammi pushing an empty swing, laughing and chitchatting with her invisible companion. Other young children had imaginary friends and they simply outgrew them—Aria was aware of that. Maybe she'd talk about it with Sammi's godfather, Matthew Hobbs, a respected spiritual counselor, when she was in San Diego. He'd surely have some good insight.

There's nothing to really worry about—it's just my nerves. She knew she was prone to high anxiety anyway—it was inherent in her job as a film producer: something her coworkers referred to as "production anxiety." One of her friends had informed Aria that, in her opinion, her perpetual state of nerves stemmed from her perfectionistic personality, not wanting to be negatively judged. There was probably truth to that.

Curiosity finally got the best of her. *Okay, I need to check this out.* Wiping her hands on her knee-length khaki capris to dry them off, she stood at the open patio door to watch and listen. At least Sammi seemed happy, almost joyful, when she talked with her friend. Aria often found her singing a song at the top of her lungs, laughing, or making goofy faces. Even as a baby, she'd lain in her crib waving her arms in the air, bursting into giggles like she was being entertained by someone or something.

Like most parents, Aria and Jonathan were obsessed with capturing Sammi's ever-changing growing moments with their camera, and, to their surprise, many of the photos revealed orbs surrounding her. When Aria had searched the Internet about the phenomenon, she'd read that some people believed that orbs were the energy of spirits, while others thought they were specks of dust on the camera lens. She wasn't sure if it was either.

Sammi jumped off the swing, still singing show tunes from *Annie*, and cranked the handle of the outdoor faucet to the on position, holding the heavy hose in both hands to water the flowers. The love Aria felt for Sammi washed over her, instantly dispelling all her concerns.

"Are you having a good time?" Aria asked as she pulled open the screen door and stuck her head out.

"Yes, Mama, we're having fun."

"Would you like a snack?"

"Sure." She squirted the hose once more and turned off the faucet.

"Okay, be right back." Aria returned to the kitchen, cut two pieces of the warm pie, and placed the plates on a wooden tray along with two small glasses of water. She slid the patio door open, took the tray outside, and set it on the backyard picnic table.

"Come sit next to me and taste my pie. Who are you talking to?" Aria said. "Are you talking to one of your friends that Mommy can't see?"

Sammi, wearing a poufy tulle tutu and her pink cowboy boots, fluffed the netting behind her to make it easier to sit on the bench next to Aria. She innocently looked up at Aria, fluttering her thick, silky eyelashes and said, "He's right here, Mama. I don't see him like I see you, but I feel him and hear him. You didn't bring any pie for him," she said with a touch of disappointment in her voice.

Aria set two small dessert plates with pie in front of Sammi and herself, then said hesitantly, "Well, I thought since he was invisible, he could eat invisible pie."

Between bites, Sammi said, "That's okay, Mama. I'll share mine with him."

"That's nice of you to share your snack with him. So it's a little boy who's our friend?" Aria asked quizzically as she took a forkful of pie.

"He isn't little."

"He's not?"

"No, he's grown up. I knew him before you were my mommy."

Aria inhaled sharply and smacked her hand against her chest. Why would her little girl invent a grown-up friend? She wondered what that meant. For sure she was going to talk to Matthew about it.

Sammi took another bite of pie and licked her lips. "This is yummy."

"I'm glad you like it. You may not know this, but sour cherry pie is Grandma Lizzie's favorite. Baking makes me think of my childhood with my own mother and grandmother. When my heart feels kind of achy and I miss them, I bake a pie. Would you like to learn to bake a pie? Very few people do that now."

"No, thank you, I'm only five. Maybe when I'm a teenager."

Aria laughed. "Okay, maybe you'll change your mind. Your daddy used to love to cook when he was your age. We'll take a pie and a bouquet of flowers to Grandma and Grandpa when we drive to San Diego tomorrow. Are you excited to see them?"

"Yes, but I wish Daddy was going too."

"He'll be gone another week or he'd come."

"I wish you didn't have to go away to work so much, but you and Daddy like making movies, don't you?"

"Most of the time we do, but it isn't always the exciting process some people think it is, and we certainly don't like to be away from you! So ... what does your friend want, Sammi?"

Sammi waited to reply until after she'd licked her fork clean. "He doesn't want anything. He just likes to come visit and talk to me and play. He calls me Christina."

With her French-manicured fingers, Aria picked at the pie crust Sammi left on her plate and ate it. "That's a pretty name. When I was a young girl, I had a good friend named Christina. She had the loveliest green eyes. Did you tell your friend your name is Sammi?"

"He knows I'm Samantha *now*, but he knew me when I was Christina, and he likes to call me that. His name is Nate. He made me a little sad, though."

"Why? What did he say to you?"

She put her fork down and stared straight into Aria's eyes. "You're not going to like it."

Aria furrowed her brow. "I'm not? Why not?"

Sammi dropped her eyes and didn't respond.

"Why not? Why wouldn't I like it?" she repeated, slightly raising her voice.

"Don't be upset," Sammi said tentatively.

"Okay, I won't."

He said, "Christina, I'm so sorry I killed you."

Chapter 2

THE NONPHYSICAL WORLD

Nate

Yes, I do exist—Sammi's not imagining me. I'm the one she's been playing with. I'm what's known on Earth as a spirit, and I currently reside in a nonphysical dimension, meaning I don't have a physical body. One of my favorite ways to spend my time is to visit with Samantha, although I know her best as Christina.

For some reason, it seems odd to people in the physical dimension when a young child has a connection with a spirit. Unfortunately, there's so much misunderstanding about us. People often refer to us as imaginary friends. I do understand how they think that, and sometimes that might even be the case, but other times, it's actually just one of us spirits visiting.

Sometimes we're referred to as ghosts, but I don't like that connotation. I'm not a scary ghost as often portrayed in movies and books. I'm not spooky, and I don't haunt. On Earth, the media sometimes makes us sound like evil beings, but I think that only perpetuates a feeling of fear. Trust me, no one needs to be afraid of me; I'm really a nice, loving soul.

A ghost is a spirit that stays earthbound, which I'm not, but I do visit occasionally. Everything in the universe is vibrating energy, but on Earth, most folks are restricted to only five senses and that limitation doesn't allow them to fully pick up on all the various subtle energies that exist. They only register a tiny part of the enormous range of vibrational frequencies that are out there. Some people can tune in to various energies better than others, but the limitation of the five senses is a drawback as it narrows the knowledge of all that is available in the vast cosmos. Humankind thinks that what they experience is all that exists; they'd be surprised to learn that's not true.

Young kids aren't afraid of us because they're still able to easily transition between different dimensions. Even Sammi's dog, Maggie, is aware of my presence, but she isn't afraid of me. Most young children are extremely open to the world of spirits. If the child's imaginary friends are actually guides or guardians, they're there to love and protect. They'll cause them no harm and are there to help.

I'm a spirit, but not a spirit guide. Sammi's father, Jonathan, had recently been a spirit guide, but he's now incarnated to do some work on the Earth plane. Considering how "open" her dad is, it isn't unusual that Sammi would also have a direct connection with the spirit world herself.

Everything seems real to a child. They haven't been conditioned yet by society on real versus imagined or right versus wrong. And more and more open children, those who are more spiritually aware, more sensitive, are currently being born into the world. The separation between the physical and the nonphysical realms used to be huge, but now they're integrating. It's happening fairly quickly now. Consciousness is changing—a shift is occurring, and it's a major one.

Some children, like Sammi, easily see through the veil—the line between the different dimensions. Simply put, dimensions are just different states of consciousness, and people vibrate at frequencies that jibe with certain dimensions.

The whole process of incarnating on Earth is a fascinating one that most people aren't even aware of. It helps to understand that the soul learns different things in different dimensions. The planet Earth has functioned in the third dimension for a very long time, but it's evolved through the fourth into the fifth dimension. The people who inhabit Earth can now increase their personal vibrations to catch up to those levels of consciousness—they call it "waking up" or "awakening." A person in the process of awakening resonates at a faster and higher vibration than others; however, they'll feel a sense of disequilibrium until they fully raise their consciousness. If they are fearful of change or unable to scrutinize their beliefs, they won't fully wake up. Although it seems complicated, it's really not.

Souls choose to come to Earth to learn from the experiences that are offered. The method for learning comes through making choices and dealing with the consequences of those choices. There's duality, or contrast, on Earth, and the learning comes from experiencing the contrast. For example, to truly appreciate a healthy, fully functioning body, one may need to experience what it's like to be disabled or unhealthy. The experience of seeing and learning both sides of the coin helps people to understand the human condition.

So on Earth, people experience negativity and suffering that they don't usually encounter in other dimensions. Suffering can actually be a teaching tool. We choose our lessons before we're born with the purpose of expanding our soul. When we're given opportunities to experience both sides of a situation, the soul has the opportunity to make choices, and through that comes learning.

Most people experience a temporary amnesia of the nonphysical dimensions when they're born on Earth. I've been to Earth many times; some incarnations were for short periods of times, some for longer. During my last life, I retained quite a bit of my memory of the spirit world and was able to share my love and positive energies with so many souls in my life.

Sammi's a dear friend of mine. She's part of my soul group—souls who vibrate at similar rates of energy and who come back again and again to live lives together in different roles. I resonate with her energy, meaning we vibrate at a similar speed. We've traveled on many Earth journeys together, and we choose to incarnate in different roles again and again. I just feel bad that she's having nightmares about our last sojourn together, and I'm determined to find a way to make things more peaceful for her.

I'm preplanning my incarnation now with a council of souls who vibrate at a higher level than me. I'm looking at the various families I can choose to be born to, since different families will provide different experiences. So many choices. So many opportunities to choose from. When I finalize the lessons I need to help grow my soul, that'll determine the best environment for me.

Personally, I think I'm a loving, gregarious soul. People probably think, *Sure, right. Then why did you kill Sammi, or rather ... Christina?*

Chapter 3

November 9

She had never so looked forward to a day off from work. Aria's theory? A satisfying life requires a delicate balance between work and play. After producing a short documentary film for sixteen days straight, she was relieved to finally be home and excited to be doing something fun with Sammi. She always looked forward to these nonstressful days. Thoughts of relaxing in a warm bubble bath, reading a good book in the hammock in the backyard, and having silly time with Sammi had dominated her mind for the past week.

Aria had given Sammi the choice of going to the zoo or the museum, but she'd already known what her choice would be. Animal lover that she was, Sammi seemed to have a strong psychic connection with the animals at the zoo, often sharing their thoughts with Aria. Her favorites were the gorillas, and both Aria and Sammi were excited to see the new baby.

Aria wore watercolor-print shorts with a mauve sleeveless blouse, while Sammi dressed herself in a white sundress with ... her pink boots. They arrived at the Los Angeles Zoo early, happy they held a season pass to avoid the long lines. They had a set route they liked to follow—the gorillas, the koalas, the lions, the giraffes, and then finally the elephants. Sometime during the day, they'd usually fit in an ice cream break. It was their routine. Even though it was early November, it was unseasonably hot, so they knew the animals would be less active, but they still looked forward to their adventure.

First stop—the Gorilla Reserve. Aria loved how the habitat allowed them to see the animals so close up through the observation windows. They stood in front of the glass, watching the powerful creatures searching for treats of onions and pinecones.

"Mama, that gorilla is eating a watermelon," Sammi said, as she pointed.

"I wonder if he knows it's your favorite fruit. Did you know gorillas like to eat roses?"

"I wish I could feed him one. Oh, how cute. That one's carrying the baby on her back. They're so much like people. They love their children," she cooed. "And their babies look just like them. How come I don't look just like you?"

"You're the spitting image of your father. I guess you got all of his genes."

"You look like Grandma Rosina. You're both tall and thin with gray eyes. But Grandma's hair is white and yours is shiny black."

"Grandma had black hair when she was younger, like me."

"Do gorillas go gray when they're old?"

"Hmm ... I don't know. We'll have to do a search on that. I do know that when they live in the wild, they might live to be around forty, but at the zoo, they can live to be fifty!"

"That's really old. They have cute faces 'cause their noses look squashed in, but I like my nose better."

"You have what's called a celestial nose: pretty with a gentle upturned tip. Mine is called a duchess nose with a straight-edge."

Sammi pressed her hands and nose against the observation glass while she talked. "Gorillas are mammals. Do you know all the groups of animals?"

"Probably not. Do you?"

She turned to face her mother and proudly announced, "Amphibians, birds, mammals, insects, fish, reptiles."

"Very good!"

"Mammals are the smartest. They are warm-blooded and that means their bodies stay at the same temperature most of the time."

"I'm impressed. You're sure learning a lot in kindergarten."

"We're going to learn about insects next. My favorite insect is the butterfly. I love them. But I also love bees. Bees are very important, and we have to save them."

Aria placed her hand on Sammi's shoulder. "You're my wise little girl. Should we head over to the koalas now?"

"Yes, but would it be okay if we had an ice cream cone first?"

"Sure, chocolate this time?"

"Yes, please."

They strolled past the flamingos, marveling at their pink color (of course!), and headed over to the snack bar. After waiting in a short line for their cones, they sat at a wooden picnic table in a shady area near the gorillas, happy to enjoy some cooling refreshment on a warm day.

Sammi licked the ice cream dripping on her fingers and pointed at the juvenile gorilla. "Mama, he's trying to talk to me."

Noticing the mess, Aria took Sammi's cone, wrapped a paper napkin around it, and returned it to her. "What's he saying?"

"He'd like to play with me. I told him I can't. I love to visit them, but I wish all the animals could be free. Can I ride the carousel today?"

"Of course."

"Will you ride with me?"

"I sure will. It's one of my favorite things to do at the zoo."

"Here, Mama." Sammi handed Aria her empty ice cream cone. "I'm done. Next I want to see Reggie the alligator and the tarantulas."

Aria threw the cones into the already overflowing trash can. "I'm not very fond of the creepy-crawlies, but I'll go if you want."

After their ice cream treat, they waited in line for the Safari Shuttle. As part of their routine, they liked to ride the shuttle to the top of the zoo and then walk back toward the entrance because it was mostly downhill. Sammi was already dragging her feet, and they had a long day ahead of them. Aria thought her pink boots were getting too tight, but Sammi insisted on wearing them because she said they were comfortable to walk in.

"Mama, I like to walk around the zoo. But sometimes I wish I could float."

"Like in a swimming pool?"

"No, like in my dreams. When I go walking with Nate, we kind of float."

"Tell me more about him, sweetheart."

Sammi plopped on a bench, resting her legs. "Can we get lunch first? I'm still hungry and want pizza."

"Sure. You're certainly your father's daughter." She laughed, thinking of Jonathan's love of pizza. "The café is over there," she said as she pointed, "so we'll be next to the giraffes, and we can watch them while we eat."

They resumed their walk, stopping at the Mahale Café, where Aria ordered two slices of pepperoni pizza, with pineapple for Sammi. They found a shady place to eat the cheesy treat at a table alongside the giraffes, watching as the long-necked creatures munched leaves from the tall trees.

"There's this place in Africa that Mommy and Daddy visited when we were there called Giraffe Manor," Aria said as she dabbed the gooey cheese on her lips with a napkin. "It's the most unique hotel in Nairobi. While we were eating breakfast, they'd stick their heads and long necks right through the open window. When I was up in my room on the second floor, one of them stuck his tongue between the bars on my bedroom window expecting me to feed him a snack. Can you imagine? They have very long tongues that are about twenty inches in length! Someday we'll take you. You'll love all the animals."

Sammi picked off each piece of pepperoni, nibbling on them one by one. "That would be so great, Mama."

Aria didn't want to overwhelm Sammi with questions, but she wanted to gently probe a bit more about her invisible friend. "Okay, you were going to tell me more about Nate. So what does Nate look like?"

"He looks like light to me when I see him, but sometimes I just hear him. He said that the last time he was here he was Daddy's age, a little shorter than Daddy, with curly brown hair and a beard and mustache. He calls himself by his name then. It was Nate."

Aria raised her perfectly waxed eyebrows, surprised at Sammi's response. "Why does a man Daddy's age come and play with you?"

"We knew each other before. Before you were my mama. My mommy then had blue eyes and yellow hair. I like to visit with him. He makes me laugh."

Aria didn't respond. Suddenly she didn't feel like eating. *Is this something Sammi is making up, or is it possible it's real?*

"He was with me for one life and he died, and then he came back quickly right before Daddy was born, and then he was Daddy's friend."

Aria folded up the empty pizza plates and stuffed them into another overflowing trash bin. She didn't understand why she got a sick feeling in her stomach whenever she thought about Sammi's imaginary friend. She'd talked with Matthew Hobbs when she was in

San Diego, and he'd assured her there was no reason for concern and had given her suggestions and questions to ask Sammi to encourage her to open up and talk. Aria knew she had to control how she responded in order to keep Sammi from shutting down. Unfortunately, she found it hard not to be overly reactive.

After finishing their lunch, they headed off hand in hand, en route to the koalas. Aria decided to continue with her questioning. "Are you thinking of Daddy's friend, Nate, who drowned in Mexico? How do you know about him? Did Daddy talk to you about him?"

"No, Daddy didn't tell me about him. He likes to be called the name Nate, though, because that was his name last time he was here. And he has pretty colors of light around him. The colors are sparkly."

"Did Grandma Lizzie talk to you about Nate or show you a picture of him?"

Sammi shook her head. "No, Mama, no one talked about him to me."

Aria was puzzled. *How could she know about Nate? Someone had to have told her about him. I'll have to ask Jonathan.*

Although Aria had some understanding of the spirit world, she didn't think it could really specifically be Nate's spirit visiting. Sammi must have overheard someone talking about him, or she'd seen a photo. Why wouldn't he visit Jonathan? Why choose Sammi? Aria decided she needed to get better informed. She rarely had time to read for pleasure, but she knew she needed to learn more about what was happening with her daughter.

"Hmm ... let's talk to Daddy about him and those dreams you're having. They seem very scary, and you're getting them more often now."

"Yeah, I don't like to talk about the dreams," Sammi said, clearly wanting to change the subject. She scuffed her boots on the ground as she walked. "I think you should give Grandma Lizzie a call. She isn't feeling very well."

"Really? What makes you think that?"

"I don't know. I just do."

"Let's give her a call when we get home and check on her."

It was such an enjoyable day. They covered the grounds of the zoo, seeing all their favorite exhibits, holding hands, and giggling at the funny conversations Sammi held with each of the animals. Finally, at the end of the day, feeling exhausted, they decided to head home— but only after their favorite part of their adventure.

The carousel was on a hill overlooking Elephants of Asia, and the loud nontraditional music called out to them: *come ride me.* Sammi jumped up and down with excitement while waiting for their turn. "I'm going to ride the unicorn today. I love him—he's my favorite. Which animal are you going to ride?" Her eyes sparkled as she spoke.

"I feel like riding the honey bee today, I think. Let's have fun!"

They took the three-minute ride two times, then headed home, with Aria feeling satisfyingly destressed and Sammi anxious to tell her dad her animal stories.

It was 9:00 p.m. when Aria and Jonathan, both working in the den, heard Sammi crying frantically from her bedroom.

Aria jumped up. "Jonny, she's having one of those nightmares again!"

They both dashed into her bedroom. Sammi was sitting up with her hands clasping her throat, gasping as though trying to get air into her lungs. Jonathan lifted her off the bed, cradling her to his chest, then sat her on his lap, gently stroking her matted hair.

With her eyes still closed, Sammi rocked her body back and forth in his arms, yelling, "Oh no, oh no."

Jonathan continued to run his hand through her hair, soothing her. "Wake up, baby. Wake up now. Everything's okay. Daddy's here. Mommy's here. You're okay."

Sammi finally opened her red, tear-streaked eyes, instantly quieting as she thrust her head against Jonathan's chest. The rhythmical caressing of her hair calmed her until her breathing returned to normal.

Aria, sitting on the edge of the bed, frowned and shook her head. "Jonny, I'm worried. This seems to be getting worse." She wished there was something she could do; she felt so helpless.

She turned to Sammi. "Honey, can you talk about your dream and tell Mommy and Daddy what's happening?"

She vehemently shook her head. "No. I don't want to talk about it. It makes me sad." Aria noticed that Sammi was trying to self-soothe by sucking her thumb—something she hadn't done since she was a baby. She decided not to push her to talk if it was so upsetting.

Jonathan continued to hold her, waiting for her shuddering to subside. "I think it'll make you feel better, though, if you talk it out."

"Not now. I just don't want to," she said as she pushed her head further into his chest.

"Okay, you don't have to talk about it," Jonathan said.

Aria disappeared into the bathroom and returned, handing him a cool wet washcloth. Jonathan dabbed it on Sammi's eyes and face, kissed her gently on the forehead, then tucked her back under the covers. "I'll just curl up here next to you until you fall asleep again, sweetie."

Once Sammi had fallen asleep, Jonathan returned to the den with Aria, sitting side by side on the leather couch. Aria couldn't help but feel upset whenever Sammi had the nightmares because she had no way to comfort her. *I think it stresses me out as much as her!*

She placed her hand on Jonathan's thigh. "Any idea what's going on?" she asked.

He reached over and gave her a one-armed hug. "My best guess on this is she's experiencing a past life trauma. Sometimes the soul energy splits off and gets trapped, often during the death from that life, and resurfaces in dreams in the current life. I think we may need to take a trip down to La Jolla and have Matthew talk to her in person to see what he thinks about the nightmares."

"Good idea. Would a past life regression possibly work for her? I know Matthew helped your godmother so much when he did that regression on her. I remember reading that in your book, and then Sophie briefed me on all the details. It was an amazingly powerful experience." Aria didn't really know if she believed something like that could work, but she was willing to give it a try.

"I know. It was! But past life regression isn't usually done or even needed on young kids," he said, giving her a reassuring wink. "We can see what ideas he has for her. If we can help release that energy that's traumatizing her, we'll all feel great relief. Let me give him a call."

Sammi seemed fine the next day, and Aria wondered if she even remembered what had occurred the night before. She carried on, singing and playing like nothing had happened.

At dinnertime, Aria and Sammi sat on the stools at the granite-topped kitchen island, making a salad for dinner. They made a great team, with Aria cutting the carrots into coin shapes and Sammi tearing the lettuce into pieces, putting them one by one into the wooden salad bowl.

As though she were reading Aria's thoughts, Sammi said, "Mama, don't be upset about Nate. You know I've been here before, right? You're the best mama ever, but sometimes I worry about my other mommy who I lived with before you. I think about her sometimes."

Aria's skin tingled and she released a small gasp, her eyes forming instant tears that rolled down her face. She felt ridiculous thinking it, but she didn't want to hear more about another mommy than her, so she didn't respond. Was it weird being jealous of a ghost?

Sammi continued tearing small pieces of lettuce, not acknowledging her mother's reaction.

"So did you call Grandma Lizzie?" Sammi asked nonchalantly.

"I didn't, but Daddy did. You were right. She has the flu or something and hasn't been feeling well at all. How do you do that? Know what's going to happen, I mean?"

She shrugged. "I don't know, that's just me. Mama, can I have a drink of water?"

"Of course," Aria said as she poured each of them a cold glass of water. "I guess you just tune in to her energy."

"Probably. But I have some good news." She swiveled on the stool to look at Aria, laughing and beaming and said, "Nate told me he's watching our family before he's born again. He thinks he's going to pick us to be his family. Just like I picked you and Daddy! He thinks we're pretty special. And if he chooses us, he's going to be my brother this time. I'm so excited, and I think it won't be long until you have a baby!" She giggled and clapped her hands.

Aria's was taken aback at her statement as her glass of water slipped through her hand, smashing into smithereens on the floor. She wondered—was this another one of Sammi's accurate predictions?

Chapter 4

THE NONPHYSICAL WORLD

Pneuma, a spirit guide, a disincarnate spirit who guides the life of someone on the physical plane, works at a computerlike monitoring device designed to help assist in guiding a person's life path. The greenish-yellow color of light emitting from his light body indicates his level of consciousness. He's Sammi's main spirit guide, who personally requested his position after serving as an intern guide—under the tutelage of a senior guide named Malach—for her dad, Jonathan, when he was growing up. Pneuma's new intern is starting work with him, and they communicate their thoughts via telepathy. In the unearthly dimensions, there isn't linear time—everything exists in an ever-present moment.

He works at the monitor, controlling the device by moving his light-hand in a pattern on an invisible wall as though he's playing a piano without touching the keys. He zooms in on Aria and Sammi and sends his thoughts to Neshamah, the new intern spirit guide entering the monitoring area.

Neshamah: I'm honored to meet you, Pneuma. I know I have much to learn. My last incarnation on Earth was a rather short one, but I experienced a great deal of learning during that time period. I think I'll be a good fit here. They temporarily moved me here to work with you to learn some lessons about love.

Pneuma: Welcome. I'm pleased to be working with you. I need to catch you up a bit on what's going on. You can review it all on the monitoring system, but I'll give you a brief overview.

Neshamah: Thanks. That'll help.

Pneuma: Where I came into this family scenario was when one of our spirit guide team members, Nephesh, had decided to incarnate to Earth to help a couple of souls through some rough times. Nephesh, when he'd incarnated, became Jonathan, Sammi's father. Jonathan had wanted to incarnate on Earth to help some soul friends—in particular, his godmother, Sophie—go through a tragic loss, as well as other loved ones in his life.

Neshamah: Weren't you the intern for the guide named Malach then?

Pneuma: Yes, he'll be checking in on us. He's a very enlightened soul. So Sophie, Jonathan's godmother, had ended up working with a spiritual advisor on Earth, by the name of Matthew Hobbs, to get her through a traumatic time. She'd ended up marrying him. He's now Sammi's godfather. You following all of this? It's complicated but gets easier.

Neshamah: So far, so good.

Pneuma: Jonathan and his mom had had a hard time after his dad, her husband, died, but Jonathan had worked through the trauma, remembering his life purpose in the process. Now he's married to Aria and they have a little girl, Samantha—Sammi. I'm one of her main guides, and now you're here to help.

Neshamah: Eager to learn. The monitoring system is very complex and may take some time to learn. What's our role here? How much do we assist?

Pneuma: I'm not sure of your level of knowledge at this point, so forgive me if I state things you already know. There's a plan that's created by each incarnating soul before going to Earth. It's like the framework of a house; the bare bones give it structure and shape. The person, while he's living his life, then adds to the frame—the walls, the finish, the decorations. He does that through his experiences and the choices he makes. If he gets off track from his purpose, we help. We're always available to assist. This family is very spiritually evolved, so I haven't had to get all that involved.

Neshamah: Okay, it's making sense.

Pneuma: I assume you're aware of the different dimensions in the universe. A dimension isn't a place you visit—it's a level of consciousness. Each dimension has a game plan, a playbook, specific to it. When we go to a certain dimension, we're obligated to live within those rules. Even though many of the people on Earth still function in third-dimension consciousness, they can gain the experience of other dimensions if they raise their awareness and awaken. Some of the more evolved souls who've gone to Earth have appeared to create miracles on Earth because they're able to tap into the laws of higher dimensions.

Neshamah: So, depending on their level of their consciousness, some people may require a lot of assistance, some less, some none.

Pneuma: And some are not open to receiving guidance from us at all. You'll find people who seem to be stuck in a rut—living in a box of rigid beliefs. Those individuals are usually very negative, playing the role of a victim, absorbed in self-pity, and shut down to hearing the thoughts of others—those people are the most unevolved. Their free will is restricted because they're held back and suppressed as they learn how to obey and comply with societal beliefs. They can't or won't believe there's something bigger out there in the universe.

Neshamah: Got it.

Pneuma: So back to this situation, on the last scene I viewed, Sammi is having nightmares bleeding through from a previous life. She's also receiving visitations from a spirit she knows as Nate, who only wants to provide her comfort. Her mother, Aria, is concerned about her invisible friend, but he's a good spirit who has experienced many lives with the spirit of Samantha.

Neshamah: So on the Earth plane, does Sammi see the spirit of Nate?

Pneuma: As spirits, we're able to keep our form transient in nature, and we can shift how it appears to people. How we present to people on Earth depends on their personal beliefs and level of consciousness. People functioning with lower vibrations can't see us. Those with higher vibrations are able to. Sammi, who's an evolved soul, sees Nate as a sphere of light or sparkles.

Neshamah: So for me, I should …

Pneuma: Learn all you can and assist me when necessary. Watch and learn. We're here as support for when they desire help. Now in this situation, typically I might send Aria an inspiration to find someone to assist Sammi through the rough patch she's going through, but Sammi's dad, Jonathan, will take the lead in that. We're working with spiritually aware people, so we don't have to do as many "spiritual nudges" as I call them.

Neshamah: That makes things easier.

Pneuma: We do our best to let everyone direct their own lives with gentle guidance to keep them on the path they intended, so with this family, things are pretty easy. Like I said, we're working with advanced souls. However, there's something we can nudge a bit to move it forward. With Sammi's life plan, some people are meant to meet each other, and it hasn't happened yet as things have gotten slightly off course. So … Matthew Hobbs is going to speak at a course in Los Angeles. There's someone I want you to give a spiritual nudge to attend. I'll show you how to do it and then you can start.

Neshamah: Ready to begin.

Chapter 5

November 8

No, it wasn't exactly the Federal Witness Protection Program, but Olivia Buffet simply had to disappear. She'd recognized the moment she'd been waiting for, dropping everything and vanishing from the life she'd known. She'd even picked out a new name—Olivia—after a woman she'd admired, and the last name Buffet—because it sounded French, like *boo-fey.*

She'd turned thirty-two on her last birthday, and she was pretty sure she wouldn't have made it one more year if she hadn't left home, seemingly evaporating into thin air. It hadn't been easy starting from scratch, beginning life anew. But Olivia had known that sometimes you had to do unthinkable things to survive.

Her plight had been a domestic abuse situation—a circumstance so unbearable that there had been no other choice but to plan her disappearance. As if it were fate, her husband had been convicted and *finally* put in prison for armed robbery. What had been bad news for Curtis had been a golden moment for Olivia. As soon as he'd begun serving his jail term, she'd immediately pounced on the opportunity—

what she'd thought would be her only chance—to run away and reinvent herself. In the recesses of her mind, she'd always worried that back in the year 2014, there'd be a newspaper headline that would read: TWENTY-FIVE-YEAR-OLD WOMAN FATALLY STABBED WITH KITCHEN KNIFE BY ABUSIVE HUSBAND.

She'd tried to forget those dreaded memories, although she couldn't help but think about them at times. She remembered how on one hot July afternoon, after he'd beaten her so badly she couldn't leave her bed, he'd warned her that if she ever left him, he'd kill her. Now that she was safely hidden away, she hoped to God he'd never find her, because if he did, she was sure she'd die. However, that was something she didn't want to think about; those nightmares needed to be put to rest.

It wasn't just the nightmare about Curtis—other bad dreams often plagued her. After many fitful nights of sleep, she'd resigned herself to attending counseling sessions to resolve the intense fears that manifested as night terrors, sometimes so violent and extreme that she'd find herself unable to fall back asleep, leaving her feeling exhausted and frazzled the next day. Not wanting to take any pharmaceuticals, she'd been eager to try alternative methods, so the therapist had suggested using hypnosis for anxiety reduction.

During one memorable hypnosis session, she'd felt an unusual internal energy shift—one that seemingly transported her to another time and place; it had been the oddest feeling. The therapist had said he'd seen that happen in his practice before, and after some research, he'd come to some conclusions, suspecting that what she'd felt and seen while under hypnosis had been energy remnants of a previous life.

Now, as she sat on a chair in her apartment kitchen, drinking a cup of stale coffee from her favorite chipped mug, she shuddered as she thought about the haunting memories of her past. While she'd been married to Curtis, her name had been Leticia—a name she actually hadn't minded relinquishing when she'd left home.

While growing up in Georgia, she'd always had a penchant for helping others and had felt grateful for the scholarship she'd received to pursue her Master of Social Work degree. Reducing people's phobias had become her area of expertise—maybe, in some way, this assisted the healing of her own fears and personal issues.

Reports she'd read suggested that abusive husbands often tracked down their runaway wives via their careers. In an effort to protect herself in her new life, she'd decided to alter what she did for a living so Curtis had less of a chance of finding her. With yoga as one of her lifelong passions, opening a studio seemed the right choice to fill her days, and to avoid the lonely feelings that seemed to surface in the evenings, she'd doggedly pursued her calling to study clinical hypnotherapy; she'd been sure it would be a great adjunct to her training in phobia counseling.

San Diego had been the perfect place for her to begin her new life; she'd been heading to Mexico, but her fear of coping alone in a foreign country, where she didn't speak the language, had motivated her to remain in the USA. Maintaining a low profile for obvious reasons, Olivia had mostly kept to herself. Sometimes it was a solitary life, but she'd made the best of it, grateful for the moments of introspection that had helped to heal her. She'd often found herself remembering the day she'd had her intense experience under hypnosis where she'd unexpectedly delved into a past life. Hungry to explore more of that evocative world, she'd felt compelled to study past life regression hypnotherapy. She'd signed up and loved the classes, finding the training stimulating, with thought-provoking possibilities.

As she finished her second cup of coffee, lost in her musings, Olivia glanced around at her three-bedroom apartment, realizing that she loved the new life she'd created. Opening a yoga studio in a nice part of town had been a dream come true; the previous owner had needed to sell the studio quickly, allowing Olivia to cash in on a great opportunity at a reasonable price. She'd been glad she'd secreted away the generous amount of money her great-grandmother had left her in her will upon her passing. She knew Grandma Pearl, who never had liked Curtis, would have been happy the money had gone to Olivia's escape fund, affording her a comfortable life.

Most of the yoga classes Olivia offered were mixed gender, but by special request, she'd recently opened two more classes geared toward silver foxes—ladies a bit older, who weren't as flexible as the twenty-year-olds.

During her Monday-morning yoga class, one of her clients, Sophie Hobbs—wearing a flowered headband to keep her auburn hair off her face—gently dabbed at her glistening cheeks with her sports towel as she approached Olivia during the break, asking her if she could leave some of her husband's brochures on the table in the foyer of the studio. Sophie's husband, Matthew, was listed as one of the keynote speakers at the Living with Awareness Conference in Los Angeles. Olivia cheerfully grinned at Sophie, accepting the brochures she handed her, briefly perusing one.

She glanced up at Sophie and smiled. "Hey, Sophie, I didn't realize you were Dr. Hobbs's wife," Olivia said. "I'm actually a big fan of his. This conference looks intriguing to me—I just might go. I've read his books."

Sophie's green eyes lit up. "Oh, you have? That's so interesting. You know, I've personally heard his talk a couple of times now and it's fascinating. You should go. And thanks for letting me leave these here. See you on Friday, Olivia," she said as she departed the studio through the glass doors.

Olivia read the first paragraph of the brochure in greater detail and immediately got a tingling sensation down her spine—an intuition she recognized indicating she should attend the conference. It was scheduled on a Monday, so she'd have to ask another instructor, Marilyn, to cover her classes for her, but it sounded like it was geared to her interests, and ever since she'd read his books, she'd hoped to have a past life regression with Dr. Hobbs one day. It was like an opportunity shining right in her face. *Meant to be.*

Wanting a partner in crime for the event, she made a beeline to her studio office to call her best friend, Jax Radcliffe, to coax him into attending with her. Normally, she didn't make friends with her clients, but when she'd met Jax at one of her Wednesday yoga classes, she had been surprised at their instant rapport. Charming and playful, he just seemed to bring out the best in her. Being very careful not to reveal the secrets of her past, she purposely was a bit aloof with people—but she trusted Jax.

Surprisingly, her call didn't go directly to his voice mail as it usually did. Normally, in his role of a nurse at a local hospital, his phone time was restricted during work hours.

"Hey, Livie, what's up?" Jax said in a hurried voice.

"I'm shocked you actually answered. I have to remember now why I even called you." Realizing the conversation might take longer than she'd anticipated, she plopped down on the desk chair in her office, putting her feet up on the wooden desk.

"I'm on break, so I'm checking my texts."

"Feeling open-minded?"

"Depends. Spill. What's going on?"

"I want you to drive to Los Angeles with me and attend a conference in three weeks. The keynote speaker is a guy I just happen to want to meet for professional reasons. You know how much I hate driving in LA traffic, so I was thinking ... if you could arrange a day off on November twenty-ninth, you could go with me for an adventure, as well as playing the enjoyable role of my chauffeur."

"What's the conference about? Crop circles? UFOs?"

Anticipating a smart remark from him, she replied, "Yeah, sure. Of course you're going to poke fun at me. No, past life regression and karma."

"Wow, something I've always dreamed of attending."

"Your sarcasm is dripping all over me. You might find it interesting. Besides, it would be fun to hang with you. Mini road trip."

"I actually have a five-day breather from the hospital coming up. No nursing for me for one whole week. I was thinking of going to Tahiti or Baja, or binge-watching TV shows with burgers and beer, but why not LA instead?"

"So you'll go?"

"Motivate me."

"I'll bribe you with food and pay for the gas. That always works. I'll make you five nights of dinners. If I like this speaker, I'm going to ask him to regress me with hypnosis. Past life regression. There are a few things from my past that I want to understand."

"Umm ... don't you already do that? Why don't you regress yourself?"

"Unfortunately, I don't go as deeply into a trance when I do self-hypnosis. Doesn't work as well for me. Dr. Hobbs mentioned in one of his books that children—younger ones, ages two to seven—are able to vividly remember previous lives without regression therapy, and I wanted to talk with him further as that's my finding. A mom who attends my yoga class asked me if I could work with her little girl, who keeps talking about a different dad than her current father. I thought I'd exchange techniques with Dr. Hobbs if he seems interested."

"If you promise not to do any hocus-pocus on me, I'll go with you."

Still a bit sweaty from her class, Olivia dabbed at her flushed cheeks with a towel she kept in her desk drawer. "But, my friend, you're in greater need of hocus-pocus than anyone I know."

"True. Text me the date so I'm sure I have it off. Gotta get back to work."

"Will do, and get back to me soon so I can sign us up."

Now that the twenty-ninth had finally rolled around, Olivia was excited at the thought of attending the conference, feeling appreciative that Jax was going along: that alone would make it a fun day. She hadn't slept well the night before—more nightmares—so she'd woken up too early at 5:00 a.m. and gotten ready in thirty minutes, not knowing what to do with herself while she waited an hour for Jax to arrive. A hot cup of coffee and a Sudoku puzzle helped her pass the time. She glanced at her watch. Where was he? She hated to walk in late to events. She decided to wait out front to save time. Twenty minutes later, Jax pulled to the curb in his 2013 Mercedes-Benz coupe.

Feeling slightly annoyed, Olivia opened the car door, leaning in to speak to him. "I thought you forgot. You're really late."

"Not that late. Sorry my alarm didn't go off, but we don't need to allow that much time to get to LA."

"Well, you never know. Sometimes it's easy and other times you sit in gridlock." She glanced down at her discount-store slacks, blouse, and jacket, feeling underdressed compared to him. Always interested in fashion, he looked trendy in his fitted khaki blazer, striped button-down shirt, and black slacks with a slight sheen to them.

"You're looking pretty dapper in your fancy pants there."

"You like these?"

She glanced down at his feet. "Yeah and what ... are those the Ermenegildo Zegna loafers you mentioned?"

"A guy's got to be stylin' when he's hanging in Beverly Hills. Come on, get in, Livie. Let's rock and roll."

She slid into the passenger seat, laughed, and jokingly wagged her finger in his face. "Alarm didn't go off, my ass. You stopped at Deja Brew for coffee. You didn't even hide the evidence—you have powdered sugar all over your face from some treat you ate. So, where's my coffee and treat?"

He brushed his beard with his fingers, trying to remove the sugary remnants. "Ye of little faith. It's in the coffee carrier in the back, along with a bag of your favorite mini vanilla scones."

She strapped on her seat belt. "Oops," she said apologetically, "now I feel bad that I was mean to you. I apologize. You really are the sweetest guy I know."

He cracked his knuckles and arched his muscular upper body as he prepared for the drive. "I am. Now let's get this show on the road."

Olivia observed her friend as he drove, studying his features, noting how he looked younger than his thirty years. Stylish hair was important to Jax, and fortunately he was blessed with a head of thick, dark hair, full on top and slightly long in the back, touching his collar. The shallow cleft in his chin that she'd admired when she first met him was now covered by a full beard. His nose was classic Greek, and his rich cognac-colored eyes always seemed to have an impish spark to them. Although he wasn't an intellectual type, per se, his tortoise-shell glasses gave him a bookish look. But the thing she loved the best—his most distinguishing feature—was his tranquil, amicable countenance. So many people walked around wearing a face that appeared pinched, uptight, or angry at rest. Not Jax. He looked serene—she envied that about him.

The ride to LA was an easy drive after all, and they arrived fifteen minutes in advance of the conference start time. Not wanting to search for parking in the very congested area, they took advantage of the valet parking at the hotel, signed in, and pinned on their preprinted name tags. Surprisingly, the room was packed with more people than Olivia had expected.

No better place to people-watch than a conference, she thought. Observing the myriad types of people who were attending a conference of a metaphysical nature—from young people to older adults, both men and woman—fascinated her. What had brought all of these people to a conference like this? She was glad she'd remembered to bring a stack of her business cards with her. After a meet and greet of coffee and bagels—she'd thought they'd be serving kale smoothies and quinoa muffins—they picked out their seats, deciding to sit up front. The first half of the conference, with its vast array of different speakers addressing topics such as children's perceptions of the afterlife, was intriguing, but it was Matthew Hobbs's talk that she really wanted to hear. Of course his speech was scheduled in the late afternoon; she hoped she wouldn't drift off to sleep.

After several hours, Olivia felt her stomach growling; she looked around the room hoping no one else heard the grumbling sound. She'd made prior reservations for their lunch break at the Blushers Café in Hollywood—a place she'd always wanted to try but had never made reservations far enough in advance to get in. After dismissal for lunch, they walked a short distance to the café and were immediately seated outside on the patio. It was the perfect spot for watching and learning what was currently on trend in Beverly Hills.

"Look at all the 'glam' walking by us. It almost makes you feel like you've been transported to some exotic location," Olivia said. She kicked off her shoes under the table; wearing heels was not in her DNA.

Jax chuckled as he looked around at the people sauntering by. "Finally, we're one of the cool people. Maybe someone will ask for my autograph."

She critically eyed Jax. "I wish you'd shave," Olivia said. "I just noticed you still have powdered sugar in your beard from your doughnuts this morning. You're covering a handsome face with that beard. I'm surprised they let you have that at the hospital."

His hand automatically went to his chin. "I like to conceal my facial expressions. Adds an air of mystery to me. Makes you focus more on my sexy brown eyes."

"You're pretty transparent, even with that full face of hair."

Olivia read the menu out loud. "What's with everything in lettuce wraps here? I forgot this is still the land where no one eats carbs. I thought that trend died out years ago. A girl could totally get hungry living in this city."

"It's just a way of life, you know? You'd fit right in. Yoga, crystals, past lives, fillers, spin class, cleanses ..."

"You forgot plastic surgery. I don't do cleanses, and I haven't done fillers either."

"Maybe you won't ever need it. A Harvard study said that about twenty percent of black people have a 'younger gene.' Maybe you have it."

"Ahh, yes, the miracles of melanin."

"You do have beautiful skin, Liv—a gorgeous toffee color. Unflawed. And I really like how you let your hair go natural. Love the dark curls."

"I had no choice. Those harsh chemicals I used were causing me rashes. But thanks for the compliment. It's weird how our world becomes more and more focused on healthy lifestyles, yet we just sat in your car on the drive up with you blowing cigarette smoke in my face."

"And I live in a cloud of guilt about it. But it helps keep me trim, and it's my only vice."

"Yeah, sure … besides excessive sex and drinking. And there are better ways to monitor your sexy physique than smoking, my friend. Better ways."

"There's no such thing as excessive sex."

"I'm just teasing you. I like that you express who and what you are." She set her folded menu on the table. "It all looks tasty, but I think I'll have the falafel lettuce wrap and a side of sweet potato fries. Sounds good. Whatcha having?"

"Well, look, Livie, they have beef on the menu. I'm going to have the Kobe beef burger. And let's have a drink."

As soon as Jax closed his menu, their waitress—a buxom blonde wannabe actress—took their order, leaving them a bowl of crudités and yogurt dip.

Swiping a carrot stick into the dip, Jax asked, "How much time do we have?"

"An hour and a half. So what do you think so far?"

"Of the conference? A complete waste of three hours of my life."

"What? Really?"

"No, I'm kidding. So, it's holding my interest. I'm actually intrigued. That one teenager who talked about his past life was convincing to me. I really was fascinated, and I'm not just saying that. I thought I'd be laughing at the whole thing or catching forty winks, but it's interesting. You'll need to catch me up a bit more on this stuff as I'm not versed in it at all. I was feeling kind of lost in parts, and I'm not sure I buy into a lot of it."

Olivia responded between bites of celery and sugar snap peas. "You don't have to buy any of it. Just have an open mind to hearing it. I didn't learn this stuff overnight—just kind of a process that evolved over time. Experiences—that's what's led me in this direction, and I was driven to read a lot of metaphysical literature over the years. I can tell you one thing for sure—I wasn't raised this way. Born, one of six kids. Went to Baptist Church. Dad ruled the roost. Mom cooked, cleaned, and did the womanly chores. We didn't believe in this kind of stuff in my family."

"Well, we sure didn't at my house. 'Jax,' my mom would say, 'don't be taunting the devil with those thoughts of yours.'"

After their cocktails were served, they laughed as they both simultaneously reached for their limes, squeezing them into their gin and tonics. Olivia took a sip and sighed as the relaxing elixir coursed through her veins. "Sounds familiar. But reading about it wasn't what changed me. My actual life experiences, followed by tons of reading, changed the direction of the path I was on. I'm not saying you have to believe anything—you don't. The word *belief* seems too static and permanent to me. 'This is what I believe' sounds so written in stone and immutable. Finite. To me, I see the world and my part in it as fluid and ever changing. Continuous change allows for learning and growth. I want to be open and see past my own family-embedded beliefs. I want to stretch myself to see something new. That's why I challenge my internal monologue all the time."

"Problem is, dear Livie, you challenge mine too. I'm content with my thoughts just the way they are." The smell was enticing as the waitress placed their plates of food on the table. "And all I want to do is bite into this big, juicy burger and think happy thoughts of cheesy beef."

Olivia stared at Jax's burger, hoping she wasn't salivating. "Now that looks delicious. I should have ordered the same thing."

He cut off a piece for her. "Here, enjoy. I'm just a sharing kind of guy. When the speaker was talking about breaking away from labeling others and appreciating differences, I was interested, but I'm not sure human beings can ever fully do that."

"Oh, Jax, now you have a big gob of cheese hanging in your beard. Ugh," she said as she dabbed at his face with her napkin. "But it's already been happening. The world is evolving very quickly, and it's just a matter of time and process. I know I don't want to be a label. I think we'll move beyond doing that over the years. The trend is there—we're moving toward more unifying behaviors. I don't think of myself or define myself as a middle-class, physically strong, single black woman."

Jax backed away from her hand—not wanting to be babied in front of people—and finished mopping his own beard with a napkin. "I bet you'd like it if I labeled you *sexy*."

"Umm ... no, that's your obsession. We fasten labels on each other like they're some kind of flashing neon sign. I don't want to be stereotyped and pigeonholed—I've lived enough of that. We're born into certain belief systems that are thrust upon us depending on our family, our culture, our schooling, our religions, our race, where we live. From the moment we're born, we're taught to believe *very* specific things, and our challenge throughout our lives is to break out of those constraints. We're all in a box."

"And maybe you just think too much. Want another piece?"

"No, thanks. And it's not the first time I've been accused of that. By the way, I don't think of who you are as gay. I don't label you by your choice of sexuality. Changing even the simplest of labels can have an immeasurable impact on nearly every aspect of our lives."

"Well, *I* think of me as gay." He squirted a thick glob of ketchup on his burger.

"There's more than one way to show up in the world. To me, labels are a trap. The jocks, the cheerleaders, the popular people, the nerds, the Latinos, the Asians, the whites. Labels cover the person's real identity. It's so limiting."

"I don't mind it. I think of it as an easy way to describe people, and you know where you fit in."

"But we're so obsessed with highlighting our differences. We distrust anything different. People are multidimensional—not one-dimensional."

"It's what we do as humans. I don't agree with negative labels, but we do it to belong in a group and feel accepted. We have a compulsion to be categorized. And it's easier to get on the back of a tiger than get off one."

"I still think we're evolving away from that."

Now Jax picked at the french fries on her plate. "So you're saying labels are for soup cans."

"Any can. Not just soup."

"My work, and I'm referring to the medical field here, is all about riding on the back of the tiger. Jumping off is a big no-no."

"I agree." She laughed. "I don't even know why I like you at all."

He shrugged. "It's just my magnetic personality, I guess."

"Yep. You're weird."

"Hey, you just labeled me. By the way, you never told me you were one of six kids. Holy crap, did your mom ever take a break? Where are they all?"

"Scattered throughout the country."

"When that first lady in the seminar was talking about the past lives thing, a part of me just rejected the concept—it just doesn't sound possible. I'm not much into the supernatural."

Olivia pushed her plate to the edge of the table, crumpling her pink cloth napkin alongside it, and concentrated on her cocktail. "Who defines what's possible? The limits of your mind? Mystic, supernatural, paranormal ... I don't think of it as supernatural. It's very natural to me. I've had a certain knowing of the nonphysical world since I was a little girl. Never felt I fit in with others. My parents scolded me for things I said, so I clammed up, but it didn't make my thoughts about it go away. I had an awareness of my nonphysical home and remembered some of the past lives I've lived. It's just part of my experiences."

"Well, I haven't had those experiences."

"You probably have, you're just not tuned in to them. Most people forget the spiritual world they came from when they incarnate in order to cope with the new world they'll live in. But I'm open, and I have some memories of other lives and roles other people have played in them. They're very vivid. I'd like to remember more of my lives because it's fascinating to me how things interconnect. Healing something from the past often heals something happening now. Makes me more aware of so many things and how they impact this life. If we allow it, we're always awakening and learning more."

Jax stared at the lone french fries on her plate that she'd rejected. "So how do you know you're not just fantasizing? Or have a good imagination?"

"When I imagine and fantasize, the emotion doesn't go with it. When I remember past life events, the emotions are pretty intense."

"I'm open to learning, but I'm not there yet. I'm not understanding the whole rebirth thing. Grew up Catholic, but I don't practice it. I should have read some of the books before coming."

"Like I said, just don't prejudge it. The concepts out there are so distorted. That's why I tend to avoid terms like reincarnation. It creates thoughts of something hocus-pocus, new agey, or weird for some people. Read about it before deciding it's not possible."

Jax finished his delectable burger and looked her up and down, smirking. "So were you Cleopatra in a past life?"

Olivia snorted and reached across the table, belting him with her purse. "See? That's what I mean about distortions. That's a stereotype people use. Fame on Earth is not relevant in the nonphysical world. Of all the past life regressions I've done on people, not one person was someone famous. I mean, famous people reincarnate too, but I haven't come across one yet."

"To change the subject ... want a new purse?"

"What? No ..."

"Why don't we bolt and go shopping on Rodeo Drive?"

"You can if you want to, but Matthew Hobbs's part is coming up, and that's what I came for."

"No, I don't have any spare cash to fancy shop anyway. And I want to hear this guy too."

"So do you want me to explain a bit about past lives before we go back in?"

Jax stuck out his arm, putting his hand in her face. "No. Stop. On overload. Shutting systems down. Save some room in my brain for his talk. But wait ... can I finish your fries?"

"Sure. Ready to go back?"

He quickly stuffed the remaining fries in his mouth. "Yep. Hope I can stay awake."

After returning to the hotel, they sat through the afternoon lectures, waiting for Dr. Hobbs's talk, scheduled at the end of the conference in the two o'clock time slot. When Dr. Hobbs was done speaking, Jax excused himself to go to the restroom, while Olivia stood in a long line with other attendees who wanted their books signed, patiently waiting. She liked his look—tall and attractive, with the most incredible aqua-colored eyes. *Here's another man who simply looks serene and at peace*, she thought.

When it was finally her turn, Olivia extended her hand to him. "Dr. Hobbs, I'm excited to meet you. My name is Olivia Buffet. I met your wife, Sophie, in my yoga class."

He shook her hand. "Ah yes, Sophie mentioned you. Pleased to meet you. Thanks for attending today."

"Of course! In your lecture, you were talking about how regression isn't usually necessary in order for kids to remember past life events. Well, I work with kids and I agree with you, but I have some other techniques I use that I find effective." She handed him her business card. "I don't want to hold up the line here, but if you're interested in talking further, please contact me."

"I'm very interested, Olivia. I'll be in touch with you."

Bad traffic! She knew it would happen and was ever so grateful that Jax was driving. The return trip home was clearly going to take twice the time it had taken to get there. When they hit gridlock, Jax pulled off the freeway to stop for a gelato, waiting for traffic to subside. The shop was bustling with people who'd probably had the same idea they did. They waited in line, reading the board listing all the flavors.

"You know all these fun places wherever you go," Olivia said.

"Because I grew up here. I recommend the spicy chocolate: it's really good. All the flavors are good."

"I'm going to get the sweet cream, I think."

"Okay, but that's not very daring."

"So be it."

"I'm getting the chocolate, cardamom, fig."

They ordered their desserts and looked for a place to sit. Jax pointed to a table for two in the corner. "Let's go over there to that empty table while we let some of the traffic lighten up a bit." He offered her a spoonful of his gelato.

She took the spoon and licked the dense, thick treat. "Oh my, but that's *really* good! I should just always order what you do. Thanks for going with me and driving: much appreciated. I hate maneuvering through the LA traffic at rush hour."

"My pleasure. I haven't had this much fun since I lost my virginity."

"Not sure how to take that."

"Hey, it's all good. I was thinking about this karma stuff Hobbs talked about, and I'm intrigued."

"What do you find intriguing?"

"All of it. I just might delve into it a bit more," he said as he dipped his spoon into Olivia's bowl for a sample.

"Get out of town! I'm shocked to hear that, but it's a good segue for me to talk to you about something I've been meaning to tell you for a long time. Okay ... get ready for my big reveal." She paused for dramatic effect, leaning into him and speaking in a hushed tone. "I'm dealing with balancing some karma in my own life right now. There are some things I haven't told you, and you're the only one I trust to share them with."

Jax clapped his hands and rubbed them together. "Oh, good, spill the juicy bits to me."

Olivia glanced around the room and licked her lips. "This is going to sound weird, but I'm kind of living a secret life. Not kind of—actually, I am. I'll need to tell you about it. I have to start being able to trust people again."

His eyes widened. "A secret life? I knew it. I knew you had a shady past. Now do tell. Spill, girl."

"This is serious. I have to know I can trust you. My life depends on it."

"Yikes. That's a lot of pressure. Your life and all. I've known you for a couple of years. What's left to tell, and why now? Just who are you, Olivia Buffet?"

"That's an interesting question. Who am I? I could give you resume info, like my age, my schooling, my jobs, my gender and so on. Or tell you some of my personality traits—like I'm partial to king-sized beds and buttered popcorn. I like salt on the rim of my margarita, blended, not on ice. I don't like talking on the telephone, and I secretly watch reality shows—"

"Wait ... you watch reality shows?"

She ignored him. "I love meaningful tattoos. I'm a problem solver. I see auras around people, and sometimes I see things in my dreams that actually happen. But that's just a description of things. Who I am, though, is simple—a spirit in a human body. Same as you."

"Well, I like all the descriptive parts. That's what's interesting to me."

"And one more thing. I can trust you, right?"

"I swear my loyalty to you." He hooked his pinky finger into hers. "Pinky swear."

"Okay ..." She gulped. "I'm a runaway wife. And I'm in hiding."

Jax slammed his plastic spoon on the table, breaking it in half. "What? By the look on your face, I'd say you aren't kidding, are you?"

She shook her head. "No ... no, I'm not. But I'll tell you about it when you come to dinner one night because it's a long story, and I have to think about how I'm going to explain this. It can only be between you and me. My life depends on it."

"Geez, Liv. It's like impatiently waiting for next week to arrive for your favorite TV show to air. The suspense will kill me. We have a long ride in the car. Why not start then?"

"'Cause I'm tired and I think I might fall asleep."

After Jax retrieved a new spoon, they finished their gelato, and it was time to get back on the road again. The traffic was finally moving at a faster pace, and within five minutes the motion of the car had lulled Olivia to sleep. She stirred when Jax stopped the car at her apartment.

He reached over and gently shook her shoulder. "Home sweet home, my lady."

She woke feeling groggy and a bit grumpy. "So sorry I fell asleep. I wasn't good company. I've just been so tired lately. Thanks for going with me, my friend. You're the best." She leaned over and kissed him on the cheek. "Have a good night."

Jax got out of the car and walked her to the entry door, leaving her with a big hug and a garlic-scented kiss.

"Love ya, girl. No matter who you are."

"Right back at ya."

Olivia flicked on the light in her kitchen, noticing the old, worn wallpaper was peeling in various spots. *Time to renovate*, she thought. Painting her tiny kitchen a bright yellow color would open up the space and make it more cheery. She microwaved a cup of Sleepytime tea and sat at the kitchen table, contemplating her day. She hoped she had done the right thing in telling Jax. She'd just needed to share her situation with someone. *Secrets burn holes in your pocket.* She'd lived many years now feeling alienated and alone. She needed to talk it out with a close friend, and she knew she could completely trust Jax. After all, he had those wonderful trustworthy eyes. There were some odd things happening in her life, and she hoped he could help her problem-solve them.

She was starting to think she was crazy.

Chapter 6

November 25

Jonathan finished loading up their new car—a Tesla SUV—for their family trip to San Diego. After driving Matthew's Tesla, he was all-in; he didn't think he'd ever get bored with those double-hinged falcon-wing doors. *How do we have so much stuff to haul for a one-day trip?* he wondered. It didn't matter: after all, it was Thanksgiving. He could almost smell the turkey roasting.

When his mom had first asked them to come, he'd hesitated, knowing he had a deadline on a project he was working on, but he was also craving some family time, and family time won. Besides, it was his mom's favorite holiday, and he tried to make it to their house for the celebration whenever he was in town. *I can't disappoint her ...* Plus, it would be a good time to talk to Matthew Hobbs about Sammi, and he hadn't seen his mom, his stepdad, Mark, and his godmother, Sophie, for several months. Time was always slipping away so quickly: it was one thing he wished there was more of. Tending to get overly absorbed in his work—often feeling downright guilty—he'd made a concerted effort to set aside more time for his family and friends.

Sammi, dressed in a denim skirt, a navy cable-knit sweater and her pink boots, walked her dog, an adorable black-and-brown Yorkie Poo, to the car. After Jonathan opened the back door, Sammi unclipped the leash. "Jump up, Maggie. Get in the car." The dog hopped in the backseat, seemingly excited to be included. "I'm glad we can take Maggie with us, Daddy. Grandma Lizzie loves her."

"I know she does. We couldn't leave her alone on Thanksgiving, could we? We had a dog when I was growing up. Two, in fact. Einstein and Betty Rose. Another dog, Cadbury, when I was older. We'll see Grandma and Grandpa, and Sophie and Matthew too. They've really been missing you." He glanced at his watch. "We'd better get on the road."

"I love dogs," Aria said. "I never had one growing up." She placed a retro Tupperware carrier with her pies on the floor of the passenger seat, leaving sufficient room for her feet.

Before getting into the car, Jonathan turned around in front of Aria, showing off his new double-breasted navy blazer. "How do I look?" he asked.

"Fashionable as always and stunningly handsome." She kissed him on the lips. "Do you want me to drive?"

"No, I'm good."

"Did you bring the wine?" Aria asked as she got into the passenger seat.

"Yep, we're all set."

Jonathan slid into the driver's seat and turned to glance in the backseat. "Everyone in? Seat belts on? Sammi, you seem to be all settled in your booster seat. Doors are going down now. Off we go. I wonder who will get the long half of the wishbone this year? I bet it's me!"

Sammi put her hand over her mouth and giggled. "I think you're wrong, Daddy. I think it will be me!"

*

The drive was surprisingly easy considering it was a holiday weekend. *Most people are probably already at their destination*, he thought. After a few hours of freeway driving, they arrived in La Jolla. As Jonathan pulled into the driveway of his childhood home, the crunching sound of the gravel under the tires stirred memories of the past. He thought it was interesting how certain sounds and smells were memory triggers for him. He suddenly felt very emotional. *Whenever I come here, I miss my dad.*

Lizzie and Sophie didn't hear him knock, and with the door open, he entered. He stood bracing himself against the doorsill between the dining room and living room, taking in the sight—watching his mom and Sophie making sweet potatoes in the kitchen—while smelling the scent of the cherrywood in the BBQ: the wood that his dad had always used when he smoked a turkey. It felt bittersweet as tears from long-ago memories gathered in his eyes. It reminded him of the final Thanksgiving with his dad before he'd died. In spite of being only five years old, Jonathan so clearly remembered his dad telling him that he was going on his *last* assignment and then he'd stop his traveling, instead working in town at a nearby hospital. Both his mom and dad had worked as humanitarian aid workers: his dad as a surgeon, his mom as a pediatrician. One more assignment, his dad had said—one he couldn't refuse. But then his dad had been murdered in the Rwandan genocide of 1994, and Jonathan's world had been inverted.

Most days, he had an awareness of his dad's spirit and was able to find ways to communicate with him, but what he missed was his physical presence—most of all looking into his soulful eyes. He was always astounded at how much information he could glean about someone just from looking into their eyes. For some reason, Jonathan could hear his dad laughing. Whenever something had struck David as funny, he'd laugh deep from his gut and slap his thigh. Jonathan would give anything, anything at all, to have his dad appear for just a day to have dinner with them and hold his little girl, Sammi. He'd been a fantastic father and would have been a loving grandfather. To many, including Jonathan, David Cohen was a hero, dying while attempting to save the life of a coworker. But hero or not, losing his dad had been a tragic life-altering event.

Jonathan had been happy when his mom had married Mark, Matthew Hobbs's brother, because he hadn't wanted her to be lonely, and he knew Mark to be an upstanding human being. Their decision to stay in Jonathan's childhood home hadn't been a hard one; the location was perfect for both of them.

As he walked around the living room, touching familiar objects, he could still feel his dad's energy lingering in the house; yet in some ways, it seemed like it had been a different life.

The despair he'd felt that winter day in 1994—the day his dad had tragically died—momentarily crept through him like icy water coursing through his veins. He slowly padded up the steps to his old bedroom, now a guest room, stopping to look at all the photos lining the wall of the staircase. Overwhelming memories and emotions flooded his body. His breathing was shallow and rapid—his head felt dizzy. In one photo, his dad had held him, riding on his shoulders with his legs wrapped around his neck. They'd both had their heads thrown back, laughing with pure, unrestrained joy. Feeling a lump under his shoe, he bent down and noticed something glimmering on the wooden step. At first glance, he thought it was a piece of aluminum foil, but when he picked it up, he realized it was an old coin. His muscles tightened and his heart pounded as it always did whenever he found a coin. It was his dad's way of giving him a message that he was present—his personal sign.

I knew you'd be here today, Dad. I just knew it. The power of all of our love is an energy that called to you. I hope you can visit a bit with our little girl, Sammi today. I miss you every single day, Dad. I love you.

He released a deep shudder. Tears rolled down his cheeks, and he brushed them away with the back of his hand. How many tears had he shed over the death of his dad? Too many to count. He'd come to a place of peace, understanding, and acceptance about why he'd died, but he still missed him. He looked around his old bedroom, pocketed the coin, and walked downstairs.

Wiping the sadness off his face, Jonathan pasted on his famous smile. The familiar, wonderful scents wafting from the kitchen provided him with a sense of comfort and contentment. Like old times—wonderful old times—he watched as his mother and godmother interacted in the kitchen, preparing the holiday meal. Seeing his mom looking so joyful made him feel content. Together, he and his mom had forged through the turmoil and pain of the tragedy of loss, forming a strong mutual bond between the two of them. She had a good life with a supportive, loving husband, kept busy with her career as a pediatrician, involved herself in her charity work, continued to stay active with her skiing and running, and even sold a few of her watercolor paintings on a website she'd created. She certainly didn't look in her sixties—youthful as ever with her long blonde hair, still worn in a ponytail, and a sparkling vitality in her eyes.

"Mom, we're here," he announced as he stepped into the kitchen. He gave Lizzie a huge bear hug and kissed her, lifting her off the ground. "Mama Bear, so good to see you."

Tears of joy welled up in her eyes. "Oh, sweetie. It's so great to see you. How was the drive? Where's my darling little girl?"

"Traffic wasn't bad. Aria and Sammi are taking Maggie for a little walk before bringing her in after the ride. It'll calm her down a bit."

Sophie ran over to Jonathan and threw her arms around him. "Give me one of those Jonathan hugs I'm always craving. This godmother of yours has been running on empty for too long; I haven't had one of your hugs for a while." She eyed him over. "You're looking your usual handsome self."

He stepped back and glanced at Sophie. "Are you crying, Sophie? Ha-ha ... I know you are—you always cry when you see me."

"Always happy tears: seeing you, touching you, makes me feel very emotional. I'm always immensely overjoyed to see you."

"And I'm always happy to see all of you. It's been too long. Let me say hi to the guys, and I'll be right back to help."

Lizzie laughed as she turned to Sophie. "You know he won't be right back to help, don't you?"

"Of course."

They both chuckled and returned to their food preparations.

Jonathan sauntered into the backyard where Mark and Matthew were watching football on the outdoor flat-screen while smoking the turkey. He was surprised at how similar the two brothers looked as they aged. Maybe it was because they had the same aqua-colored eyes, or maybe it was because they now both had gray hair. Looking around to see what had changed, he noticed how the backyard trees—the ones he'd loved climbing as a kid—had gotten huge over the years, and the patchy grass, where Betty Rose used to run and play, had been replaced with artificial turf due to the drought. But other than that, it seemed the same to him.

Jonathan approached the guys with a big grin on his face. "That smell! That smell is making me salivate. Mark, Matthew—I've missed you guys."

They each gave him a one-armed hug while holding a can of beer.

"Matthew, you're using the same wood my dad used to smoke the turkey. The smell reminds me of him."

"Yep, he taught me how to do it, and I've used it ever since. I'm making the turkey his way, in his honor. Sit down. Take a load off. What can I get you? What are you drinking these days?"

"Actually, I brought a few bottles of the best chardonnay you'll ever taste. It's like butter, so smooth. I got it at the Napa Film Festival. Aria brought them in."

"Crank 'em open and let's taste it," Mark said.

It seemed as though a tornado had whirled into the yard when Sammi entered the gazebo with Maggie, running around in circles and barking.

"Grandpa!" Sammi threw herself at Mark as he picked her up and twirled her around.

"Hey, I love those awesome pink boots! I missed you, baby girl. What have you been up to?" Mark asked as he beamed at the bundle of energy before him.

She covered her mouth with her fingers and giggled. "I've been up to everything, Grandpa."

Matthew bent down with open arms. "And how about a hug for your godfather? I have something for you."

"What is it?"

He reached into his pocket and handed her a glass heart. "I got this when I was in Italy. For your heart collection. I saw it and thought of you. It's a Venetian Murano glass heart necklace."

Sammi examined the heart, turning it over in her hand, stroking the blue veins with her index finger. "It's so beautiful. I love it. Thank you. Please put it on me now."

Matthew fastened the necklace on her. "You're stunning."

"Thank you. I'm going to go cook now. Sophie and I are going to frost cupcakes."

"Wait, cupcakes? Aren't we having pumpkin pie?" Matthew said, looking baffled.

"Yes, Mama brought *lots* of pies, but we're making some cupcakes too. For me!"

She scampered off to the kitchen, and Jonathan followed her in order to gather up a few bottles of the special wine to take out back. He stood still for a moment and watched Aria as she laughed and joined Sophie and his mom in the cooking frenzy. *I still love to watch her after all these years.* He knew how much she enjoyed the family Thanksgiving tradition, but it did make her miss spending holidays with her mom and dad in Italy. He made a mental note: he'd have to take her on a vacation to see her folks. With their varied schedules, there just never seemed to be enough time.

Sammi pulled a stool up to the counter to help cook, and Jonathan could see Sophie's eyes mist over—he knew cooking with Sammi made her feel nostalgic, reminding her of the days when he'd sat on the counter as a little boy, helping her bake cakes. It seemed so long ago.

Sammi pivoted on the stool, wooden spoon in hand. "Sophie, Daddy said you've been Grandma's best friend for a long, long time."

Sophie stood on a chair, removing serving platters from the back of the upper cupboard. "That's true. I've known your mom since I was eleven years old."

"Wow, that's forever! Can I go see your cake shop sometime? Mama said I would go crazy there."

"Crazy about all the goodies?" Sophie asked.

"Especially pink cupcakes," Jonathan said, taking the platters from Sophie and setting them on the counter.

Sophie grinned at Sammi. "You know, we can make the frosting for these cupcakes a beautiful pink color. Do you want to do that?"

Sammi clapped her hands. "I do! I do! How do we do that?"

Sophie put her index finger to her lips and looked around the room. "Okay, shhh … nobody is listening, are they? It's our secret, and you can't tell. We'll use a little beet juice."

Sammi's eyes twinkled. "Oh, now I know an important secret."

"You do."

Jonathan grabbed three bottles of the wine from the refrigerator and took them back to the gazebo to open them.

"Matthew, it's been too long since I've seen you in person. Virtual-Time is great, but seeing someone in the flesh and feeling their energy mix with yours is the best. Nothing replaces that."

Jonathan noticed Aria wandering back to the patio and thought it might be a good time for them to talk to Matthew while Sammi was busy in the kitchen.

Matthew poured wine for everyone and took a sip. "You're right about this wine, Jonathan. It's got a silky, elegant texture. Delicious! So how's it going with that script you're working on?"

"Great. I've been pounding it out, and I think I've got a good product. I made quite a few changes from the first draft I sent you guys. I think you'll like it."

"I totally got into it. Looking forward to seeing the changes." Matthew lifted the cover of the smoker to check the turkey, permeating the entire area with its enticing smell.

"I'll send them over to y—sorry, I'm so distracted by that unbelievable smell!" Jonathan said.

"I know. We're all salivating. So you and Aria have some concerns about our little Sammi? Tell me a bit more about what's going on while she's in the kitchen. Aria briefed me a bit last time she was here."

Jonathan took a sip of his wine, savoring it as it rolled over his tongue. "As I mentioned, Sammi's been having really bad nightmares, and she isn't open to talking about it with either of us. I'm sure she has trapped traumatic energy from a past life, but I think you mentioned that a regression probably isn't needed with a child her age. I've told you about how she talks to a spirit named Nate who refers to her as Christina. I'm positive he's the spirit of my friend who drowned, and she's also aware of her spirit guide, Pneuma. As you well know, Pneuma helped guide me when I was growing up. Of course, Sammi's very open. Sees auras clearly. Is able to easily tap into some past life stuff. I was wondering if there was something else you could do to help her release the trauma, or do you think she should be regressed? I need suggestions on how to get her to open up. She's holding back from talking for some reason."

Jonathan could almost read Aria's mind as she leaned against the gazebo pillar, listening. He knew she was hoping Matthew would have some good ideas to help her little girl find relief. She took it hard that she couldn't do more to soothe Sammi—she didn't like feeling helpless, unable to resolve her daughter's sadness.

Matthew opened his arms to her. "Hi, Aria, come give me a hug. How are you?"

She returned the hug, smiling at the man who was always so supportive, welcoming, and kind to her. "I'm doing great, Matthew. You're looking well. Life's been good to you."

"It certainly has. I may be a bit grayer than I was yesterday, but I'm doing well."

She sat down at the table while Jonathan poured her a glass of wine. "Mmm, sweetie, this is so good," she said to Jonathan as she tasted it. "So, Matthew, how do we release this trapped energy you're talking about?"

Matthew returned to the bar stool at the grill station, sipping his wine as he thought. "Well, I've been thinking about this. Children are so open they can often remember their past lives spontaneously without hypnosis or prompting. Their memories aren't buried away, and they aren't under the full amnesia yet. In fact, it's interesting, but I met a woman at my last conference who works with just this very thing. She lives here in San Diego. Imagine the synchronicity of that. She even gave me her business card."

Jonathan turned to Matthew and lowered his voice so Sammi wouldn't hear. "Although we often naturally find ways to release the old traumas, I think she's a bit stuck. I'm not sure why she won't talk about it with us. Maybe protecting us in some way?"

"So how do you unstick things, then?" Aria interjected.

"We know, from records of past life regression sessions, that trauma from a previous lifetime can leave what they call 'a footprint in the unconscious mind.' Does she spontaneously talk about anything from a past life?" Matthew asked.

"Yes, she talks about another mommy with blonde hair and blue eyes, but not much more than that." Aria said quietly. "As Jonny mentioned, for some reason she says she doesn't want to talk about it. I haven't been able to get her to open up. I tried using some of the ideas you talked about with me, but I wasn't very effective."

"I can give the lady—her name is Olivia—a call and see if I can talk to her about Sammi, if you'd like. She specializes in kids." Matthew looked directly at Aria and gently said, "I don't want you to be so worried, Aria. We'll get to the bottom of this and find some resolution. It may require a little bit of perseverance and patience."

She nodded in response. "Thanks. I do understand that."

Jonathan helped himself to the bowl of peanuts on the table, popping one at a time into his mouth. "I like that idea. Of course, Aria is aware of all this stuff because of me and the book I wrote as well as my life experiences I've shared with her, but as she lives it out, she really is worried and freaking out a bit because it's just so hard to console Sammi," Jonathan said.

Aria nodded in agreement.

As though on cue, Sammi emerged from the kitchen to set the large oak table in the backyard. As Jonathan and Aria relaxed in their patio chairs, Sammi approached them and handed Aria a basket with silverware and Jonathan a stack of napkins.

"Here, you can help me," she said. "Mama, please set a place for Nate tonight. It'll be nice for him to spend some time with Daddy."

Aria accepted the basket. "Since he doesn't eat, do we really need to set a spot for him?"

She nodded. "I just think it would be nice."

Jonathan turned to Aria. "You can set his place next to me. And Aria? Let's set one for my dad too." *It'll be nice to have Nate and my dad join us in spirit.*

The aromatic scents seduced everyone to the table, the gathering spot for the family feast.

"It certainly smells like Thanksgiving. I can't wait for the pumpkin pie," Mark said.

"Oh-oh … let's not forget an important family tradition. Jonathan, you still need to make the secret sauce for the turkey," Sophie said.

Sammi looked quizzically at everyone. "What's the secret sauce?"

Lizzie laughed. "When your daddy was about your age, he started the tradition of making secret sauce, otherwise known as gravy for the turkey. He'd dump in the grossest spices and things into a bowl to add to the gravy. Later as he got older, he'd actually perfected his sauce. Sophie had said he should market it. It would be a winner."

"I think you should teach Sammi the secret recipe so it's handed down over time," Sophie said.

Sammi turned to Jonathan with a pleading look. "Will you, Daddy?"

"Of course. But the secret is, you have to change the recipe every year. Let's go make it!" They walked hand in hand, back to the kitchen.

While the others chatted over wine, Jonathan and Sammi made the famous secret sauce and brought it to the table in an antique gravy boat while Lizzie finished adding some final touches to the platters of food before dinner was served.

"Aria, who are the extra place settings for?" Lizzie asked, as she perused the table.

Aria pointed to one of the place settings. "That one's for Sammi's imaginary friend."

Jonathan cringed at her response, knowing Sammi felt upset whenever Aria said Nate was imaginary.

Sammi scowled. "Mama, I told you he's not imaginary. He's real."

"What's his name?" said Sophie.

"Nate. I knew him before I came to this family, and he was a friend of Daddy's before too."

"Mom, you remember Nate," Jonathan said.

"That's cool. Of course. I remember Nate very well. I still miss him and will never forget him. I'm thrilled he's in contact with you. How is he? What do you two talk about?" Lizzie asked.

"Oh, just lots of things."

"The other place setting is for my dad, hoping he'll join us in spirit," Jonathan said, glancing at his mother. Lizzie bit her lower lip and nodded, gazing at him with tears in her eyes.

The feast was finally ready, with an abundance of steaming platters artfully arranged on the table. Matthew carved the succulent brown bird at the table while everyone watched. "Here's the wishbone," he announced after he finished carving. "We need to let it dry before making a wish, though."

Forks clinked, chatter filled the air, wine flowed freely, and a loving energy was shared by all. With everyone feeling satiated, they sat back in their chairs—a few of them unbuttoning the top button of their pants—to relax after the feast and make room for dessert.

"Did Nate enjoy his dinner, Sammi?" Sophie asked.

Sammi took a final spoonful of mashed potatoes, licking it like an ice cream cone. "He just likes to be with us. You know, Nate's been watching our family and deciding. He's going to be born, and he's making plans. If he goes to our family, he'll learn certain things, but if he goes to another family, he'll learn other things."

"Those are pretty big decisions to make. Very important ones," Lizzie said.

"I wonder what his other choices are," Jonathan said.

Sammi shrugged. "They're important, and I'm excited because he told me good news. He made a decision."

"Can you tell us what it is?" Mark said.

She climbed up on her chair, stood, and threw her arms straight up into the air. "Yes!" she exclaimed with pure joy. "I'm so excited. Nate decided he's going to be my brother." She laughed and clapped.

The room was quiet with all the adults peering around at each other with blank stares. Jonathan immediately turned to Aria with a puzzled look. *Could Aria be pregnant?*

Aria shook her head. "I don't think so, honey."

"You're going to be surprised, then, Mama, 'cause there's a baby inside you right now!"

The room was rendered silent.

Jonathan noticed that no one knew what to say after Sammi's announcement. Maybe Aria was pregnant, even though she was on birth control. He played the concept over in his mind. He rather liked it. He loved being a dad, and having another child would be a welcome addition. He glanced again at Aria, but he couldn't read her facial expression. He knew some of the concepts involved in all of this spiritual information were hard for her to accept, but she'd been doing a lot of reading and asking questions and seemed more at peace with various ideas. He knew it would all work out as it was meant to be. But no one said another thing about it.

Sammi climbed down from the chair, delighted with the news she'd shared. Searching through Aria's purse, she found the pack of playing cards she'd brought along. "It's time to play Go Fish, my favorite card game," she said. After three rounds of the game, Lizzie announced it was dessert time: pie and coffee, with pink cupcakes for Sammi. Jonathan noticed that everyone was feeling the sleepy effects from overeating and the relaxing impact of the wine. He hoped he was awake enough to make the trip back to LA. Seeing all the smiling faces, hearing all the laughter, smelling the traditional scents of the season, tasting the comforting flavors, touching and hugging his loved ones—it was exactly the medicine his soul had craved. A part of him didn't want to leave.

But it was late, and they needed to get back on the road as Jonathan had an important breakfast meeting in the morning. As though she could read his thoughts, Aria pulled him aside. "Jonny, I'm wide awake and only had one glass of wine ages ago. I'm happy to drive us home, and you and Sammi can sleep on the way."

He looked at her lovingly, rubbing his hand on the small of her back. "Thanks, babe. I appreciate it." He kissed her on the lips.

"Sammi, can you get Maggie on her leash, and we'll take her outside for a walk before the ride back?" Jonathan asked.

"Sure, Daddy." She hooked the leash onto her collar, and Jonathan, Sammi, and Maggie took a stroll down the block together, while the others began the not-so-enviable chore of cleanup.

*

The night air was nippy, and Sammi stared up into the semi-lit sky. "Daddy, look at the moon!"

"It's so bright, isn't it? At least half of it is. We're looking at a half moon, so we're seeing exactly half of the moon all lit up while half of it is in shadow."

"I love walking while the moon is shining on me."

"Me too, sweetie. Me too." He held her right hand while she held Maggie's leash in her left hand.

"Daddy, are you excited that Nate is coming back to be with us?"

"I am, sweetheart. I'm glad you're happy too."

"Oh, look at this," she said. She bent down and picked up a shiny object from the sidewalk.

"What is it?"

"It's a silver coin. Can I keep it? I like it."

Jonathan's eyes welled up again, and he nodded. "That's the spirit of your Grandpa David giving you the message that he's here with us. He leaves coins as special signs for me." He paused briefly, absorbing the significance of his dad's gesture. "Now he's leaving one for you too."

"Thanks, Grandpa David," she said. "I love it." Sammi put it in the pocket of her skirt as they headed back for the journey home.

Could he feel more full and content? It was the perfect day.

Thanks, Dad. Happy Thanksgiving. I love you.

He blew a kiss to the heavens.

Chapter 7

The Nonphysical World

Malach, a spirit guide vibrating an indigo color, enters the monitoring area. He comes to mentor Pneuma and his intern, Neshamah.

Pneuma: It's good to see you, Malach. I need some guidance. This is my intern, Neshamah.

Malach: A pleasure to work with both of you.

Pneuma: Neshamah, Malach is Jonathan's main guide and my mentor. I've learned so much from his training.

Neshamah: Nice to meet you.

Pneuma: To catch you up on what I'm doing, Malach, look at the monitor. There were three opportunities to get this person on track with her life plan, and she hasn't taken any of them, so should I get involved here and give a nudge now, or wait for more opportunities to show up?

Malach: Let me take a look at what's been going on. Hmm ... yes, I see a simple remedy here. Watch the monitor. Observe the lines of possibilities as they light up. See if you see it.

Pneuma: Ahh ... sure I do. I need to get her to Olivia Buffet's yoga class and things will be back on track.

Malach: Yes, please proceed.

Pneuma: Thanks.

Malach: All's looking good. Nice job.

Chapter 8

December 3

At the end of her busy workday, Margo Phillips plopped down on the brown leather couch in her living room, grabbed her laptop, and sent an email to Thomas, her friend in Colorado. She knew she could go online and chat with him on Virtual-Time, but she was feeling lazy and didn't want to fix her hair and face—she was still wearing remnants of mascara, but other than that her face was devoid of makeup. She'd met Thomas online in a grief and loss forum, finding herself pleasantly surprised at how quickly they'd established a strong connection. At first, she'd been amazed at the level of friendship she could develop with someone without having ever met in person. *Maybe it's the anonymity that provides the security people need to open up and share their intimate thoughts. I guess that's how all of those catfishing scenarios on dating sites happens,* she thought.

It had been fascinating how much she could tell about a person's personality simply by their online style of writing and interacting. A whole year of emailing, texting, and Virtual-Timing had gone on before they'd physically met for the first time. What a relief when they'd discovered the same attraction in person that they'd had online. It had felt comforting to find a friend who had a similar outlook on life and some common interests. But meeting him had opened up a part of Margo that had long ago been closed off. She realized she'd been lonely: how odd she hadn't been aware of that before.

She'd learned on the forum that when people feel an instant rapport—that instantaneous click you sometimes feel—it often stems from remembering that person's soul from another life. Both she and Thomas had felt it, even if it was over cyberspace—the bond was definitely there.

At her age, Margo had never thought she'd meet someone romantically. *You never know what life has in store for you. There are always unexpected twists and turns.* Thomas was coming to town again—to take her out for a belated birthday dinner—and she felt as nervous as a young girl going out on her first date with the high school football quarterback.

Thomas had told her that after his wife had died, he'd experienced vivid dreams—dreams of visitations from her. His curiosity had gotten the best of him, and he'd just had to do an online search. He'd come across the grief and loss forum and had watched and observed the interactions of the members for half a year before he'd decided to become a contributing member. What a pleasant surprise when Margo had joined: finally someone else his age!

Margo had loved the way he wrote his posts—articulate, yet so loving and gracious. He was mellow and kind and had a great sense of humor. He lived alone, basically retired, but still doing speaking engagements as a motivational speaker.

In spite of her insistence on avoiding a birthday celebration, Thomas had planned the trip to San Diego in hopes that she'd change her mind and allow him to honor her seventieth birthday, and for that, she'd appreciated his thoughtfulness. Her birthday marked the tragic day her family had died—how could she possibly ever celebrate on that date! But, she'd figured, a special dinner on a different day would be acceptable.

She'd spent so many years living alone that she sometimes thought she'd forgotten how to be social. Not that she minded living alone. Not at all—it suited her. But she did enjoy having a companion for social events and an occasional dinner and a show. And of course it would be nice to have someone to travel with—she'd always wanted to see a bit of the world.

Turning seventy seemed mind-boggling. Where had her life gone? When had she gotten so old? She thought she was physically aging pretty well—and, thankfully, she didn't mentally feel anywhere near her age. She still colored her hair a golden blonde—no gray for her—and kept herself in good physical shape. Okay, maybe a bit of aching in her knees and hips at times, maybe a bit of high blood pressure ... but otherwise, she felt ten years younger than she was. She did note how she avoided looking in mirrors more than she had years ago. Discovering new wrinkles bothered her; she wasn't looking forward to the day when she might look like an apple doll.

Apple dolls had been so much fun to make when she was a young girl. Each autumn, she'd spent hours making them with her sister. Firm McIntosh apples made the best ones. They'd carefully peel them, exposing the white flesh, and then whittled them with small paring knives into faces with eyes, nose, mouth and ears and maybe a few laugh lines. Briefly soaking the heads in lemon juice and sprinkling them with salt preserved them for drying. The next step was to hang then out in the sunshine for about a month. Almost like magic, they'd turn into wizened faces, every one unique, ready to be made into a witch doll, a Santa Claus or a little old man or woman.

Each had their own personality; some ended up looking cantankerous and ornery, while others looked centered and at peace, as though they smiled with a twinkle in their eyes. To put the finishing touches on them, her mom had spent hours on end sewing bodies and clothing for the dolls. The most fun part had been decorating them with something that made them unique: maybe some white hair; maybe a hat or scarf and miniature glasses; maybe a touch of blush on their cheeks and lips. If she turned out looking like a wrinkled apple doll, Margo hoped at least it would be one that looked happy—she didn't want to end up a cranky old woman.

Although it seemed amazing to most people, Margo still worked every day except Sundays. She'd been a hairdresser since she was in her twenties and eventually bought the salon when it went up for sale. People were surprised she could stand all day on her feet at her age, working with her hands, but she loved it, thoroughly enjoying her interactions with clients—many of whom had been customers for years. Many days, she'd felt she had a common bond with bartenders and therapists as she listened and advised people on their loves and losses in life. Her manner was always considerate and warm, and people opened up to her easily.

Both she and Thomas had experienced so much loss in their lives, and she recognized that in many ways trauma can be a bonding experience—knowing each other's pain without having to explain it was very comforting. They'd already spent time writing and talking about their personal histories. Hers was something she rarely shared with other people—it was still hard for her to talk about those deeply agonizing events.

She'd had a complicated past. At the tender age of eighteen, Margo and her nineteen-year-old boyfriend had been forced by their parents to marry after reluctantly informing them that she was pregnant. She'd been scared and embarrassed—her parents, horrified.

It was essentially an old-fashioned shotgun wedding, so she hadn't been surprised when her husband had run out on her the day the babies were born. He'd had no desire to be a father. They'd had twins—a boy and a girl—but he'd never met them. Margo had known it would be too much for a nineteen-year-old boy to handle a responsibility of such colossal proportions, so she hadn't felt disappointed he'd left. She'd never loved him, so it really hadn't felt like a big loss when he'd walked out. But with twins, it had turned out to be more than she could handle on her own at her young age. With their devotion and love, her parents had taken her and the kids in to their home to provide her with the support she needed. She'd always been Daddy's girl, and her father had been particularly supportive of her. Her mother had died in a tragic car accident when she was only twenty-two, and that loss bonded her even closer to her dad. Although he'd remarried a few years later, their special connection had never been broken.

She'd ziplined through her life, and it wasn't until the past few years that she'd realized time was beginning to run out. One New Year's Eve, she'd made the resolution to live her life more fully—whatever was left of it. She hadn't been looking to remarry, but seeing a bit of the world with a companion would be a dream come true.

Paris. Paris was her dream. Paris in the springtime. Paris anytime. She imagined herself eating pain au chocolat at a sidewalk café, strolling through museums—utterly mesmerized by the artwork—and lingering for hours at sidewalk cafes, drinking café au lait and watching people stroll by. Maybe someday … but someday better show up fairly fast.

She'd placed her life on hold for a long time after the family deaths. It was something she still found difficult to verbalize. What was there to say when your children and father were there one day and gone forever the next? After their deaths, it had taken her a long time to get to a place of reconciliation with life. In the beginning, she'd wondered what kind of supreme being would allow such cruelty. Was she being punished in some way? In the immediate days after the tragedy, she'd sometimes sit in the dark in the corner of the kitchen, her back pressed against the wall, as she'd tried to make peace with her loneliness and pain. She'd cry until her very soul felt empty, but later, she hadn't been able to produce tears and that bothered her even more. The agony had eventually turned into a Novocain-like feeling of numbness. Sometimes she'd just sit, perfectly still: there'd been no reason for her to move. She'd craved hearing the sounds that were missing from her life: giggling and laughter, hearing someone say "Mommy," the gentle sounds of the children's breathing as they slept at night. She'd missed it so much.

She'd had a very hard time facing the world while emotionally living in a desperate space. But Margo had become wiser over the years; her aloneness had allowed her to spend time in internal thought and healing. It had been a process, of course—all growth is a process. But as she approached seventy, she'd decided to open some doors: take some classes, make some friends. It was time to move on. What motivates someone to come to that place suddenly one day, she didn't know.

She'd wondered if it was divine inspiration, because one day when she'd been meditating, she'd received a strong inspiration—kind of a jolting sensation in her head—to search online for some meetups in her area of San Diego. She'd found one not too far from the hair salon where she worked. It was at Olivia Buffet's yoga studio, with classes specifically for silver foxes. Secretly, Margo hated that name. She wasn't a silver fox in her mind, but she knew she wasn't limber enough to join the classes with the twenty-and thirty-year-olds. So she put her big toe in the water and signed up on her lunch break, paid her enrollment fee, and planned to stop on the way home and get a mat and some yoga pants.

Margo's birthday fell on a Friday—her first day of yoga class. *I'm just going to treat this day like any other.* She felt an overall sense of anxiety, a feeling she'd experienced every year on that date. After work, she'd entered the studio, finding herself impressed. It was contemporary and clean and had a meditative, Zen-like quality to it. The walls were mirrored with bars attached, and the floors were shiny, with green plants lining the perimeter. Her first class had gone well, but she could feel how tight she was, especially in her hamstrings and back muscles. Olivia had assured Margo she'd see a dramatic change in her flexibility in a short period of time. She hoped so. She didn't want to live on painkillers as she aged.

Until today, Margo had had no idea Olivia had read over her sign-up card and had noticed her birthday was coming up, apparently thinking she'd surprise her as she did for all her clients.

She had been shocked when Olivia had ended the class five minutes early—announcing they had a special birthday to celebrate after class—while Sophie Hobbs wheeled a magnificent cake she'd created out on a cart. Tears rolled down Margo's cheeks. She felt conflicted—touched that someone would do that for her, but also feeling she should never celebrate her birthday. After Sophie cut the cake, she pulled Margo aside.

"What's wrong? Are you okay?" Sophie asked.

Margo wiped her tears, swiping with her thumbs. "You're so kind and thoughtful. I'm just feeling emotional. I haven't celebrated my birthday for years. It just touched me, and I appreciate the kindness. It was a traumatic day for me many years ago. People in my family died on this day."

"Oh no ... I'm so sorry to hear that. So no celebratory plans for today?" Sophie asked with a solemn tone of voice.

Margo looked down at the floor and shook her head. "No, I don't do special things on this day."

"My husband is out of town giving a lecture," Sophie cajoled, "so let me take you out to dinner. We won't celebrate. We'll just have dinner together. Why don't we change and we'll go? I'll drive and bring you back later for your car."

"I walked here today. But I'm not sure ... I don't think so."

Sophie gently touched her on the elbow and looked her in the eyes. "Of course we must. I won't take no for an answer. You shouldn't be alone on a day like this."

Sophie's kind gesture touched something deep within Margo's heart. Although she felt conflicted, she decided to step outside her box of self-imposed rules and join Sophie for dinner. *Why not?* Always up for trying a new restaurant, she agreed when Sophie suggested the Vagabond—a relaxed, funky little place with bohemian artifacts and décor. It was quaint, dimly lit, cozy. A Peruvian dish of fiery peppers and fall-off-the bone lamb on buttery rice sounded good to Sophie, and Margo decided on sea bass wrapped in bok choy. They swooned over every last bite.

"You're very kind to take me to dinner, Sophie. It touches me."

"Well, I'm just a sucker for birthdays and a firm believer in celebration, even though we aren't really officially celebrating. I believe we need to find our joyful moments. It's the business I'm in, my passion."

"Your cake business does sound like 'happy work' to me. It's just hard to celebrate on a date that was so tragic in my life."

"I understand how those dates stick in our minds. My first husband committed suicide in our garage on August twenty-first, 1987."

"Oh my," Margo said as she shook her head, "my year was 1979. Sophie, I'm so sorry to hear about your husband. How did you get through handling a suicide? What a horrific tragedy."

"With the help of some very special friends. My current husband, Matthew, worked with me on the healing process. He did a past life hypnotherapy session with me where I regressed to a past life as a Native American woman. My son was killed in that life at a young age, and I'd never gotten over it. The spirit of my son in that life is now my godson, Jonathan. He came to me in this life to teach me that the soul is eternal—he's the living proof. It was the most powerful, healing event of my life. Truly profound for me. Changed my whole viewpoint on life and death. From my healing process, I learned forgiveness. Another very powerful tool in the arsenal of life."

"Actually, on my grief and loss forum, several people had talked about having an awareness that their loved ones who passed on were people they previously knew in a past life. The idea is intriguing."

"If you still feel unresolved issues, you could try working with my husband. He's a very good spiritual counselor if I do say so myself."

"But it wasn't a past life—it was this life. However, I would like to release some of the guilt and anguish I feel. Would he be able to help me contact them from the spirit world? I've moved on over the years and learned a great deal, but I'd love a sign or message from them."

"Well, my husband's death wasn't a past life either. I'm not sure if he could make contact with them or not. Each case is different. Do you want me to check, or do you want to call him?"

"Oh, thanks, I'll give him a call. You know ... I do believe grief and loss are great teachers. It makes us stop the distractions going on in life and look at what is real."

"Yes, grief is extremely powerful and usually catches you when you are totally unprepared."

"Unprepared? Absolutely. I reached a point, though, where I didn't want to wallow anymore. I didn't want to miss the purpose of this life and to have to repeat lessons I didn't learn. Once is enough for me. One must not consistently miss the point of a lifetime," Margo said.

"That's the value of delving into past lives for me. You learn things that help you get through this life with, maybe, less suffering. I learned that from my Native American life experience."

Margo took a couple of sips of her pinot grigio. "Me? I'm an overachiever. I just want to get on with the lesson, learn it, and move on. I was that way in school too."

"Call him—my husband, I mean. It's worth it to see if you can heal further. The release is so fantastic."

"Oh, I don't know if there's any point at my age. It's a bit late in the day for that."

"Nonsense. It's never too late to heal and grow. I think the third chapter of your life is the best time to finish old business that's yearning to be resolved."

"Maybe so. I used to feel the presence of my kids near me, but less so now. I wish I could hold them once more. They were gone too soon. People talk about closure, but to me, there's no such thing. But I didn't get to say goodbye, and for some reason I just want to say it."

Sophie gasped. "Wait, Margo. I had no idea you lost your *kids* ... more than one?"

Margo nodded and turned her head away from Sophie, attempting to regain her composure.

Sophie noticed her distress and attempted to distract her so she didn't have to endure publicly releasing a flood of tears. She reached out, grasping the back of Margo's hand and gently squeezing it.

"I think I'll change the topic since I still don't seem able to verbalize what happened. Dessert?" Margo asked.

While they studied the dessert menu, Margo composed herself again. All the talk about loss with Sophie took Margo's thoughts back in time all those years ago. "People say they move forward from tragedy. But how do you do it? What I learned is you must open yourself and release. Feel the emotions, the pain, the suffering, and open up and release it. Stop the resistance. Accept and bend when the wind blows instead of fighting it," Margo said.

The waiter delivered a decadent-looking dessert, two spoons, and two cups of coffee. Sophie dug her spoon into the chocolate lava cake, scooping out the decadent, thick goo. "Oh my God, this is so good. Dig in and share this with me." She handed Margo one of the spoons. "Yes, what you're saying is so true. As soon as we stop resisting, everything changes. I call it 'let life.' Just let life. The problem is still there, but our perspective changes."

Margo took a spoonful of the dessert Sophie offered. "This is scrumptious! I do hear what you're saying. Grief is an insistent beast and simply demands to be listened to. It's the bridge we use to cross over to new lines of thinking. When we're in a place of discomfort or pain, we're much more driven to find the answers that give everything a more profound meaning."

"Oh, I agree that adversity is a moving factor. A powerful one."

"So I'm curious," Margo said. "Was it love at first sight for you and your husband?"

"If it was, we weren't aware of it. He was intent on his role as a spiritual counselor, and I was so stuck in my trauma. A point came when I realized I'd been in love with him for a long time, but I didn't see it then. You simply must meet him. You'll like him. Everyone does."

"Oh, heavens, I'm so full!" Margo said, shoving her plate to the side. "Well, you've been very kind. I should get going. Busy day tomorrow. Thanks for the evening, Sophie. It was cathartic to me."

"Anytime, Margo. I had a lovely time."

They left the restaurant and Sophie drove the short distance to Margo's house, pulling up to the front of the house to drop her off.

Margo exited the car, hesitated a moment, then leaned in to speak to Sophie. "Thank you for driving me. Do you want to come in for a decaf?"

Sophie paused momentarily, then said, "Sure, for a few minutes."

While Margo made the coffee, Sophie stood in the kitchen, looking around. "I love these old houses in this section of town. What year is this?"

"It's a 1925 three-bedroom, two-bath Craftsman bungalow. I know it's in major need of renovation. Especially the kitchen—I'd love an upgrade in here. I remodeled the two bathrooms a few years ago." She noticed that Sophie had picked up a photo of a small dog from her knickknack shelf.

"What a cute dog," Sophie said as she returned the frame to the shelf.

"That's Brewster. He was my dad's dog. Gosh, he loved that dog so much. They had a very special kind of bond. It was funny to see my big dad with a little dog like a Boston Terrier. After my dad died, I took care of Brewster until he passed on. He was such a great source of comfort for me. It's like he looked out for me, and I always felt safer with him around."

They sat at the kitchen table with their steaming cups of decaf, contemplating life.

"So you chose not to remarry?" Sophie asked.

Margo shook her head. "I never felt like I could open myself up to it. I married young because I was pregnant. The baby-daddy was only nineteen, and the day our twins were born, he took off. Then a couple of years ago, I re-met a man at my pottery class that I had dated years ago. He seemed interested, but I just wasn't open to a relationship at that time. Then, I met a very interesting man online in the grief and loss forum—Thomas. He's going to be in town in a couple of days."

"Oh, that's wonderful. You know, I'd love to meet him sometime." Sophie glanced at her watch. "I've had a nice time, but I need to get going. We have to do this again." She rummaged through her wallet, then pulled out a business card and handed it to Margo. "Here's my husband's card with his phone number. Do give him a call. You'll love him."

"Thank you. You're beyond generous and kind."

"It was my pleasure. Happy birthday, Margo. See you at class."

Chapter 9

December 3

Even though the kitchen in her apartment was very organized, Olivia couldn't find where she had stored her tortilla press. Thinking it was somewhere in the back of one of her cabinets, she rummaged through the bottom cupboard, taking everything out and stacking pots and pans on the terracotta-tiled floor to find it. She couldn't believe how much useless kitchen paraphernalia she'd collected. *There it is—in the far back corner!* She figured she should have just bought a package of tortillas at the store like everyone else would do. But she'd learned how to make them in a Mexican cooking class and decided to try them out on Jax for the first of his promised dinners. *He probably won't even notice they're homemade.* While humming a song that had earwormed itself into her head, she pressed each ball of dough in the press and then cooked them over medium heat in a large nonstick skillet. She stacked the hot tortillas in a basket, keeping them warm with a cloth napkin.

Jax arrived thirty minutes late, as usual. She'd made beef brisket in the slow cooker for the tacos and was whipping up a bowl of her favorite guacamole when he rang the bell.

Olivia opened the door to find his arms loaded down with bottles of wine, and he leaned in and kissed her on the cheek. "Hey, sweetness. What smells like a slice of heaven in here?"

"Beef brisket for tacos. What did you bring? You didn't have to bring anything."

"I did have to. Have you ever known me to come empty-handed? No, you have not. I brought some great wines. Hunter and I recently went up to Temecula for a wine tasting and came back with a few cases. We're going to use one of the wineries for our wedding wine and put our own label on it."

"That's a great idea. Come sit down at the table and talk to me while I finish up here. So how are the wedding plans going?"

He plopped down on one of the kitchen chairs. "Livie, we found this incredible home near the winery to rent for the venue. It's perfect! I'll show you some pictures on my phone. Sit, sit, and come look."

Olivia joined him at the kitchen table as he scrolled through the photos. "These are really great photos. You do have an eye for photography. This house is unbelievable."

"Look at this. This is where we'll have the reception and dancing. Isn't this an awesome room? Pitched wooden ceiling, chandeliers, harlequin-tiled floor, low banister all around closing it all in. French doors to the outside. It sits on a five-acre landscaped garden. It has ten bedrooms, so some people—special people—can just sleep there that night."

She flicked to the next photo. "Oh my God. That master suite! You guys will stay there on your wedding night, right?"

"That's the plan."

"I want to stay in the room with you! Look at that master bath. Three steps up to soak in that massive tub. That would be one glorious bubble bath. That's awesome."

"I know. And look at this tropical spa room. And the waterfall and pool."

"That's a great house. What a cool idea, and right there in wine country. I'm sure glad I'm invited."

"It's exciting, but making wedding plans shows you a person's true personality. I seem to have little say in this. That's okay, though. For me, I've always thought of weddings as the biggest exercise in narcissism there is, but it's important to Hunter, and he knows just what he wants, so I'm letting him run with it as he wishes. He's adamant about every detail and, honestly, I just don't care as long as it makes him happy and the wedding is sexy."

"A sexy wedding. Hmm ... I've never heard of that as one of the criteria for a wedding. Well, let me talk to a lady in my yoga class who makes the best cakes. You must use her for your reception. I kid you not. Best cake ever."

"Sure, if I can get approval from the boss. I think if people make it through the wedding, the rest of the marriage must be a breeze. I didn't realize how bossy Hunter can be."

"I've seen some interesting personality traits emerge from friends who have planned their weddings. Hunter's just a take-charge kind of guy."

"Well, I've heard of bridezillas, but not groomzillas. He wants a Renaissance masquerade wedding, and before you say it, yes, he's serious."

"With all the guests wearing a mask?"

"Yes ..."

"That's different."

"I know, right? He has a fascination with it. It's his dream wedding."

"I never heard of it before. For a wedding, I mean."

"Me either. He said in the 1300s, masquerade balls were these far-out elegant pageants that they used to celebrate marriages and other medieval court events. In fact, the first known masquerade wedding in history took place in 1393 to celebrate the marriage of some lady-in-waiting of some French queen in Paris. They sounded like they were these ostentatious costumed dances that were reserved for the uppity-uppities. I guess they're a part of history."

"I can't imagine people in this day and age going to the trouble of dressing up. People are kind of lazy about that stuff. Sometimes it's hard enough to get them to even go to the wedding at all. One of my coworkers invited a hundred and fifty guests to their wedding, and only about seventy-five showed up. People even RSVP'd they were coming and then didn't show."

"Well ... you don't know our friends. They'll most definitely come in costume and mask. Most are into the Renaissance fairs like we are and many make their own costumes. Anyway, the part I love is that the theme behind wearing masks at masquerade events is hiding one's identity. That's just so me, isn't it?"

"It sure is."

"I like being mysterious. In the old days, at the masked balls, no one would reveal who they were until well after midnight. This tradition goes back to Venice, Italy. Apparently it was a time when anonymity was hard to come by and being judged by others was pretty commonplace. You couldn't be shady without someone knowing who you were. The mask gave them a bit of the privacy they craved along with an opportunity to hide their true personality. The masks will let everyone feel free to say and do what they want without judgment."

"That's interesting. But I don't think a mask will eliminate the judgment. I think I could get into it, though. I have a bunch of mask ideas floating around in my head already."

Jax found the battery-operated wine opener, removed the cork from the bottle, and poured two glasses. He clapped his hands and rubbed them together. "Okay ... here's my big request. I want you to be my best man, woman, best person at my wedding. Please say yes."

Olivia assumed a thinking posture. "Let me think ... do I have to throw you a bachelor party?"

"Of course, and it needs to be down and dirty."

"Oh Lord. I'm not sure I'm the best person to set that up for you."

"My friend, James, will help you. Just say yes."

"Of course I will. Makes me tear up that you asked me. Thank you. It's all coming together, Jax. I'm so excited for the two of you."

"Thank you. Now I can't wait another minute to eat. That smell is driving me crazy. Are we ready?"

"We are. I set up a taco bar on the counter, so you can make your own and add whatever you want. There's cheese, lettuce, onions, homemade guacamole and salsa. And of course, the beef."

"Can I make myself five?"

"Make as many as you like."

He picked up a few tortillas and created his tacos. Jax took a bite, then put his plate down and approached Olivia, standing behind her—hugging her around the neck while planting a kiss on her cheek.

"What's that for?" she asked, turning her head to look up at him.

"I'm blown out of the water. These are genuine homemade tortillas. Did you make them?"

"I did. Proof is in the dishwasher—my tortilla press."

Jax returned to his seat, taking another bite. "Don't talk to me for a minute. I'm busy feeling euphoric. These are out-of-this-world incredible. I'm now spoiled forever. You know the tacos are delicious when you start wearing them on your shirt." He dabbed at the dripping juices with his napkin. "I wonder if I can get Hunter to make these."

"I imagine you have ways of persuading him," Olivia said as she plopped a huge spoonful of guacamole on her taco.

"Oh, I do, I do. So you think I knew him in another life?"

"Possibly. Probably." Olivia tilted her head to the side and bit her lip. "You both have a thing for that time period. Making costumes and dressing for the Renaissance and all. And you said there was an instant connection between the two of you. More important, do you think so?"

"I guess. But honestly, why would we bother to come back over and over?"

"To teach. To learn. To balance our karma. To grow our souls, advancing level after level."

"Oh, like the Candy Crush game. We can't go to the next level until we learn the nitty-gritty of the one we are on and pass it. I got so addicted to that darn game."

"Yeah, and some levels are much harder to pass than others. And coming back again gives us a chance to clear our karma with each other."

"Honey, I don't give a damn about karma. Really. Why do we even care about karma?"

"That's okay if you don't. But I do. That ol' unbalanced karma is going to stop me from reaching my full potential. The purpose of karma is to help you become a better person."

"I already am a good person. And so are you."

Olivia shook her head.

"What? Are you judging?"

"Not at all. You're a really good person. I was just thinking about what you said. That's me. That's my life. One big masquerade event.

And it must be after midnight, because I'm taking my mask off and revealing myself to you. My mask has given me a chance to hide out for many years now."

Jax helped himself to another taco. "So are you ready to tell me the details?"

"I've thought about it, and I am, but I'll do it another night. For some reason I feel beat tonight. Too many sleepless nights. I'm just so exhausted."

"Really? I'm worried because you've been tired an awful lot. I hope you aren't sick or something. I'll try to be patient, but the suspense is getting to me. I don't have to work for a couple of days, so I thought we'd be up late chitchatting tonight."

"Sorry about that," Olivia said as she leaned over and patted his cheek.

"I may go in tomorrow anyway. My favorite patient, George, has been in and out of the hospital, and I'd kind of like to be the one who takes care of him. He always asks for me."

Olivia held her index finger in the air in a moment of thought. "Oh, that reminds me. Remember that hat I had knit for you that he liked so much?"

"Yep, he almost stole it off my head. He said a bald guy needed a nice hat like that more than I did."

"Well, I made him one. I even wrapped it in a box with a bow. Remind me to get it for you before you leave."

"Aww ... that's so sweet, Livie."

"So, in keeping with my Mexican theme, I made us some mini churros for dessert. Do you want coffee with them?"

"You have any decaf?"

"I do. I'll make us each a cup." She placed a coffee pod in the machine and brewed two cups.

Olivia brought a plate of the sugary cinnamon churros to the table, laughing out loud at their shape. "Hot out of the deep fryer. Well, by now I guess they're just warm."

Jax picked up one of the odd-shaped objects, turning it over in his hand, examining it. "What happened to them? They look like a Chernobyl experiment gone wrong. They're usually a long, fluted fritter. I think these exploded or something."

"I know, right? I made the mistake of adding baking powder and the recipe didn't call for it, and the dough seemed to grow when they hit the hot oil. They're delicious, though. Taste it."

He bit into it, spraying cinnamon and sugar in the air. "You're right. They're wonderful. Thanks for going to all this trouble for me."

"No trouble. It was fun."

"I like this idea of you cooking dinner for me. Let's make more deals like that."

"We don't need a deal. My kitchen is always open for you."

"Okay, but don't put me off on telling me your secret again. I want to be there for you and hear your story, okay?"

"I promise. I just need a good night of sleep without any nightmares."

Jax reached into the pocket of his jacket, hanging on the back of his chair, and handed Olivia an envelope.

"What's this?" she asked with a puzzled look on her face.

He gave her a Cheshire cat smile. "Open it and it will no longer be a mystery."

She opened the fancy silver envelope to retrieve a beautiful gold invitation with a narrow pearl-embossed filigree border.

"It's an invite to our house for a grand Christmas dinner. We're having it catered, Charles Dickens Christmas style. Roast goose with sage and onion dressing. Plum pudding with hard sauce for dessert.

Bring a unisex wrapped gift of around twenty-five dollars for our Secret Santa game."

She raised her eyes to look at him. It had been so many years since she had spent Christmas with anyone; it almost didn't bother her anymore. The invitation touched her in a way she didn't expect. Jax was like the silver lining in her cloud. "I'm honored for the invite, and put me down as a yes."

"It'll be more fun than you can imagine. It's Hunter's and my first holiday dinner we're hosting as a couple."

They ate their dessert and chatted another hour until Jax caught her yawning. They said good night, Jax took George's gift with him, and Olivia decided to clean up the next day. She didn't feel any relief as she *still* hadn't told Jax.

I wonder why I keep procrastinating about telling Jax my story!

Chapter 10

December 3

She was shocked; there was no doubt about it. Aria drove home from the doctor's office deep in thought as she recalled how surprised she'd been during the Thanksgiving celebration when Sammi had stated that Nate was joining their family as her brother. In her heart, she hadn't believed it, but Sammi had said it with such conviction. At first she'd hoped she wasn't pregnant because she didn't know how she'd fit a second child into her busy life, but on the other hand, she felt very excited at the thought of welcoming another baby. *Do other women feel as torn as this?* She hoped, for some reason, that if there was a baby, it wouldn't be someone they knew in a past life, but Jonathan said it was highly likely the baby would be from their soul group and have past connections, whether they were aware of it or not.

But when Aria missed her period, she began to wonder what was going on. After all, she'd planned this out with Jonathan. They'd have one child. She was on the pill. She knew there was a failure rate with them, but she was surprised it could happen to her. It was a bit of a shock to see that her home pregnancy test was positive. *Really, how could Sammi know this?* She'd decided to confirm it with the doctor before saying anything. Now, having the results validated, she knew Sammi was right. She was pregnant. *Is Nate really coming?*

Once Sammi was asleep in bed, Jonathan and Aria sat in the family room on the love seat, drinking tea and eating a late-night omelet, when she told Jonathan the news.

Jonathan jumped up, pulled her to stand, and hugged her, lifting her feet off the ground, spinning her around. "This is awesome, Aria! When are we due?"

She laughed, then sat back down and took a bite of her omelet, twirling the melted strings of cheese with her fork. "August twenty-sixth. I'm very excited, but I'm not sure how this happened," Aria said, her voice shaking with emotion.

"Well, you know the pill isn't one hundred percent effective, but I'm surprised. It sounds great to me. Meant to be. You're acting kind of odd. You're not really happy?" He took her free hand, placing his hand over hers, massaging the back with his thumbs.

She hesitated for a moment. "I am. Very much. It's just that—"

"Just what?"

"Oh, nothing. I mean … nothing."

Jonathan waited for her to continue.

"I love the idea that it would be, could be Nate. I mean, I know it's not Nate as the baby will have a different personality and body and all, but I'm glad the spirit of Nate is coming to us. But why am I having such a hard time grasping that could really be true?"

"Babe, you don't *have* to grasp it. Maybe you're just not ready for that. In the end, it doesn't make any difference, does it? He'll be a new personality. Don't even think about that. Just enjoy the pregnancy the same way you did with Sammi. Don't worry about who is what. Once he's here in the flesh, Sammi won't be thinking of him as Nate any longer."

Aria shook her head. "I've been ruminating about this jealousy thing I seem to have going on. It's not very attractive. Or healthy."

"So did you come to any conclusions?"

She exhaled the pent-up emotions she'd buried in one long drawn-out sigh. "I think it started when I was a kid. I was the first child in the family, and I knew, from hearing about it so often when I was growing up, that my parents had wanted their firstborn to be a son. My dad was very disappointed I was a girl. When my brother, Joe, was born, there was such celebration. They were overjoyed to have a boy, and there wasn't a day that went by where I didn't feel that he got special attention. I was positive they loved him more than me."

"I didn't realize that. I'm sorry." Jonathan continued to lovingly rub her hand.

"I hadn't really thought about it. Then one day, all of these painful thoughts surfaced. I still feel he's their favorite child! I thought having one child would be a good idea for us. There wouldn't be any favoritism going on. I never would want to do that to a child of mine."

"Were you disappointed your first child wasn't a boy?"

"Oh no, never for a moment. Truly, I just wanted a healthy child. My hope and wish came true. How about you?"

"The gender just didn't and doesn't matter to me."

"Now that I'm aware of that, I think I can work on letting it go."

"That's great, Aria. Shining light on our darkness is very healing."

"Jonny?"

"Yeah?"

"Thank you for that." She instantly felt better. He'd taken the pressure off of her. "Sammi said it's going to be a boy, and we should name him Tyson. I looked the name up, and the personal characteristics associated with that name are creativity, optimism, and happiness. I love those qualities."

"I agree. I actually like it. But if I know you, you'll be making lists of names."

"Probably ..."

Unfortunately, Sammi's nightmares had returned, once again causing all of them sleepless nights. Aria wished that Sammi felt comfortable enough to talk about it without fear of hurting her feelings or upsetting her. For some reason, Aria felt guilty that she couldn't personally ease her anguish.

Jonathan was frowning when he emerged from Sammi's bedroom after soothing her back to sleep. He returned to the couch next to Aria while she poured them another cup of tea.

"I used to have lucid dreams that sometimes freaked me out. I'm not sure of the best way to get her to resolve the trapped energy. I think we should see that lady Matthew talked about," Jonathan said.

"She talks about everything! Why does she not want to talk about it?"

"I still think she worries it will upset you."

"Then she should talk about it with you."

"Let's see if the woman, Olivia, can get her to release the traumatic energy. I'll call her and see if we can sync our schedules for an appointment. I'm really booked solid for a few weeks but will figure a way to fit this in."

"Please do, Jonny. We need to put these nightmares to rest. This needs to be resolved."

Chapter 11

December 22

It was a gray morning with a light drizzle when Margo picked Thomas up at the bustling San Diego airport, where no matter the time of day, there was always a traffic jam. Airport authorities didn't allow drivers to pull over and sit at the curb to wait for their arrivals, so she'd already driven around the airport loop five times waiting for him to materialize from baggage claim. After her sixth loop around, she saw Thomas emerge from the terminal, pulling his navy-blue suitcase behind him. Her breathing quickened. *I'm really excited about his visit!* Finally, she saw a vacant spot and pulled to the curb to pick him up, waving at him until they'd made eye contact. She glanced in the rearview mirror to check her makeup and fluff her hair.

He's so good looking, she thought. Such a nice full head of white hair and riveting, electric-blue eyes. He wore a world of experience on his face, with a soft expression and an affable smile. She pressed the key fob to remotely open the rear tailgate of her car and hopped out to greet him, leaving the keys in the car, motor running. They gave each other an unfettered embrace and kiss. *Mmm, he smells like a mixture of sunshine and beach sand.* She felt a bit nervous about how to act due to the newness of their developing relationship but decided to simply drop the worries and live in the moment, with every intention of thoroughly enjoying his visit.

As Thomas slid into the passenger seat, Margo returned to in the driver's seat, diligently watching over her left shoulder, waiting for the cars to pass so she could inch out from the curb. "I'll be less stressed once I get away from this traffic mess," she assured him. "It's just so good to see you! Your plane made it right on time. Good flight?"

He affectionately placed his hand on her knee. "It's great to see you too. Yes, it was a good flight and everything went well. You have no idea how much I've been looking forward to this visit. Thanks for picking me up. So I decided to stay at the Sheraton this time. It's near here, right?"

Margo glanced out of the corner of her eye at him, a bit trepidatiously, as she slowly merged into her lane. "I don't want to seem too forward, but you're welcome to stay with me if you're comfortable with it. I have a guest room you can use. It would save on back-and-forth driving."

"Thanks. That's not too forward for me. I just don't want to be an imposition."

"You won't be. I've been excited about this visit as it's been quite a few months since our last get-together. What's new since we last chatted?" Margo asked. "I feel like we haven't talked for so long."

"I'll fill you in. Want to stop for a coffee over there? I could use some caffeine. And I'll make a call and cancel my hotel reservation."

"Sounds great."

They stopped at the Deja Brew coffee shop, deciding to sit outside, under the patio umbrellas, in spite of it being a bit damp. Thomas ordered and brought her a salted caramel latte. She took a quick sip of her coffee, burning her tongue. Her cheeks warmed as his gaze lingered on her. She hoped she didn't have lipstick on her teeth.

Thomas slowly tore open a yellow packet of sweetener and stirred it into his black coffee. "I find I'm liking this partial retirement thing more and more. I love the flexibility of being a consultant, especially because I can arrange my own training schedule. I enjoy being a motivational speaker, but I like it even more now that I schedule my own calendar. I feel kind of guilty, just doing whatever I want since Nadine passed. I never thought my wife would die before me—let alone from dementia. When she was still alive, I always felt I shouldn't be away for too long, even though she didn't remember who I was when I visited. Dementia is really hard on the loved ones. It's different now being on my own. Feels a bit lonely, I guess. And neither you nor I have grandkids to visit," Thomas said.

"Yes, I know loneliness. I imagine it was heartbreaking to see your wife and not have her recognize you. And I was just thinking the other day that I'm missing out by not having grandkids."

Thomas nodded and lowered his voice as he expressed his reflections. "When we found out Nadine couldn't have children, we thought about adopting, but we never followed through with it. I can't imagine how tough life has been for you, losing your family."

"We all go through loss, don't we? I was talking with a lady friend of mine, and we agreed we all want just one more day with our loved ones."

"Isn't that the truth?" Thomas said between sips of his hot beverage.

"To say things we wish we had said, but didn't."

"That's why we should always say things to people and not hold back. Tell them we love them and appreciate them, because you never know if you'll get another opportunity."

Margo removed the lid of her coffee to let it cool. "Before the accident, as I was putting my daughter to bed, I saw one of the drawings she'd made that day. She loved to color, and I found a drawing she'd made of her and me. It was the oddest thing. I was front and center in the drawing, and she was far off in the distance in the upper right corner of the paper with a halo of light around her head."

Thomas raised his eyebrows. "And she said it was her?"

"Yes, and before she went to bed, she said to me, 'Mommy, remember I don't want you to be sad.' I said, 'I'm not sad, my love.' The next day my life changed forever, and I became acquainted with sorrow."

Thomas reached out, placing his hand on top of hers and gently rubbed it. "That's so powerful! Margo, please know this. I'm not afraid of your pain and sorrow—it doesn't scare me."

Margo reached up and pushed her hair out of her eyes. She knew her face couldn't hide the reality that her heart couldn't bear. She nodded, pressing her lips tightly together in hopes of preventing tears.

Thomas noticed something on her arm he hadn't been aware of before as she reached up to her hair. He shook his head. "I guess I didn't notice before, but is that a tattoo on your inner wrist? How did I miss seeing that?"

"Yes. It's an infinity tattoo." She turned her arm over to show him. "Most of the time I wear a watch that covers it. Around this loop I have three hearts—one for my father, one for my daughter, one for my son. One of the loops of the infinity circle spells love." She rubbed her wrist. "I'm a heart collector. Hearts are a symbol for me that the love connection is never broken. I find them in all sorts of magical places, like they're little secret messages to me. Did you know that in Ancient Greece, they thought the human heart contained a person's soul?"

"That's interesting and strange. Nadine collected hearts too. I have her collection in a box in the attic."

Margo smiled, showing her recently whitened teeth. "Sounds like Nadine and I had more in common than just liking you. Are you ready to head out?" Margo asked as they finished their coffee.

Thomas glanced at his watch and gulped down the remainder of his coffee. "Sure. Would you mind if we didn't go directly to your house? I planned a few things at the Hotel Del Coronado for us, and I didn't realize the time."

"Sure. What're we doing?"

"It's a surprise." He wore a mischievous grin as he reached for her hand, walking her back to the car.

As they drove along the harbor, the sun began to peek out from the gray clouds and Thomas donned his black-rimmed sunglasses. "Now I feel like I'm in California! So tell me a bit more about your birthday. You said you'd fill in the details when we got together. I know you weren't looking forward to that day."

"Actually, it was really pleasant. One of the women in my yoga class made me a beautiful cake and then insisted on taking me to dinner. I hadn't celebrated my birthday for years, but it felt nice. And of course you sent me that beautiful bouquet of flowers."

"Well, we're going to celebrate too. A bit belated, but how does a fancy dinner sound? I did a little investigating. I was thinking of starting with drinks at Babcock and Story bar, then dinner at the Coronado Sheerwater Restaurant."

Oh, a man who can actually plan a surprise. "Sounds fantastic."

"We can relax at an umbrella table on the patio overlooking the ocean, under a nice warm heat lamp, and then go for a long walk on the beach."

Her eyes sparkled. "Let the festivities begin."

*

It was Thomas's first visit to the Hotel Del, and as expected, it was all decked out in holiday splendor: a true winter wonderland. The enormous, festive Christmas tree in the lobby looked magical with its tiers of twinkling lights. They spent time exploring the shops before dinner, weaving down the pathway, arm in arm, when Thomas suddenly hesitated as they walked past a store called Spreckels Sweets & Treats.

"What's up?" Margo asked.

"I must confess a guilty pleasure of mine."

"What is it?"

"Fudge! I'm going to duck in here and get a quarter pound of chocolate fudge to take home with us. You want anything special?"

"No, I'll share with you whatever you get."

Thomas purchased his fudge, and Margo tucked the bag into her purse.

"This is a grand hotel, isn't it?" Thomas asked.

"It sure is, and it's over a hundred and twenty-five years old. When it opened in 1888, it was the largest resort hotel in the world. You know, they filmed *Some Like it Hot* with Tony Curtis and Marilyn Monroe here."

"What year was that?"

"I'm not sure. Around 1959, I think."

Thomas stopped walking and took Margo's hand in his. "I didn't know if you would want to do this or not, so you can say no. But I booked us a couples massage at the spa. I read it's one of the top twenty hotel spas in the world."

I'm being treated like a queen, she thought. The sensation of holding hands felt comforting, yet simultaneously exhilarating. "That sounds excellent."

"Good. Let's head over."

*

After being thoroughly relaxed from the massage, Margo felt as though she was in a heady trance. They continued their dive into relaxation oblivion with drinks at the bar and then headed over to the restaurant for dinner.

Margo marveled at the perfect setting. Their table was on the outdoor patio overlooking the ocean, where the sunset formed residual streaks of pink and orange cloud wisps across the sky. It was breezy, but pleasant, and her sweater and the heat lamp were sufficient to keep her comfortable. They pored over their menus, finding it hard to settle on one choice.

"I have to order something from the sea. I'm thinking about the peppercorn-coriander-crusted Ahi tuna. What about you?" Thomas asked.

"The rib eye is calling me. Want to share our entrees?"

"Great idea."

After an impressive dinner of mouth-watering flavors and stimulating conversation, they headed down to where the sand met the surf for the anticipated walk along the beach. As the ocean water rhythmically licked the shore, Margo kicked off her shoes and waited as Thomas removed his shoes and socks and rolled up his pant cuffs, readying himself to wade in the chilly water. As she drank in the heady perfume of salt and seaweed, she was surprised at her own reaction as a somewhat familiar tingling sensation vibrated up and down her spine when Thomas reached over to take her hand. She loved the sensation of the grains of sand giving way beneath her feet as she stepped, each little particle hugging and massaging her tired feet. As the ocean waves retreated, so did her anxieties.

"Wow, when the sun goes down, it gets a bit nippy. This evening has been incredibly relaxing for me," Thomas said, shivering slightly.

"For me too, and you're completely disarming me and shattering all of my silly dating phobias," Margo said, glancing up at him demurely.

"Good. I want to make you light-headed and smitten," he said as he pulled in for a kiss. His touch felt so comforting and warm, allowing a sensation of safety to wash over her, along with an openness to whatever was going to happen. *Imagine at my age, feeling these sensations.*

In spite of it being late, they returned to the car and took the long scenic route back to her house. Trying to delay the ending of a perfect day, Margo made them each a cup of decaf, when she found her nerves hit full tilt. *I can't believe how awkward this is to deal with our sleeping arrangements!* She'd previously decided to set Thomas up in the guest room and whatever came after that, did—she was determined to allow things to flow at will. They both awkwardly said good night and turned in to their rooms.

But as Margo crawled under the covers, she decided she didn't want to be alone—she'd spent a lifetime of lonely nights, and she felt an overwhelming desire to be with him. *Enough with trying to be proper or coy.* She thought she'd make herself available to him, just in case. After taking a swig of mouthwash, she applied a light pink gloss on her lips and sprayed a bit of Falling In Love cologne on her wrists. She walked barefoot into the guest room and stood in the doorway in her nightgown, hoping she looked seductive. "Is there anything I can get you before I say a final good night?" she asked flirtatiously.

He was sitting up in bed reading when he glanced up at the lovely sight in his doorway. "You're beautiful," he said as he gazed at her.

She blushed.

"I was hoping you'd join me ..." He extended his hand to her.

"I was hoping you'd ask ..." She placed her hand in his. She began to tremble. With the intense excitement she felt from his touch, she surrendered to her desires.

But there was one thing she knew for sure—it was going to be a life-changing visit.

Chapter 12

January 6, 2022

Jonathan turned the sound system in the house on full blast. It was too quiet; he couldn't write when it was so silent. The house always seemed less vibrant when Aria was gone—he missed her energy. She was out of town working on a movie for a few weeks, and he found himself longing for her company. The loneliest time for him was at night, when his bed was empty. His first sign that he was in love with Aria had been when he'd realized how solitary he'd felt when she wasn't with him. In the beginning of their relationship, he'd patiently wait for her to fall asleep at night, watching as she gently blew air through her pursed lips, before allowing himself to fall sleep. It was a protective gesture of his, and he'd felt fulfilled when he saw her, peacefully asleep, safe in her dream world.

Jonathan conscientiously worked on his laptop, editing a script, while Sammi sat at her child-sized desk, busy coloring, a pile of half-peeled crayons in a box next to her. He watched her with her tongue sticking out of the corner of her mouth—something she did when she worked intently. As soon as the music started, Sammi joined in and sang, her vocalizations reverberating off the walls: free, unrestrained, and deep from her heart. He marveled at how centered she was, how at peace with her world. Except for those darn nightmares, she was a happy child.

She stopped singing and brought her paper to Jonathan. "I'm done, Daddy. I made a picture of Nate and you when you were fishing."

He inspected her work. "You're a good little artist. That looks like both of us. Let's hang it on your art wall in your bedroom."

He stood, found the tape, and fastened it to the wall. "Well done. I really like it. But, honey, it's time for bed."

"Okay, Daddy, but I do want a story tonight."

Jonathan turned down her bed while Sammi got into her honeybee-patterned pajamas. "Would I forget to tell you a story? No, not me, not ever. Stories are my thing." He gave her a tickle. "Don't forget to brush your teeth."

"Daddy, when's Mama going to be home?"

"Not for another week, cupcake. She's got a project going on right now. So Daddy's going to read you a story and put you to bed."

"Daddy, instead of reading me a story, can you tell me a story about Nate? I'm excited Nate's going to be my brother. He was a good friend of yours, he said. And before that, he was in a life with me—so he decided to be in a family with both of us this time."

"I wouldn't be at all surprised if Nate came to be a part of our family. He was like a brother to me."

"He said he's recently had two short lives and this one he plans to live longer."

"He said all that? That's good. I wouldn't want a child of mine to die before me. Too painful."

"Daddy, tell me about him. How did he die when he was your friend last time? He told me it was best if I ask you. I think it's a good idea if you tell me while Mama's away."

Jonathan pondered her question for a brief moment, thinking how odd it was for a child to ask about how someone died, but he knew she was a unique and curious little girl from the moment she was born. Always wondering, always questioning.

"Why's that?"

"Sometimes things I talk about make her sad, and I don't want her to feel sad."

"Do you think so?"

"Yes, a little bit, I do." She went to the bathroom to brush her teeth and, when finished, returned to her bedroom.

"Okay, time to crawl under those unicorn sheets, and I'll sit here next to you and tell you about Nate." Jonathan sat on the edge of the bed while Sammi snuggled under the covers. "He was my good buddy for many years. We went to high school together—gosh, we had so many things in common. We both loved the ocean, to surf and fish, play pool, skateboard, party, snowboard, listen to music, simply have fun. We traveled to places for adventures, like to Baja and Nicaragua. And we both loved to spearfish. Remember the stories how I told you about how my dad and your godfather, Matthew, used to take me fishing? Most people use scuba tanks, but Nate and I did free diving. Nate loved to free dive and go spearfishing."

Sammi pulled the covers up under her chin. "What does 'free die' mean?"

"Free *dive*. You dive without a tank. A breathing tank of air."

"Why?"

"You feel free, like you're a fish or a dolphin."

"Do you catch the fish with worms?"

"No, you have a thing that's like a gun and it shoots the fish while you're underwater. I have a black speargun that looks something like my pool cue with a pistol grip. It connects to a spool of fishing line on a reel used to hand-crank a fish in. Underwater hunting, I guess you could call it."

"How do you breathe, then?"

"By taking a big long breath and holding it while you dive. We went on this great trip to the Sea of Cortez. It was so relaxing. We fished, drank beer and ate, and camped out under the stars. We stayed in a small fishing village called San Evaristo."

"Did a shark get him, Daddy?"

"No, one day we were going to go out fishing, but I had a really bad headache. It wouldn't have been good to dive with my head in pain, so I stayed back, and Nate and Phil went spearfishing. My buddy, my friend, came face-to-face with death that day. He dove down in the water and drowned. He still had a fish on his spear. Phil tried to rescue him, but he couldn't."

"Why didn't he come up and take a breath?"

"It was too late. It's this thing called shallow-water blackout. As soon as you start to hold your breath, a gas in your blood called carbon dioxide starts to go up. If it goes up too high, you pass out underwater. It happens without warning, and usually the person isn't even aware they're out of breath. And then they drown."

"You must've felt so sad."

His voice trembled, forcing him to remember that his feelings were still raw. "I felt guilty I wasn't there to do something, but Phil was, and he still couldn't help him. It was too late."

"I'm sorry, Daddy." She sat up, putting her arms around his neck, pulling him toward her and hugging him.

"Thanks for that hug of love, sweetie. I still miss him a lot. The nicest, sweetest, most humble guy ever." He shook his head and wiped his eyes.

"Did you have a funeral?"

"We had a funeral for him. The best part of our goodbye celebration was the paddle-out. When you're a surfer, the whole community comes out to say goodbye. Everyone sat on their surfboard in a circle around a boat that his family was on, and we said profound and funny things about him, wishing him well in his next life. Then his parents lovingly scattered his ashes into the ocean. Everyone on their boards surfed 'one last surf' for Nate, back to shore. I ha—" He stopped, choking on his words. "We had a band play his favorite songs and had a cookout to celebrate his life. He left behind a legacy of love."

Sammi put her hands on each of his cheeks and said, "I love you, Daddy. It does sounds like a better way to die than the time he was with me."

Jonathan's gaze lingered on Sammi. He was so happy she was opening up to him but didn't want her to feel self-conscious about it. He decided to ask her more. "How did he die then?"

"I'll tell you sometime, Daddy, but I still don't want to talk about it right now."

"My little love, you can feel safe talking to your daddy about anything. Maybe there's something I can help you with. I love you, and I'm here for you."

She leaned in to him and reached for Jonathan's hand and held it.

"I know that. I'll talk about it later, though, okay?"

"Of course."

"I'm glad he picked us for his family."

"I am too. More than likely we've had lots of different lives together before. I remember a life with him where he played the role of my dad, and he saved my life. Maybe I want to experience being his dad now and help him in some way. It balances the energy. Everything we do has an energy and it needs to be balanced. It's called karma."

"Oh, that's what he's going to do with me too. We have some energy to balance. I'm happy he'll be my brother."

"Nate died doing what he loved—he was in the ocean, fishing. For me, he was way too young to die, but he had agreed to come and have a short life to give lessons to his loved ones and friends. To many, it rattled them to the core *because* he was so young. Sometimes we just need to be shaken up. Sometimes we're just too busy being busy, and we forget what's important, so things happen to shake us up and get us on track again. We have to remember that sometimes tomorrow doesn't come."

"Thanks for the story about Nate. I'm feeling sleepy now." She sunk back down under the covers. "Good night, Daddy. I love you."

"I love you more." He kissed her on the forehead and tucked her back in.

After Sammi fell asleep, Jonathan sat on his bed with his laptop, talking to Aria on Virtual-Time. "What time is it in Spain? It's awfully early in the morning for you, isn't it?" Jonathan asked.

"It's early, but I have a meeting in an hour. How are you guys?"

"We're doing great except for how much we miss you."

"I miss you both so much," Aria said, sounding a bit forlorn.

"We had an interesting conversation tonight. Sammi was asking about Nate and how he died. I told her about it. She seems better and hasn't had a nightmare for a while—maybe she's integrating it all," Jonathan said.

"She doesn't talk about him as much to me as she did before either. Isn't she getting to that age where the amnesia sets in? So maybe she's forgetting."

"I don't think she's going to forget. She's very open. Many of the children born now are a new breed of kids. Some, known as rainbow children, are coming to Earth for the first time, so they don't have karma. Sammi does have karma that she's talked about, but she has such unique abilities, like seeing orbs and sparkles, knowing when someone is going to call or come over, and she's so kind and loving. Always seems advanced beyond her years."

"I missed talking to her today. I'm glad for technology to keep us connected, but as of right now, it can't give you the physical feeling that a hug and kiss gives you."

"Aria?"

"Yes?" she said, hesitantly.

"I think Sammi is clamming up and not sharing things because she senses she's hurting your feelings in some way. I think she's holding back to protect you." He blew out a long sustained breath. "You know, love is not in limited supply. Love is expansive. The more we love, the greater our ability to love even more. She's probably had tons of moms over various lifetimes. Right now you're her mom, and she couldn't love you more. Her feelings about Nate, her feelings about her other mom, are nothing you should feel hesitant or jealous about. She will not love you any less than she does. Please know that and think about it so she feels free to share with you. Nothing can ever take away the love she feels for you."

Aria was quiet.

"Babe, I say that out of *my* love for you."

"I know that. I was quiet because you're right. I'll think about why I have these jealous feelings—I know I need to work through them. Thanks for telling me that. I just want to be home right now. I miss you both."

"We miss you. Call you tomorrow, okay?"

"Love you."

"Always."

Chapter 13

January 6

Another night of insomnia! It had become more than annoying. She just wanted to sleep—sleep through the night like a normal person. *Is that too much to ask?* Olivia was downright exhausted again, but it was payoff dinner number two for Jax, so she couldn't just serve a bag of potato chips for dinner. It had been a hectic day at her yoga studio. One of her longtime clients, who happened to be at the end of her pregnancy, had assumed a modified sun bird pose, and the groaning soon-to-be-mom had ended up reclining on the studio floor, announcing that she was beginning labor. Everyone had gathered around, fussing over her and giving her directions on what to do while she waited for her husband to arrive. The incident had set the class back about an hour, throwing off the schedule for the rest of the classes. When the day was over, Olivia hadn't had time to stop at the store and make dinner. She was sure Jax, being such a compassionate guy, would understand.

She set the kitchen table with paper plates and two boxes of hot pizza that the delivery boy had just dropped off. A few minutes later, the bell rang. It was Jax, this time, loaded down with beer.

He walked in, sniffing the air as he set the bottles on the white-and-yellow laminate counter. "Livs ... ordering pizza doesn't count as making me dinner. That's clearly cheating."

In jest, she stuck her tongue out at him. "I disagree. I didn't say home-cooked. I'm providing you with dinner. Besides, I got the breadsticks you love. So beer or wine?"

"Since I brought a ton of cold beer, that's what we're going to have. It sure smells good. Did you get it with extra cheese?"

"Yes, and one pie has everything on it like you like it. Sit and let's dig in. I'm so hungry."

They sat at the kitchen table as the enticing scent of oregano, pepperoni, and melted cheese permeated the room.

"So I'm dying to hear this secret story you have to tell. So juicy! And why did you decide to tell me about it now at this point in your life?"

"Because some weird things are happening, and I need to pass this by someone. You're the only one I trust. I've been feeling anxious and not sleeping well. Having insomnia is awful. It takes a lot of energy to hold on to secrets, you know."

Jax pushed his chair back from the table, stood, and went to the counter to secure several paper towels.

"I'm here for you. What weird things?" He handed her a paper towel.

"I do have napkins, you know ..."

"These work just as well. Save your napkins for fancy times. So tell me."

"Well, you have to know the story before you understand why they're weird. In a nutshell, I married the wrong guy. I was young, dumb, and naïve. As a kid, I had really bad self-esteem, was too easily influenced, and unfortunately got caught up with some bad people. I'm not proud of some of my past behaviors, which I'm not going to get into right now. My worst mistake was I ended up marrying Curtis."

"Holy crap."

"He's a deeply troubled person. Always has been. He's dealt drugs, has taken drugs himself, and got off on shaming me and controlling me. It got progressively worse over time."

Jax jumped up from his chair. "He didn't beat you, did he? Tell me he didn't beat you."

Olivia averted her eyes. "He started coming home every night, raging at me verbally and shaking his fist in my face. Mad at this, mad at that. He really resented me getting a good education. Then he started pinching me and bruising me in areas covered by clothing. Soon after that, he began punching me in the gut. And there was always verbal abuse. Always."

Jax sat down, returning his pizza to his plate. "Oh God, I'm feeling sick."

"He was obsessive-compulsive or something. He had bizarre rules he forced me to follow. Always wanted the bed made exactly just so. Shirts folded a certain way. Socks rolled and sorted by colors. He made me organize the spices alphabetically. Although he did things that went against that OCD behavior—like he'd eat out of the ice cream carton and leave one spoonful in it. He knew it aggravated me, so he did it on purpose. More of a control freak than obsessive-compulsive, maybe. I don't know if he was never diagnosed, to my knowledge."

"You must have felt terrorized."

"He had horrific anger issues and started to knock me around. I can't tell you how much his rage frightened me. He'd usually hit me in places where no one would see bruises and red marks. And the alienation was awful because he took great pains to isolate me from my family and my friends. Except for working, I felt like a prisoner. He could kill me with a simple move of his hands if he wanted to. After all, he was a master of the martial arts, and his weapon of choice to hit me with was his collapsible bo staff."

Jax grabbed her hand and held it, his eyes filled with tears. "Oh God, Livs, this breaks my heart to hear this."

Olivia purposely ignored his emotional response, intent on getting through her story without breaking down. "Bruised ribs and chest became the norm for me. He'd come home mad at the world and beat me instead. There's nothing as horrific as misplaced anger."

"Why did you stay? The unanswerable question, right? You thought you deserved it?"

"Never. I never once thought I deserved it. But he told me he'd hunt me down like the bitch that I am and beat me to a pulp and bury me alive. I believed him. And of course he threatened to kill my family by burning their house down at night."

"Unbelievable! Did you tell anyone?"

"No, he'd watch me. Checked my phone and computer. Surprise visits at home —sometimes even at my classes. He had ways of spying on me that I have no idea how he did it. He'd always been pretty tech-savvy, so who knows? He could hack into my computer and phone. I couldn't risk it."

"So you never called the cops?"

"No, and I don't know what they would have done anyway, but I was always looking for an opportunity to leave. My prayers were answered when he got busted for dealing drugs and went to jail. That was my opportunity to escape—I figured it was my only option. My plan had been to go to Mexico, but when I got here in San Diego, I decided to stay. I mean, I didn't speak Spanish, so that would have been a deterrent. I'd sent my sister a note when I left and, thankfully, she wired me money, and I'd been secretly saving up some over the years."

"So you had to just up and leave everything. Wow. Name, job, all of it right?"

"Yep. Just glad I didn't have to hide a kid as well."

Jax approached her and pulled her to stand. "Come here and let's hug it out." He embraced her, while she dabbed at her eyes with her paper towel.

"That's okay. I'm okay."

"Well, I'm not." He grabbed her again, even tighter, and she started to sob. After the tears subsided, he stepped back at arm's length to look at her. "See my jaw hanging down here on my chest? I'm gobsmacked, Livie, gobsmacked."

"I know. Sorry I didn't tell you before. Let's sit down and eat this pizza before it's cold."

They ate their pizza in silence for a few minutes as Olivia let Jax absorb the information. *I wonder what he's thinking about all of this?*

He shook his head. "I'm so sorry that this all happened to you. I can imagine you're scared shitless that he'll find you. I won't say a word to anyone. Thanks for trusting me. Let me know if there's any way I can help you. Can I tell Hunter about this, though?" Jax said.

"Not yet, please. I went to a woman therapist for a few years, which was very empowering—she really understood domestic abuse. Then I went to a person who did a past life regression on me, and wow—now that was eye-opening. She said I was working out some karma from the past."

"Interesting ... so what weird things are happening now that worry you?"

"It's bizarre, but I have the strongest sensation I'm being watched and followed. When I left the studio the other day, someone was leaning out of their car window, snapping photos of me. Odd things like that. I had a coffee at Deja Brew and, again, someone was sitting across from me, clearly watching me."

"Is there some way we could put a private investigator on Curtis and see where he lives and where he's going and what he's doing? I would chip in on the cost with you. Or at least you could come live with us."

"Curtis has been out of jail for years, so I have no idea where he even lives," she said with downcast eyes.

"That's the point of getting a private investigator."

"I don't know. I'll think about it, okay?"

"What about what I said? Come stay with us."

"I can't. I can't keep running. I like my own place, and I don't want him scaring me off from that."

"Please think about it. I want you to feel safe and be safe."

"Thanks, I know you do."

A small blue vein throbbed aggressively on Jax's forehead. "Do you see horns growing out of my head? Do you see a pitchfork in my hand? Do you see flames coming out of my shoes? This has brought the devil out of me, and I want to hurt this guy and hurt him bad! I want to do something to help this situation."

"I know, I know … I've felt that way many, many times. Help me while I prepare dessert. I need to take a break from talking about this for a minute. It just gets too overwhelming for me."

"Okay. I can do that. What are we having?"

"Homemade gooey brownies, kind of crusty on the outside like you like, but soft on the inside. We'll top them with cinnamon ice cream. I'll cut the brownies. Can you get the ice cream out of the freezer? A new container right up front."

He opened the freezer and grabbed the pint-sized carton. "Okay, got it. Where's the scoop?"

"In the far drawer by the fridge."

"I think I—" Jax stopped after he opened the ice cream container and stared into the carton. "Houston, we have a problem. Who gets this little bit that's left in here? You or me? It should be me, since I'm the guest."

He tipped the carton for her to see. There was one scoop of ice cream left in the bottom of the carton.

"Didn't you say this was new and full? Are you sleep-eating?"

She took the carton from him and stared into it. "Yes, it was full, and I didn't eat any of it."

Then it hit her—Curtis. *Is it possible?*

She dropped the carton on the floor and felt her warm pee as it trickled down her leg.

Chapter 14

THE NONPHYSICAL WORLD

Neshamah: Even though I'm here to learn the ropes of life on Earth, I'm finding that it's more complicated than life in other dimensions. At least that's how it seems to me.

Pneuma: It may appear that way. It's important to understand that Earth is in a state of ongoing change. Think of dimensions as levels of consciousness, and each dimension has a certain energy vibration. Know that there's constant motion and fluidity between all of the dimensions. Earth is known to be mostly third-dimensional, and that happens to be a very low frequency. The way people learn in a 3-D existence is by experiencing duality. Opposites. Up/down. Failure/success. Black/white. Another thing unique to the 3-D world is the illusion of linear time, which we don't have in our dimension. One more complication is that people are born to the 3-D world with an amnesia, which we refer to as the veil, where they don't remember other parts of the universe and other dimensions.

Neshamah: My understanding is there's been a shift of consciousness going on.

Pneuma: Correct. The frequency of the Earth is now in flux, always shifting from one dimension to the next. As human beings expand their consciousness, they're able to move interdimensionally. They'll still experience time and space but will also be able to tap into fifth-dimension qualities like unconditional love, wisdom, compassion, and instant manifestation.

Neshamah: Kind of like upgrading your computer operating system. Can anyone on Earth shift to other dimensions?

Pneuma: If they raise their vibration, yes. A person has to vibrate in resonance with the specific frequency of each dimension. Bottom line? How they vibrate is how they experience their reality. Each dimension essentially has a different set of rules and conditions.

Neshamah: Okay, different rules for different dimensions ...

Pneuma: That's correct. Earth, as a 3-D density, has had very rigid beliefs and rules. On Earth, people have experienced fear, conflict, corruption, suffering. The people who vibrate to that lower frequency will not be able to experience the higher dimensions. If a person is inflexible in their belief system, they won't experience a complete amplification of consciousness.

Neshamah: Enlightenment is the goal?

Pneuma: Partially, but enlightenment is not necessarily what people think. It's really the disintegration of all that is false. Many people vacillate between dimensions—they can move back and forth and not even realize it. It's very liberating to transition from the limitations of a 3-D world to the more expansive dimensions. Many people are aware of this, and they refer to it as an awakening. As the veil continually thins, people are seeing what is real since they are no longer contained in restrictive 3-D beliefs. Not everyone will awaken, and they don't have to. If people are open to the possibility, they will.

Neshamah: And the benefits of that are ... ?

Pneuma: Moving out of a place of fear, karma, and duality to a state of well-being, beauty, connectedness, and love.

Neshamah: I see ...

Chapter 15

January 7

Olivia woke up the next morning with Jax on her mind. He'd insisted she stay at his house until she figured things out about Curtis, but she felt the need to stay in her own home. *I simply can't live my life on the run.* She'd assured Jax that the ice cream situation couldn't have been Curtis—clearly it had been her imagination—but Jax had demanded she give him a spare key to her front door, just in case. She worried her karma with Curtis was going to get her killed. Panic of the worst kind kept bubbling up from her gut to her throat—she hoped he hadn't found her. She knew she hadn't eaten that ice cream. Or wait—had she forgotten to get a new carton when she'd gone to the store? She couldn't remember.

She didn't want to live life feeling scared again and have to pick up, leave, and start all over. In the still of the night, the last thing she wanted to worry about was that someone else was going to end her story. She could hear her heartbeat pounding in her ears. Did other people live with the kind of fear she felt? It wasn't the way she wanted to live—it needed to stop. Perhaps there was a way of working out their issues and balancing the energies they had created without it coming to some tragic end, like her death. She had read something about that, and Dr. Hobbs had touched on it briefly during his lecture. Had she forgotten to buy ice cream at the store, and it was just an old container in the freezer? Was she going nuts? There's no way he'd sneak in and eat her ice cream and leave a scoop. That was crazy thinking.

Even though her week was booked solid, she decided to free up some time so she could see Matthew Hobbs for an appointment. Maybe there was a way she could heal things over with Curtis on another level. She needed relief from the fear that enveloped her serenity.

Always accommodating, Dr. Hobbs had agreed to work her in that week due to a cancellation, so Olivia drove to his office in his home in La Jolla for her appointment. She was surprised when he answered the door himself. "Hello. I'm glad you came to see me, Olivia. Come in."

He's such a nice man, she thought. *He has a very pleasant energy about him.* "And I'm glad you could squeeze me into your schedule. Thank you for taking the time."

"Of course. Come join me in my office and have a seat. How can I help you? I did read your papers, but please tell me in your own words. So you're interested in a past life regression?"

He gestured to a comfortable-looking chair near the window. Olivia sat on the edge of her seat, crossing her legs. Dr. Hobbs sat across from her with a pad of paper and pen in hand.

"Yes. As I wrote in my papers, I'm a person who's gone through a nasty domestic violence situation with my husband. He threatened to kill me, and I took those threats seriously. When he was in jail, I made my escape. I'm here to see you, because I'm worried he's found me and is after me, but not directly. I don't know if it's a figment of my imagination or if he's trying to terrorize me. I don't want to go to the police and bring who I am to their attention if it isn't him. I have no proof of anything. It's been a long, hard road to inventing the new me. The reason I've come to you is because I was told by a medium in the past that I have karmic issues with Curtis, and I would like to absolve them in hopes he doesn't have to resort to killing me. Is that a bizarre request, and is it even possible?"

Dr. Hobbs positioned his hands in a V, fingertips touching. "That's an interesting question. Sometimes it's possible to absolve karma. It depends on many variables. Let's talk about that a bit."

Olivia told him about the ice cream carton, how she had the feeling she was being watched, and how Curtis had used surveillance technology in the past to track her every move, her every email. She struggled to maintain her composure, not wanting to be reduced to tears. She bit down hard on her lower lip as she came to the part that was hardest to share. "He beat me with a bo staff in my pelvic region until I lost my baby. His anger was getting progressively worse over time. I want to understand the karma we have and how I can absolve it without playing it out in a bad way, if that can even be done. I don't want this to come to a tragic ending."

"Well, first let's get on the same page about our understanding of karma, so we're talking the same language."

"I did hear your talk in Los Angeles, of course, which kind of inspired me to even think about this. I remember you saying the word karma has been bantered around and misused so much that everyone has become confused about what it really is. More often than not, people think of it as some kind of grandiose punishment—like an unleashing of the all-powerful wrath from an irate, pissed-off God. Karma's going to get you! But that's simply not true. The universe wants harmony, so it seeks to balance the energy."

"Well put. The universe doesn't play the vengeance game. The intention of karma is to help a person evolve to become a better person. Karma means you're engaging in experiences to further develop your soul."

"I get what you're saying."

Dr. Hobbs walked over to an object hanging in the bay window, lifted it off its hanger, and returned to his chair. "See this prism?" He held it in the air, turning it so the sun shone through it. "This one has five planes, three sides, and a top and a bottom. As you know, white light is comprised of all the colors of the rainbow, and when it passes through the prism, it bends and splits into the colors: red, orange, yellow, green, blue, indigo, and violet; karma is like the split light. When the light is balanced, it's white. The key for us is to achieve balance. Once we understand this balance, we can clear out what people call karma."

Olivia cleared her throat and ran her fingers through the curls in her hair. "I understand. We come here for certain experiences we create to help us balance our energies and grow our souls."

"Yes. Many of us come from a dimension that has a constant love frequency called agape, or unconditional love. When you're in a state of love and perfection, it's actually hard to learn lessons because there's no contrast. If you're floating around in big ol' vat of love soup, that's all you know. So in order to grow and expand, we incarnate to a place where complete love hasn't yet been achieved. One choice is our planet Earth, where we start having experiences and we react to them, causing us to make choices. Then we need to deal with the consequences of those choices. Sometimes we aren't aware of the consequences until we go back to the nonphysical dimensions. If we miss a lesson the first time around, we might decide to return to Earth in a new incarnation in order to repeat the lesson and hopefully learn it that time around. That yearning to learn is karma."

"I understand."

"Karma begins when we make choices that are out of alignment with our life purpose. It provokes change and the seeking of wholeness."

"Well, I want to stop the negative karma I've created from spilling over into something that isn't necessary: namely my demise. Harmony and balance is my goal. I'm on a mission to absolve my karma."

"Okay, let's begin the regression and see what we're up against. Since you do this yourself, you know the ropes."

"Yes, I can go under very quickly."

"I have a meditation room that's studded with crystals and dioptase, which helps bring past life memories forward and clear them. I'm going to set you up in that room."

"Great! I love using stones for my past life work—I also use dioptase since it helps facilitate compassion and forgiveness. So we preplan our relationships that were karmic in nature from previous lives and draw to us specific situations that give us the ability to release the karma?"

"The regression may let you see the truth in the relationships and help change the dynamics of it, or even enable you to allow yourself to release the other person, so both of you can move forward in your lives," Dr. Hobbs said.

Olivia followed Dr. Hobbs to a quiet and peaceful meditation room with a large recliner as the focal point. Just as she imagined, it was clean and uncluttered, with a small table, a yoga mat, lots of plants, and meditation pillows. She ran her fingers over the walls studded with crystals and dioptase. *That would be cool to do in my yoga studio. In fact, having a small meditation room would be a great addition.* Touches of nature were scattered throughout the room—jars filled with sand and seashells, fresh flowers, healing rocks. A diffuser for essential oils provided a relaxing scent, although she couldn't identify the fragrance.

"What's that wonderful scent?" Olivia said as she scrunched her nose, whiffing the air.

He gestured for her to sit on the recliner. "Oh, it's myrrh. Myrrh helps us remember past life experiences that are causing issues in this life."

"Really? I didn't realize that. I can use that for the people I work with."

As Olivia planted herself in the recliner, Dr. Hobbs made himself comfortable in a chair next to her and began the regression. His voice, so soothing and singsong, induced her into a deep state of relaxation. She allowed herself to settle into a hypnotic trance, and Dr. Hobbs led her through the regression. When it was over, she'd fallen asleep, and he let her rest until she naturally woke.

Olivia emerged from the meditation room alert and refreshed, looking for Dr. Hobbs. She found him working at his laptop in his office. "Sorry I feel asleep," she said, standing in the doorway.

Looking up from his work, he tilted his head and raised his brows. "Not a problem. How are you feeling? Would you like something to drink? We can review what happened now if you like."

"Although I'd like to at some point, I need to get going. I'm having total recall of what happened, and I need to digest all of these thoughts in my mind before I can verbalize what I think. How about I make another appointment with you to review this? Right now I want to mentally stay in this place I'm in for a while and process it. It's very powerful to me."

"I understand." He handed her a flash drive.

"I've recorded a karma-clearing program for you. You can take it home with you and use it."

"That's perfect. So I might be able to clear my karma with Curtis without something horrid happening?"

"Actually, your karma isn't *with* another person. It's with yourself. You created it, you're the one to absolve it. Others only act as a catalyst to stimulate the karmic experience from the past. And the way to do it is with forgiveness and grace. Make peace with yourself."

"I'll be working hard on this."

He stood to see her to the door before she left. "Give it a try, Olivia. Clearing karma focuses on forgiveness and love. You have my cell number, so call me with any questions or concerns you might have ... no matter what time it is."

Olivia drove by rote, hoping her car knew the way back home. Deep in thought, she decided to skip running her errands, feeling an overwhelming need to call Jax from her car. She gave the voice command to dial him, and he answered right away.

"Hey, Livie, what's up?"

"Jax, is Hunter working tonight? Are you busy? Can you come over?"

"Are you okay?"

"Yeah, I had my regression today, and I thought I wanted to be alone with my thoughts, but I want to talk about it with you. Could you come? We could make popcorn and drink wine—"

"You had me at wine. Actually, I'm not busy. Was just going to watch TV. Hunter's working tonight, and I'm done with dinner. Heading over."

Jax knocked on the door, holding a bottle of wine and a bag of popcorn kernels. He set them down on the kitchen island, then reached under the counter for the popcorn popper.

"Hey! Where's the popcorn popper?" Jax asked, looking confused as he searched through the cupboard.

"Oh, it broke. We have to make it the old-fashioned way, in a pan."

"Really? Okay, so I pour some oil into the pan with some popcorn, cover it, and wait for it to pop?"

"Shake it while it's popping so it doesn't burn on the bottom. While you're doing that, I'm going to straighten the coffee table a bit so we have room. I'm literally swimming in papers."

He raised his voice so she could hear him in the living room. "Okay. I want to make sriracha and butter topping. Does that sound okay to you?"

"Sure. I like spicy."

He poured the oil and the unpopped corn into one pan, put a stick of butter and sriracha in another, and waited. "I'm missing the popcorn popper ... this is sort of like trying to bake a pie with a flashlight."

"Honestly, Jax. Do you need me to do it?"

"Nope, just felt like complaining. So how does it happen?"

"What? The regression?"

"Yep."

"You get real relaxed and go under hypnosis. Kind of feels like you're asleep, yet awake. I go under really easy as I've done it so often. Dr. Hobbs took me back in time and suggested I choose a door to go through that would take me back to a life relevant to the karma I want to heal with Curtis."

"Does it feel like dreaming?"

"Actually, people experience it in different ways. It's kind of like dreaming to me, but I'm not watching it like I seem to in my dreams. I'm feeling it. I'm inside my body looking outward."

"It's hard for me to imagine it." He poured the popped corn and sriracha-butter topping into a bowl. "Pour the wine, okay? And let's sit in the living room."

After Olivia poured the wine, they settled in on the well-worn living room couch—with Jax wedging himself between the armrest and Olivia—eating popcorn and drinking the wine.

"Okay, spill!" he said between handfuls of popped corn.

"Well, my friend, brace yourself for this. It sounds pretty ugly." Olivia took a couple of extra gulps of wine to relax her so she could face what she was going to say.

"Oh-oh. Okay, I'm braced."

"So when I opened the door, I was back in the 1800s, living a life as a white male overseer on a plantation in the South. Following the directives of the plantation owner was part of my job, and I was told to beat the slaves if I felt they were out of control. They were considered property and treated as such. I was under a great deal of pressure to increase profits for the plantation. So I was on horseback, doing a routine inspection of the plantation along with another man, who rode along with me. We spotted a young black girl hiding from us behind a tree—I thought she was trying to get out of work. And— note how I'm cringing as I say this—she was pregnant.

"She was due to receive forty-nine whippings for that offense. She said nothing when I told her to lie facedown and expose her flesh to me. She knew what was coming. I got off my horse and ... oh my God, it's just too horrid to—" She gulped and closed her eyes as she spoke. "I ... I punished her with my rawhide whip. I raised welts on her and watched the blood trickle down her back."

Olivia didn't speak for a few minutes, attempting to collect herself so she could continue. Her hands were violently shaking.

Jax cupped one hand over his mouth as though horrified at her statement and placed his other hand on top of hers and gave it a tight squeeze.

"What's so astounding to me is I didn't even seem emotional or angry. I was just trying to maintain control of the property. How could I think of this human being as *property*? The poor girl begged me to stop, but I kept on ... I kept on ..." She closed her eyes and shook her head. "I kept on ...

"When I was done flogging her, I told the person I was with to take her back to the other workers, and I proceeded on with my inspection of the other slaves. So nonchalant. Just like something I did every day.

"When I came out of the hypnotic state, I felt horrified. I was shocked at how cold and unfeeling I was.

"I sobbed uncontrollably. This was a role I played? For what purpose? The inhumanity is mind-blowing to me. Well, here it is—the young, pregnant black girl was Curtis in that life! We had exchanged gender and race this time around. I see why we don't remember these things from lifetime to lifetime—because the memory can be unbearable. It's enlightening and truly a teachable moment, but still unbearable."

"Are you positive it was you?"

"I am! I can't describe it, but I was in that body and it was me. I'm positive. And then all of a sudden it all made sense to me. There were lessons to be learned from this experience. In this life, Curtis and I are playing out roles to balance that negative karma we created from that life. It showed me I was not thinking for myself or about what was right or wrong in the treatment of another human being. I followed the herd and did what all others did at that time. It was what I was taught. I never questioned it; I just did what I'd been conditioned to do. Blindly following. I was inhumane and callous—stuck in a rigid belief system. I'm no longer that way now."

Sitting side by side on the couch, Jax leaned into her, shoulder to shoulder. "Oh, Livie, it sounds so horrid. I'm so sorry. So it's like you're being punished now from the result of that life?"

"No, no. That's not what I mean. You're missing my point. There's no blame on anyone. There's no punishment or retribution. It's about learning through experiences, and boy, did I learn!"

Olivia couldn't help but notice that Jax's expression was similar to what she imagined if she'd just pulled a rabbit out of her back pocket. His eyes were wide and his face was sheet-white. He looked as though he might vomit.

"You okay?" Olivia asked.

"Hmm ... I'm really not sure." He covered his mouth with his hand as he slowly blew air out.

"I often dream the phrase, 'Oh, sir, please stop, please stop.' Now I know what it was from. I'm sure I learned lessons and raised my consciousness after that lifetime. For as long as I remember in this life, I have embraced the quote, 'Don't think you're on the right road just because it's a well-beaten path.' Now I think things through first before I act and do what my soul directs me to do. I felt I was a lemming in that lifetime, just blindly following the dictates of society. Treating other humans like animals because that's just what was done at the time is disgusting to me. I learned. I'm a humane and compassionate person now. But in this world of ours, I think most people don't really have much free will at all. It's an illusion we have because we're really held hostage by what we've been taught, with all the societal beliefs and the conditioning we're all exposed to. There's no free will in that!" From the look on his face, Olivia wondered if she'd made a mistake in telling Jax.

Tears welled up in his eyes. "God, God, that's so horrid. I can't even bear to hear this. I have no desire to know if I did something like that in another life. I couldn't live with myself. Why would you want to know that?"

"Because I want to know I learned the lesson and never want to behave like that again. Ever. Now or in any lifetime. I know I have evolved. In this life, I now do my best to not blindly follow social norms I feel are against the goals of my soul growth. So many times in history, as well as now, people just go along with horrifying things because it's what others do. I must think for myself. I must always evaluate if an action I take is what my soul wants. Think of all the times in history people did things because they were told to or went along with what everyone else did. The horrors! We need to challenge things we were taught—no matter who the teacher is."

"Geez, Livie, geez." He shook his head.

"I understand we need rules to function in society, but when it harms others, we need to take a stance. Blind obedience is one scary thing."

"It's so overwhelming!" Jax poured himself another glass of wine.

"So I created this karma, and apparently I'm balancing it in this life with Curtis as the catalyst. I asked Dr. Hobbs if there's a way out of it, and a way to stop the karmic obligation from continuing. I really want to ascend and experience more of my multidimensional nature, and as long as I keep creating negative karma that needs to be balanced, that will prove to be difficult. You know, it's said in other dimensions that Earth is a very tough place to live because of all the negativity here. We live in a fear-based culture. Most of the human beings here are working out karma from the past. For me? I want to break out of these karmic patterns. I think I've learned what I needed to learn, and I feel I don't have to live it out by going through this drama with Curtis."

Jax spoke in a whisper. "Oh, Liv, I don't even know what to say."

An expression of pure chagrin settled on her face. "I never want to do an inhumane thing in all my existence again. I can't describe it, but it's an internal drive in me."

"Maybe you need to be a monk to do that. Hey, maybe that's why monks are monks!"

"Dr. Hobbs said he thinks that once we fully understand our actions, behaviors, thoughts, feelings and perceptions, we can then use our free will to consciously create a different path of karma. Forming a state of grace."

"What's a state of grace?"

"It's being in balance, in harmony with people, yourself, and the spirit. It's being in a state of now, feeling gratitude, and knowing unconditional love. His feeling is that when we're able to forgive others, as well as ourselves, we can sometimes absolve our karma."

Jax continued to shake his head, as though unable to find words.

"I have greater understanding of what's happening with Curtis and me. I forgive myself for what I did as an overseer, and I forgive him for what I perceive he's done to me. They were lessons for us. I hope he forgives me too. I don't want to repeat any of this in other lives we may have together. My goal is to heal our relationship and dissolve the partnership with love and grace. I need to move on from it and discharge the karma. So maybe I can do it with forgiveness and unconditional love, and that's what I'm going to work on."

"I hear you. Stop the bad karma. Stop perpetuating more violence and suffering. But, Livie, I'm pretty sure I couldn't forgive him."

She raised her eyebrows and slightly tilted her head. "But do you think you could if you thought you planned this out together before you were born to balance energy or to play a role of teacher or student? If he was in on this plan to teach me, and motivate me to learn forgiveness?"

"I don't know. I don't think I'm there, but I guess I'll keep creating negative karma, because that kind of forgiveness isn't in me."

"I think it is. I feel like we're like magnets, and we draw people and situations and experiences into our lives to learn and release what we need to let go of and find a sense of tranquility. Bottom line is we pull people into our lives who are going to help us heal, grow, and learn. I think that's why I pulled you into mine."

Jax raised her hand to his lips and kissed it. "Even if I get the preplanning thing, why do we choose such extreme suffering, or choose to be the victim of murder, or torture, or rape? Why would anyone select that?"

"Okay, say you can't relate to the preplanning thing. Explain why you think those things happen in the world. Why do you think bad things happen?"

"There are just bad people in the world." Jax reached across the coffee table for an unopened bottle of wine along with the opener. Olivia gently placed her hand over his, returning the bottle to the table, hoping he received her unspoken message of *you've had enough now.*

"But why? So there's bad people and victims? And a few that get away with being neither? And each of these people live one life, in that one role? Why are there so many people doing such bad things?"

"I don't know. I can't think that much." He looked forlorn holding his empty wineglass.

"Through the history of the Earth there's been a ton of war, death, murder, crime, and other horrific things. We've probably all played in these scenarios. Tragedy and loss can be the strongest motivator to grow and change due to the intensity of the experience. An experience can sometimes be so powerful that it leads to a permanent change of being. Sometimes it takes reaching the point of almost unbearable suffering to make a change. Don't try to unpeel the pain—think of it as a catalyst."

Jax rapidly stuffed more popcorn into his mouth, chewed, and waited before he spoke. "All I know is I feel sick, and if there's one iota of truth in any of this, I'm just worried about you right now. This is the here and now—not the 1800s. If you won't move in with us, I'm going to get you a dog. An attack dog."

"No attack dog, please."

"I love you, Livie, and I don't want any harm coming to you. I want to swoop in on my white unicorn and ride it through the stardust to whisk you off and rescue you."

"Be there for me, support me. But I have to be the one to do this."

"But to me, with this plan of yours ... well, it seems like you're trying to boil the ocean. I'm just worried. I want to call the police."

"At this point, there's nothing to call them in for. Please don't make me regret telling you all of this. Let me work this through."

"I don't know if I can, Livie. I just don't know."

The slurring of his words and the slow opening and closing of his eyelids concerned Olivia. "You need to stay here tonight. I'm not letting you drive home. You've had too much to drink. No arguing. Call Hunter at work and let him know."

"Okay, I'm not going to argue. I'm too tipsy to drive. He's doing night shift anyway and won't miss me not being home. Livie, sometimes do you feel like you're the sledgehammer and I'm the wall?"

She kissed him on the cheek. "No, but sometimes I feel like you're the notes on my sheet of music ..."

"I like that. Thanks." A semi-smile finally appeared on his face.

"Give me a hug and go to bed. There are towels and all you need in the guest room."

Jax leaned over and gave her a deep bear hug. "Okay, I hear you. I'm off to bed. Night. Sorry I drank too much. It was just very upsetting. Love you, Livie."

"No problem. Go get some sleep. Love you too."

After Jax went to bed, Olivia sat on the couch finishing her glass of wine, hoping she'd done the right thing in sharing her experience with Jax. On a gut level, she believed it was the right thing to do. She felt lighter—sharing a burden can provide a sense of relief.

Feeling emotionally drained, she also headed off to crash in bed, hoping, finally, for a restorative night of sleep.

Chapter 16

THE NONPHYSICAL WORLD

Neshamah: So from the Earthly perspective, what's Olivia referring to? We don't deal with karma in our dimension, so I need some clarification.

Pneuma: Karma is more specific to lower dimensions—there isn't karma in the higher dimensions. There are so many misconceptions on Earth—the concept of karma is thrown around in incorrect ways. Many who are now alive on Earth reincarnated from earlier generations, except for a new group of people who've arrived without prior karma, and those who have come from other dimensions. So for them, life on Earth is about balancing energies. Karma isn't about punishment or people getting what they deserve due to their poor choices. It's about learning from the experiences.

Neshamah: Seems like a lot of the lessons on Earth are pretty harsh, at least from their perspective. And apparently no one wants to think they once played what they label a negative or bad role.

Pneuma: Good and bad is a judgment that people on Earth use. As you know, there's no judgment of right or wrong, good or bad, here.

The thing is, everyone at some time plays what they might think of as a negative role. That's duality. On Earth, you learn when you experience one side of an issue, then the other. Each person is essentially an actor who has had many roles, and some have played the role of an abuser, a liar, a cheat, a murderer. Long ago, people on Earth were vibrating at a lower frequency and weren't aware enough to learn the lessons they encountered. They didn't act in alignment with their soul's purpose and created negative karma with each other that needed to be balanced. So they returned to Earth to balance those energies. They have to change how they make life decisions. They need to develop an increased awareness in order to escape repeating the same lessons over and over. Unfortunately, many people don't realize it's a bad idea to try to get revenge or retaliate, because they'll just create more karma to work off.

Neshamah: Sounds never-ending.

Pneuma: Olivia's right about Earth. It's known as a difficult place to live. Some people, like Olivia, want to get off the karmic wheel, as they call it. She's determined to absolve her karma and elevate her consciousness. If you go through a difficult or tragic situation, when you weather the storm and emerge from it, it's very important what you do next. If you take revenge, you create more of the same ongoing negativity. If you step into a place of grace and forgiveness, and establish balance with your life purpose, you end up with soul growth.

Neshamah: I imagine karma is different in various parts of the world.

Pneuma: Good point. Very different. Where Sammi lives, in the USA, karma is different than in other countries. Most people, where she lives, aren't working off the karma for basic food, shelter, and safety, although there certainly are those who are in other areas of the planet.

Neshamah: I like living in a place of total love.

Pneuma: I know what you mean. The universal law of love is a higher law. Remember this: love trumps karma.

Chapter 17

January 17

Jax night! The apartment smelled a bit stale from being closed up all day, so Olivia opened all the windows for some cross ventilation. The night air wafting through the living room felt fresh and slightly chilly. Dressed in her yoga pants, pink T-shirt, and bare feet, she responded to the doorbell, answering it with a whisk in one hand and a wok tool in the other. She let out an unrestrained grin—she'd been really enjoying her dinners with Jax. A sense of relief had washed over her after she'd told him about Curtis—holding her secrets in for so long had been eating at her. She actually felt buoyant. Even though he didn't see the world the same way she did, Olivia was grateful to have Jax as a support system: he was always there for her with a listening and caring ear. She was perfectly fine with people going down their own path. What she loved about him was his heart and soul.

Jax pushed in through the open door with three wine bottles in hand. "Move out of the way or I'm going to drop these," he urged her. "These babies are chilled and ready to drink. I'm getting used to having dinner with you on some of the nights Hunter works. I really think we should make it a regular event. I couldn't wait to see what we're having tonight."

Olivia stepped to the side to let his burst of energy enter the room unheeded. "I'm making pad thai. I got this recipe from a coworker, and honestly, I could eat it every day."

"I didn't think I'd see you for dinner until next month, so this is great. What should I do to help?"

"Open the wine, please."

He set the bottles down, wiped the moisture from his hands onto his jeans, and grabbed two wineglasses out of the cupboard. The table was set in the dining room, near the open balcony door. He opened a bottle and set it on the table. "Spiffy-looking table setting, Livs. I feel like I'm important tonight."

She scooped the steaming noodle dish from the wok into a porcelain serving bowl. "You're always important, my friend. I just felt like cranking out the fancy china. Always a surprise with me, huh? One night it's eating out of a cardboard pizza box, another night it's paper plates for tacos. From paper plates to fine china."

"Never a dull moment with Olivia Buffet."

"Come sit in the kitchen and talk to me while I add the garnishes. Now, let's talk about your wedding plans. How is Hunter holding up under the pressure of all the decisions that need to be made?" She zested a lime to top the noodles.

Jax plopped down on a kitchen chair. "He's holding up just fine. It's me you should be worried about. He's like a human bulldozer," he said with a deep, heaving sigh.

"Nah, I don't need to worry about you. You can hold your own. Oh, and by the way, I have Sophie Hobbs lined up to bake your masquerade wedding cake. It's one of my wedding gifts to you. I just need to know what flavors of cakes you two want. How about a different flavor for each layer?"

"Let me ask Hunter if he has a preference. Our current argument is about what we should each wear for a mask. Did you find something for yourself?"

"Not yet. I might make one. I saw one online that wasn't for sale, but it was a cool mask of the moon. I might go as a moongoddess, wearing a blue tulle skirt. Not a full moon, but a crescent moon."

"Now you have me excited. You're going to make it out of what, like papier-mâché? Can I help you? Maybe I'll make one too. I want to make those masks with the long noses."

Olivia dumped some chopped salted peanuts on the top of the noodles. "Yes, papier-mâché. I'm seeing us crafting in the future. We could make them to wear, but also make some to decorate the tables and some for people who conveniently forget to bring one."

"That's a lot to make."

"Do you and Hunter have an idea of how many will be attending?"

"No, not yet. We have to send the invites out first. The invitations are going to be medieval scrolls."

Olivia placed the platters on the table in the dining room and served each of them a heaping portion of pad thai, while Jax poured from the open bottle of wine.

Jax took a bite of his dinner, releasing a loud swooning sound. "This pad thai tastes so good. Did you put crack on it?"

"What?"

"It's addictive. I could eat it all."

"Go ahead. It's good for you."

They both twirled their noodles on their forks with great relish. They caught up on the current events of their lives and finished their meal, and Jax topped off their wineglasses once again.

"Let's relax on the couch," Olivia said. She patted a spot on the burgundy-striped couch for him to sit, noticing a stain on the right seat cushion. *I really need to get some new furniture in here!*

After Jax was seated, he turned to Olivia with a mysterious grin on his face. "I'm going to give you a heads-up. I told Hunter we could ask you together—invite you over for dinner and all—but I didn't want you to be shocked."

"Hmm ... that's ominous. What is it?"

"Before I tell you, I wanted to inform you of something I think you'll get a kick out of. I told Hunter you thought he and I might have lived lives together before. Without a blink, he stepped right into it, nodding and agreeing. He's sure we did! He's had many dreams about the Renaissance period and was fascinated with it and even did a paper on it in college. I said, 'What?' How could I not know he believes this stuff! Funny, but he'd never said that to me before. He's fascinated with Her Majesty, Queen Elizabeth Tudor, who reigned from 1558 to 1603. And he thinks he could have been in the hoity-toity social circles of the Elizabethan era. That's probably the source of his fascination with the masquerade wedding. The masquerade balls were used for weddings for the upper class."

"You can always try finding out if you're really interested. Just sayin' ..."

"Maybe, but probably not. I don't want to find out I was some wretched soul who guillotined people's heads off. The whole preplanning our lives thing still puts me off a bit. Planning our lives before we were born—I just can't get past that people would choose such awful things. Being a Nazi? Being a serial killer? Being burned at the stake or other torture? Eaten by lions?"

"I've explained that I think we use pain as a catalyst to learn and grow. If we're satisfied with things as they are, we won't be inspired to make changes, so we'll only experience the status quo. Human beings usually need a strong motivator to change. Pain does that. I know I can be completely unmotivated to change if I'm comfortable in my ways. But if I'm in pain, I'm *very* motivated to change."

"Well, I can't argue with you as I can't think of another logical explanation for why there's so much negativity and suffering. I just don't have an answer. Maybe it's got something to do with the devil."

"Is the devil a concept that's more acceptable and believable as an explanation than what I've talked about?"

"I don't know. It's what I know, Livie. It's how I was brought up."

"Exactly. It's an indoctrinated belief. Like I've said, people are often afraid to entertain ideas outside the belief system they were taught as a child. To most people, it's uncomfortable to live outside the box. So I'm just curious—in your mind, everyone has one life they live, and some are just born to be horrible perpetrators and others are victims?"

"I don't know. It just doesn't make sense. I don't want to think I played the role of some bad guy."

"This is how I see it. On Earth, when we're in physical form, we can't comprehend the thought that we might actually choose to participate in despicable behaviors. But if you view it from the spiritual dimension, it looks different. In this dimension, we learn through duality and polarity. We don't know what joy is—what it truly feels like—until we experience the absence of joy. The learning part is the soul's journey. When we come to Earth, we come for the experiences. Incarnating is about *all* experiences and the opportunity to make our choices.

"In the nonphysical realms, nothing is viewed as good or bad like it is here on Earth. You learn things from playing various roles, like I did. Like an actor accepting a role in a play. One guy may play a villain in one play, and then in the next play he might play a good guy. He doesn't look at either role with a judgment. He just plays the role. We learn from experiencing different genders, religions, races. I learned so much from playing my role as an overseer on that plantation. From this perspective of my life here on Earth right now, I simply don't see the bigger picture of where I'm headed. If we agree to play out these roles with others in the name of learning and growing from the experience, then it makes sense to me. Looking at situations from different perspectives helps you understand what others go through. It helps you learn empathy and compassion."

"I guess that gray hair I see on your head is giving you a whole bunch of wisdom."

"Hey, do I have gray hair showing?" She reached up, patting the top of her head.

Jax playfully tousled her hair. "Just one. You can pluck it later. I guess I like the idea there's a positive purpose in mind behind it all, but I just don't know. But speaking of karma, I was thinking of a way you could gain some good karma. That's right up your alley, right? You want to make some good karma?"

She leaned over and whispered in his ear. "Why do I feel this is a setup for a favor?"

"Because it is. No pulling the wool over Livie Buffet's eyes."

"What is it?"

"You talked once about the idea of being a surrogate mom, and, well ... we, Hunter and I, were hoping you'd be the surrogate for us, and be the baby's mother. He or she will need a good female influence. Who better than you? We'll make you keep your somewhat crazy ideas to yourself, but other than that, you can just be who you are. No, really, I'm just joking about that. I love you exactly as you are." He laughed, then patted her knee.

"Wow, you're really jumping forward here, aren't you? Before I answer that, I just want to say something about the good karma part. If you do things that people consider to be positive or good under the impression it will balance bad karma or that you'll be rewarded in the end for doing good deeds, you need to rethink karma. The freedom, the release, the liberation, comes about from actions that come from a selfless place. There can't be an expectation of *any* reward. Okay, now, to respond to the request—you're thinking pretty far ahead here, yes?"

"Just thinking about it. Want to sign you up before you go do it elsewhere."

"I'm not signing up anywhere else. I'm glad you gave me advance warning. It's something I do need to think about."

"We'd pay your expenses, of course. Do you think you could have a baby and give it up? If it was to someone adorable like me?"

"I wouldn't need pay to do it. That's what I'd have to think about and get in touch with. I love the idea of doing it, though, for someone I care so much about. I think you and Hunter would be such loving and unbelievable parents. I love you guys. If I do it, it would be an act of love for me."

Olivia slowly sipped her wine. "By the way, I got you a pre-wedding present but didn't have time to wrap it."

"For me? Oh, good. Get it. I want it now."

"It's in the bedroom. Hold on. I've been working all day, and I didn't have time to get it together."

Olivia walked into the bedroom and let out a scream.

Jax came running. "What's wrong?"

She pointed to her bed, shaking.

"What?"

"The bed's made, and I didn't make it. I don't make my bed!"

"Wait a minute—you don't?"

"No."

"Huh ... well, do you have a cleaning lady come in?"

"A cleaning lady? Really, Jax? No. No one. I have this fear it could be Curtis."

"Why would he do that, Liv?"

"To terrorize me."

"So you've had a few drinks. Maybe you forgot you made the bed."

"I have to try to believe that. He's been out of jail for a long time now. If he found me, I think he'd just confront me and not play games."

"I just don't see this guy coming in and making your bed. He'd have to have cojones the size of grapefruits to do that, or swiss cheese for brains."

"Unless he's changed and has some plan in mind. I have to let go of this fear. It's just not healthy for me."

"I'm sure you just forgot. Really, don't worry about it." He gave her a hug. "So, Livie ... what's my gift?"

Chapter 18

January 17

He'd put it off for long enough. The nightmares were happening inconsistently, but with more intensity. It was time to deal with them and help Sammi move on. While Aria was in Canada producing a horror movie, Jonathan decided he and Sammi would fly down to San Diego with a pilot friend of his. It was time for Sammi to see Olivia Buffet—his goal being to integrate the splintered energy from her past life experience, freeing her from the nightmares. He had a good feeling about it.

After washing the dinner dishes, Jonathan sauntered into the family room, where Sammi was sitting on the floor with Maggie, brushing her coat. Between strokes, she'd hug her, pet her, and whisper loving messages in her ear.

Jonathan bent down to pat the dog. Turning to Sammi, he said, "Hey, sweetie. I have a surprise. What do you say we take a fight down to San Diego tomorrow to see everyone? Your first plane ride since you were a little baby. I want you to meet a new lady who wants to get to know you a bit. She has a great playroom, I hear. I think you'll like her."

Sammi didn't look up, continuing to brush Maggie's coat. "I want to see everyone, but I'm not going to fly. Let's just drive."

"Well, I have a friend who's flying there, and I thought it would be fun for you," Jonathan replied, somewhat perplexed.

She hugged Maggie tightly and shook her head. "No, I'm not going to. It wouldn't be fun for me."

"Why not?"

She crossed her arms over her chest and pouted. "Because I'm not going to."

"Are you afraid of the airplane?"

"Yes, I am, so I'm just not going to."

"Okay, sweetie. No worries. I'll let Jim know we made other plans. We'll drive."

Jonathan bit his lower lip and scrunched his nose. *That's interesting.* He wasn't aware of that fear—he'd never heard her mention it before. Maybe it had something to do with her nightmares. He wished he could get her to talk a bit about it. Maybe Olivia could do it. He knew how cautious Sammi had become about hurting her mom's feelings, but opening up to someone else might work. He decided not to push it any further.

The next morning they packed up the car with their luggage, along with Maggie's things, and headed south to San Diego, leaving about an hour later than Jonathan had planned. The dark gray sky had been threatening showers all morning, and small pellets of rain lightly fell, causing him to turn the wipers on low.

As they drove, Sammi, sitting in the back in her booster seat, opened the window for Maggie, who stuck her furry face out of the window seeking the wind.

Jonathan talked to her while looking in his rearview mirror. "Sweetie, can you get Maggie to move away from the window so I can close it so she won't stick her face out? I know dogs love to feel the wind, but it's not a good thing for her. Flying debris can hurt her eyes and ears, and it's just dangerous."

"Okay." She patted the seat next to her, coaxing Maggie to move from the window. "Sorry, Mags, but safety first. We have to put the window up a bit." She held a treat in her hand to entice her pup to come to her. Easily redirected, Maggie left the window and nibbled the treat from Sammi's hand.

"Okay, Daddy, she's next to me, so you can close the window back here."

"Great. Thanks. So we're on our way!"

"Daddy, we're like peanut butter and jelly sandwiches."

"We are?"

"Yeah, I'm your peanut butter and you're my jelly."

"We make the best sandwich ever, don't we!"

The sound of the wipers and the gentle rain seemed to have a hypnotic effect on Sammi. Jonathan glanced in his rearview mirror a few minutes later and noticed she was fast asleep. It reminded him of when she was a baby and had a hard time falling asleep. No matter what time of the day or night, he'd strap her into her car seat and go for a long ride, allowing the soothing motion of the car to quickly lull her into dreamland. *It seems like yesterday.*

After a couple hours when he exited off the freeway, the change in speed woke Sammi up. She rubbed her eyes. "Are we there?"

"Almost. Maybe five more minutes and we'll look for her apartment building."

"Daddy, look for an apartment building that has a red door."

"Okay, but did someone say she had a red door?"

"No, I just see it in my head."

They approached the building, and sure enough, there was a red door. They parked the car and found Olivia's apartment. Jonathan contained Maggie in her cage and set it down at the entry to ring the bell. He felt Sammi slip her hand into his, grasping it rather tightly.

He looked down at her, wearing a gentle face. "You understand she's just going to play with you right?" he said, wanting to assure her she didn't need to feel afraid.

"Okay, Daddy. What are we going to play? Can you play too?"

"It'll be a surprise, 'cause I don't know what game it'll be. Daddy needs to work while you're playing, so I just want you to have fun."

"Okay."

Olivia answered the door, greeting them with a radiant smile and extending her hand to Jonathan, then Sammi.

She has the whitest teeth I've ever seen! he thought.

"Hi, I'm Olivia. Nice to meet you, Mr. Cohen. I'm a fan. I read your book, *The Line Between*, and related to so much of what you said. I also really like your movies."

"Call me Jonathan. Thanks so much. I'm humbled."

Olivia squatted down to Sammi's level. "And it's very nice to meet you, Miss Samantha."

Sammi stood still and stared at Olivia for a few minutes.

"Sammi, say hello to Miss Olivia," said Jonathan, urging her to interact.

Her eyes welled up with tears. "Hello. Can I give you a hug?" Sammi asked.

"Well, of course you can."

Sammi hugged her and hung on uncharacteristically long.

Jonathan was concerned she was afraid of what was going to happen. "Sammi, are you worried? Miss Olivia is just going to play with you," Jonathan said.

"I know, Daddy."

Olivia invited them into the kitchen—she'd recently finished painting it a canary-yellow color and the scent of fresh paint lingered—and asked them to sit at the table. "I always like to start with us sharing some cookies and milk. How does that sound?"

Sammi perked up. "I think they're going to be chocolate chip."

"That's exactly what they are. I made them myself." Olivia offered the platter to Sammi and then Jonathan.

"These are good. Do you like them, Daddy?" Sammi wiped the melted chocolate off her lip with her fingertip.

"Delicious."

"Do you think you would like to play with me?" Olivia said.

"I do. I like you. You're so pretty now. You have such pretty skin and hair."

"Thank you, Sammi."

Jonathan mentally noted Sammi's unusual behavior with Olivia and chalked it up to nerves. She probably was aware on some level that the visit was to help her with her nightmares and felt reticent to delve into them.

While Sammi finished her cookies, Olivia pulled Jonathan aside.

"Jonathan, do you want to sit in and watch? Please know this is not a regression. We're going to use play to see if we can open things up. This may take more than one session depending on how she reacts. Some kids open up right away. Some don't. Sammi may need to get to know me better. I usually start with some music that opens the third eye while the child sits in the yoga position called the child's pose. Then I link my heart chakra to hers. After that, we'll play."

"I don't want to be a distraction. I'll sit over here in the corner so I can watch but not be in the way." Jonathan sat at the desk in the corner of the room, opened his laptop, and pretended to work.

"Great. Make yourself at home, and if you need anything in the kitchen, help yourself," Olivia said as she took Sammi by the hand to the area of the room where the dollhouses were lined up.

"Sammi, I'm going to do some work over here while I wait for you. Olivia has a pretty cool play room," Jonathan said, wanting to assure her she'd be fine.

"Okay, Daddy. So you'll be right here?"

"Yep, right here." Dollhouses might seem innocent, but Jonathan knew they were a tool counselors sometimes used to get a child to give up their secrets. Olivia had a box brimming with different dolls of varying genders, ages, races, and several styles of dollhouses. It was a delightful place for a child. She had puppets and an entire box of transportation toys. Tucked in the corner of the room was an easel for painting and drawing. *This will be interesting.*

Olivia and Sammi sat on the floor, tailor fashion.

"I work with lots of kids. But it doesn't seem like work because we play. Do you like to play?" Olivia flashed Sammi a smile that made her eyes appear as though they were twinkling.

Sammi held her fingers in her mouth and nodded her head yes.

"First we need to get nice and relaxed. Do you like music?"

She nodded again.

"I'm going to put these headphones on your ears, and you can secretly listen to my special music."

"Okay."

Olivia demonstrated a position she wanted Sammi to assume. "Watch me. Get in this position. In yoga it's called an asana. This is the child's pose. Start in a kneeling position."

"My mom does yoga."

"That's cool! Drop your butt toward your heels as you stretch the rest of your body down and forward. Like this.

"Now put your arms in a relaxed position along the floor, rest your tummy comfortably on top of your thighs, and gently place your forehead on the mat.

"I'm going to put the headphones on you, and then you listen to the music. Stay like that until you feel nice and relaxed, as long as you like. I'm going to do it along with you and do something called chakra linking. We have seven energy centers in our body called chakras that are the colors of the rainbow. I'm going to link my heart chakra, which is green, with yours during this session." She placed the headphones over Sammi's ears and clicked on the music.

After about eight minutes, Sammi removed the headphones.

"I'm done," Sammi announced.

"That's perfect. Now let's play dolls, and we'll make up stories to tell. It's going to be fun! Go ahead and pick out one of the dollhouses you want to use. Do you like stories?"

"My daddy writes stories. He said our story is very important."

"Your story *is* very important. Let me show you what I have. See all of these dolls I have? And trains and cars, and planes, and swing sets, and all sorts of things. Pick a doll."

"Can I pick more than one?" Sammi asked as she sat in front of the smallest dollhouse, making her selection.

"There are no rules when we play. You can pick whatever you like. Go ahead. Then tell me a story about them. Make up whatever you want."

Sammi pulled out a fabric boy doll from the box and rummaged to find a girl doll and an adult doll. "There's a boy and a girl and a mommy who live in this house."

"No daddy?"

"No, the daddy went away." Sammi handed the boy doll to Olivia. "Here, you hold the boy doll while I find a grandpa doll." She dug through the box of dolls until she found one that satisfied her. "I like him 'cause he looks older, but I wish he didn't have gray hair."

"We can pretend it's a different color. What color would you want it to be?"

"Brown."

"Where do they live?"

"They live in a house, but it doesn't look like this." She pointed to the dollhouse.

"What does it look like? How is it different?"

"It's not big like this house, and it doesn't have an upstairs. And there's a swing set in the backyard."

Olivia handed Sammi a toy swing set. "Go ahead and put it back there."

Sammi bent the legs on the dolls and put the boy and girl on the swings.

"Where's the mommy?"

"The mommy is in the house packing suitcases. She's upset. She doesn't want them to go on a trip."

"Where are they going?"

"On a trip with their grandpa. He flies airplanes. They're going to see their grandma."

"A big airplane like this, or this smaller one?" Olivia held up two different-sized toy airplanes.

Sammi accepted the larger plane she handed to her and looked it over. "The big one, but it had three hearts on the tail here."

Olivia stood and retrieved a booklet of stickers. "Here are some heart stickers—go ahead and put them on the tail."

Sammi peeled off three and placed them on the tail of the plane. "Grandpa will fly the plane with the boy and the girl. The mommy isn't going to go because she has to work, and the children are going to spend time with Grandma. It's her birthday. Do you have a grandma doll?"

"I do. Let me find it for you." She dug through the box and found an older-looking female doll with gray hair, handing it to Sammi.

Jonathan, watching out of the corner of his eye, noticed how Sammi laughed and giggled as she made the child dolls interact with the grandma doll.

"Now it's time for them to go home after their visit with Grandma. The boy and girl sit together on the plane. They're going home. The grandpa is flying the plane with another man. They eat the snack Grandma packed them."

"What did they have?"

"Raisins and string cheese. The little boy is very afraid, but the little girl is only a little afraid."

"What are they afraid of?"

"The sound the airplane makes when it takes off."

"What does it sound like?"

"Like roaring. They fly like this." She stood next to Olivia and held the plane and pretended to fly it through the air. "Oh, they're up in the air in the clouds. Everything looks so little down below. The children eat their snacks and color in their coloring books. It's time to land at the airport.

"Oh-oh ... what's that crunching sound? There's a big bump like this." She held the airplane and made violent jerking movements with it.

"People are screaming. 'We've been hit. We're going down,' she yells. 'We're going down. Oh no ... oh no ...'" She dropped the plane on the dollhouse. "The plane crashes and now it's on fire. The little girl and boy fly into the sky like this." She threw the boy and girl doll through the air. "So does Grandpa." She threw the adult male doll too.

"Everywhere there's fire. And then they're dead." She collapsed down on the floor, burying her head in her hands, crying, then sobbing.

Jonathan jumped up and saw Olivia look up, signaling him with her index finger to let her work it through with Sammi. *Okay, I'll let her cry it out. She needs to release it. This is so hard to watch her acting so upset, but I know she needs to release this emotion, this trapped energy. Let it out, Sammi. Let it out.*

Sammi spontaneously resumed the child's pose while she cried, and Olivia slowly stroked her fingers down Sammi's spine, relaxing her. She began to calm.

"It's okay, Sammi. It's not happening now. You're here with me. Tell me what you're feeling."

"It's really scary and the mommy is so sad." She sat up and put the mommy doll on the bed, facedown, and made crying sounds.

"You're okay, Sammi. It's all over. You're safe here with us now. It's just a story now."

"It's a sad story."

"Then what happens?"

"They go to see their mommy as spirits. She sees them. She's so sad and can't stop crying. They tell her they're okay."

"Can she hear them?"

"Yes, she does. They're dead, but the mommy's too sad, so sad. Now they need to find the mommy and tell her they're okay. They're okay."

"Who's the mommy? Can you tell me more?"

Sammi stood and crossed her arms across her chest. "I'm done playing now. I want Daddy." She ran to Jonathan and crawled on his lap, throwing her arms around his neck.

His thoughts were going a mile a minute. *Oh, my sweet little girl. So that's what happened to you! That's what's been causing all the nightmares and anxiety.* He hoped going through what she did was enough to release the energy. *I wonder who the mother is...* Obviously, Sammi had been carrying her pain and anguish from her past life to her new life as Sammi.

Olivia stood next to Jonathan as he soothed Sammi. "You're okay, sweetie. You did a good job today. Thanks for playing with me."

She looked up at Olivia with widened eyes. "I think you miss your mommy too."

Olivia was taken aback. "Yes, I do. I haven't seen my mother for many years."

Sammi nodded. "I know."

While Sammi watched the fish swimming in the aquarium, Olivia explained to Jonathan what she thought had just happened.

Jonathan noticed a subtle change in Olivia. She seemed shaken. "You okay?"

"Yeah, sure. I linked my energy centers to Sammi's to tap into the feelings, and they were pretty intense. I'm feeling a bit emotional from it."

"I haven't heard of the chakra linking before."

"I learned the technique a few years ago and have used it a few times with kids I work with."

"Hmm ... interesting." He'd have to talk about that with Matthew.

While Sammi was being entertained by the fish, Olivia debriefed Jonathan, speaking softly. "So obviously, it's a plane crash. She didn't talk about it as herself, though. She said 'the little girl and boy,' but she was clearly feeling the emotions. She seemed to be having trouble dealing with the residual anguish of the mother. I feel she's very attuned to that sadness. I can feel it myself from the linking. The trauma of flying through the air has stuck with her. I don't know where or what year, but we can try again for that, if you want. I didn't want to push beyond what she could give. But more than the crash itself, I think she's feeling pain for the mother."

"She's always been an empath, picking up on the energies of not just people, but animals as well. It can't be too far back in time that this happened. The plane had a logo of three connected hearts. I think they were flying Eros Airlines."

"I was thinking the same thing."

"And I think Eros Airlines was Air Love America and changed their name in the early seventies. I'll do some research on this," Jonathan said. "Should be pretty easy to find."

"I was feeling the sensations along with her, and it was pretty intense. Maybe jot down anything after this that comes up, or sensations or feelings she has. I've seen kids feel very tired after this, so be prepared for that."

"Okay. We're going over to my mom's house now, and it'll help distract her a bit. It's weird. Explains a few things. She refused to fly down here today. I have a friend who's a pilot who was coming down, and she empathically said no."

"Let me know what you find out."

Jonathan walked over to the fish tank as Sammi gazed into it. "Would you like to get an aquarium with fish?"

"No, I think they would be better being in the ocean or a lake."

"Sammi, how do you feel, sweetie?" Jonathan gently stroked her hair.

"I'm done crying now. I don't want to play this game again. I want to go see Grandma and Grandpa now, and I want Maggie."

"Okay. You did a really good job playing today. Maggie's in her cage in the other room. Let's go get her and be on our way."

Jonathan shook Olivia's hand. "Thanks, Olivia. We'll talk soon."

"Again, do let me know what you find out in your research. I'm very interested."

Olivia opened her arms to Sammi. "Sammi, can I have a hug goodbye?"

"Okay." She stood on her tiptoes and gave her a hug. "I'll see you. Come on, Maggie, let's go see Grandma and Grandpa."

Jonathan was glad the experience was over. He wanted Sammi to feel at peace. With the trapped energies brought to the surface, he hoped that once and for all, the nightmares were now a thing of the past.

Chapter 19

THE NONPHYSICAL WORLD

Neshamah: That was a pretty intense interaction. So the trauma from Sammi's past life causes her current nightmares?

Pneuma: Sammi didn't have all the information on the conscious level to integrate it because the experience of the actual trauma she had in the past is stored on an unconscious level. With Olivia's technique, she was able to tap into the unconscious level and retrieve that bit of information, experience the energy that was connected with it, and hopefully has now processed the information completely. It's like when a computer goes down and you need to find the lost data.

Neshamah: So when a child is displaying phobias or fears, it could be that a trauma wasn't totally dealt with and it could be related to a past life. But time on Earth is linear, so it can feel like the trauma is actually happening in their current life.

Pneuma: Yes, that's the case.

Neshamah: So did reliving the information heal that now for Sammi?

Pneuma: As they say on Earth, time will tell.

Chapter 20

February 1

Olivia was mentally distracted while she taught her yoga class—she kept replaying her session with Sammi over and over in her mind. There was something so different about that experience than ones she'd had with other children. She couldn't put her finger on it. *I need another session with Dr. Hobbs to figure this out.*

She made an appointment and, a few weeks later, drove to his office in La Jolla. Dr. Hobbs greeted her when she rang the bell and gestured for her to enter his office.

"Come in, Olivia, and have a seat. How about a cup of tea? So you want to review your session with Sammi?"

She selected the comfortable-looking chair by the large bay window and perched on the edge of the chair. "I'd love a cup. So, I asked Jonathan if it was okay if I talk about my work with Sammi with you, and he said, 'Hell yes,' so I guess that's his consent."

Dr. Hobbs poured and handed her a cup of Earl Grey tea, then sat across from her. "He told me his observations about the session. Your technique is fascinating to me, and we have to talk more about that at another time. It's so interesting what came out of it. It took nothing but a distraction using play to bring it right out of her. Plus, telling the story to a neutral party was key. Well done. Sounds like she has issues centered around her mother's feelings from that life, and Jonathan mentioned her concern about hurting her mother's feelings in this life."

"Yes, the focus was definitely on her mother's feelings. The thing is, when she was describing it, I was feeling the emotions along with her. I chakra-linked with her, connecting my heart center to hers, and that does help me tap into people's emotions more intensely, but hers were particularly powerful. I may need to be more careful with some people. She has these strong bonding feelings for the mother in her past life—she felt guilty and sad about abandoning her. I actually experienced her intense feelings of worry or anguish for her mother figure. As she was talking about the plane crash, she was grasping my hand very tightly."

Dr. Hobbs stood and stared out of his office window. "Fascinating observations. It would be interesting to see if her previous mother is still alive. Jonathan is going to research this."

"That's a wild thought. I've read about it before, but I've never personally come across it. Have you?"

He turned to face her. "I've read and heard of it too, but I've not come across it in my practice before. The universe has interesting ways of bringing people together to work out karma. It's the norm for members of soul groups to meet up again and again. They are drawn together like moths to a flame." Dr. Hobbs returned to his chair.

Olivia sipped her tea and thought for a moment before speaking. "And sometimes we're instantly aware of a connection with another individual, and sometimes we're not. I think we'd get a lot more information on this if people weren't so afraid to open up. So many people who come to me keep their sessions secret because they worry people will call them crazy. On the Internet, when people relay revelations their young kids say about past lives, it's often called *creepy* or *chilling*. Actually, I read a survey somewhere that reported that roughly one in ten people can recall a past life."

Dr. Hobbs leaned back, allowing himself to sink into the softness of the leather chair as he folded his hands over his chest, with fingers interlocked. "There was a story I read about a case from the early 1900s. I think it was where a girl named Lugdi was born in Mathura. She died a week or so after delivering a baby boy. Almost two years later, in Delhi, a baby girl named Shanti was born. When she was older, she often spoke about her husband and child in Mathura and about where she'd lived and about her family in a prior life. She was six at the time. Long story short, she ended up meeting with her husband from that life and was overwhelmed when she also met her son from that life. The husband was totally convinced it actually was his wife. Apparently, many prominent people studied the case. Imagine such a thing. Think about if you were Sammi, and you died in a past life and came back to a place where you lived before, and the person who was your mother then is alive."

"I see why we forget our previous lives when we're born, because life would be so complicated otherwise and it could cause relationship issues."

Dr. Hobbs stroked his chin. "It could. I've toyed with this concern. I know Sammi wants to connect with her former mother, but I'm not sure if we should pursue seeking out more information. I want to do it only to serve in the best interest of the people involved and not just to settle a curiosity. If it's healing to the souls involved, that may be different."

"Yes, who knows what emotions and issues it might bring up? I guess it wouldn't hurt to check into it. Maybe identify the mother, if she's alive. If she's not open to the possibility of reincarnation, there wouldn't be any point. And it could stir up some real psychological problems for the mom—start her grieving all over again."

"There's a great deal to consider. It could open a big can of worms. But that doesn't resolve the situation that you're here for," Dr. Hobbs said.

"I'm experiencing some strong emotions lately, so I'm just feeling so anxious. I've been dealing with my feelings about Curtis and working diligently on the karma-clearing program."

"Where are you with your feelings toward him at this point?"

"I've certainly transitioned through the years. At first I was filled so full of hate for him. Just an angry, raw hatred. And then I started thinking about how he grew up and what a terrible childhood he had himself. He was out on the streets early in his life, having to fend for himself, finding his own shelter and food. Day-to-day survival in that kind of environment had to be difficult. He had no good role models in his life to give him an inkling as to how to be an okay husband. He had so much anger in him, and it escalated over the years."

"Do you still feel the hate?"

Do I? She had to think for a minute to assess her current emotions. "Surprisingly, I don't. I don't hate him anymore. But I can say that now, because I'm away from him—or I think I am—and he currently isn't hurting me. If I were still in that day-to-day situation, I have no idea how I'd feel. Actually, I want to reach a point of detachment, where I don't feel any emotion for him at all."

Dr. Hobbs nodded in approval. "The intense feelings you're experiencing are a good sign. More than likely, your energy shift is in progress, bringing you to a higher vibration. The old, the worn-out, the unneeded behaviors bubble up to the surface so you can release them. Part of the ascension process you're heading on involves detaching, so know that you're on the right road. You're trying to balance yourself."

"That's good to know. I definitely am experiencing changes going on, and I feel like I'm in that void. That place you go when you let go of something, but something new hasn't come to replace it yet—so, kind of a limbo. It's a strange, almost empty feeling."

Dr. Hobbs held his index finger in the air. "I have an idea. It may be a good idea to do some energy cord work. Are you familiar with that?"

"No, please tell me."

"It would be very similar to the chakra linking and delinking you do. Often, we'll bring back past relationships with others from our soul group so we can absolve the karma. As you're well aware, they haven't always been lovey-dovey relationships, and we often reconnect with someone who may have been an enemy in another life. It's common to see that in families. We've been in many relationships over lifetimes and have created a lot of karmic ties. The goal would be to remove those negative energetic attachments. That makes it easier for you to be with them in a loving, compassionate way. Then you may not have to come back in another life together and balance it.

"As you know, your thoughts and emotions are energy. So when you talk about, think about another person, you're sharing some of your energy, and that creates an energy cord with that person, and you're probably not aware you're doing it. Someone can do the same to you. If you obsess about someone or a situation or there's something you can't let go of, there may be a cord that's linking you. Here's the good news—you can get rid of negative cords that are not serving in your best interest. The goal of cord healing is to eliminate the nonbeneficial exchange of energies."

"Sounds very appropriate for me to do this with Curtis. How do I do it?"

"You can do this in the quiet of your home. Get in a relaxed state and then mentally inspect your body and identify and find the cord that belongs to Curtis. Do a search of your body and see where you sense it. I do this by getting in a lotus position with my palms facing up on my lap. Then I visualize searching my body, looking for cords. You can ask your spirit guides to help you find the source of the cord or cords that you have with him. Once you find it, or them, look at it and describe what it looks like and feels like. You need to figure out if it's serving a purpose to grow your soul.

"If you decide to heal it, gently imagine the cord dissolving, evaporating into thin air. If you find his essence refuses to let go of the cord, you may have to be more aggressive, but if it can be done with love and peace, then gentle is the way to go."

Olivia knitted her brow as she concentrated. "If he won't release it, and I need to be more aggressive, what do I do?"

"Be sure you're cutting the correct cord, first of all. There are very valuable cords you have too. If you decide to eliminate it, choose a cutting tool. I imagine a sparkling golden laser saber that I use to cut the cord. Pick whatever works for you: your choice. I visualize slicing through the cord, then pulling the cord totally out of my body and vaporizing it. Then I send healing light to the location it originated from. Visualize the energy being released from your body. Then state your intention that the energy connection between the two of you has ended. Sometimes the other person wasn't ready to release it, and they may try to reconnect it again, so that's something to be aware of. Send them healing light from your heart chakra to theirs to finalize the procedure."

Olivia nodded. "Sounds like something I can do. I'll work on that. Actually, there are several people I could use it with."

"I find it very effective. You can use that technique with patients too. If you find you get overly attached or emotional about their issue, you can deal with that cord."

Olivia helped herself to another cup of tea. "I figure these feelings that surfaced after working with Sammi are all a part of the energy shifts going on in me. Even though I did the unlinking of our chakras, but I'm still feeling really connected to her. I don't want to cut any energy cords with her, however. I've been dreaming about her every night and have this sensation like I'm meeting up with her in our dreams. But not as us, as different people."

Dr. Hobbs lifted his eyebrows. "Tell me more about the dreams with her."

"We're usually playing together—we're probably about the same age she is now. Only in my dream, she has short curly hair, almost like ringlets, and bright blue eyes. She's Caucasian. Tall. I, apparently, am her brother, and I look just like her. Tall, with curly blonde hair and blue eyes. We're very close, very bonded. I feel like we're twins."

"How did you react when you first met her in this life?"

"An instant connection." Olivia paused for a few seconds before continuing. "There's this part of me that feels like I'm part of her story."

"Interesting ... funny thing is, I have this strong intuition that you *are* part of the story too. Perhaps, just perhaps, you're one of the missing links in this story, Olivia Buffet."

Dr. Hobbs held his finger up in the air to indicate he was thinking while he paced the room for several minutes. Olivia wondered what was going on in his head but gave him silence to process his thoughts.

"Give me a few seconds," he said.

He returned to his chair and leaned forward toward her as if he were going to share a secret. "I have this thought. What if you actually were in the same plane crash together? What if the universe is pulling everything together? You've heard of collective karma, right?"

She nodded. "In your lecture, yes. Souls with common objectives."

He nodded. "In this three-dimensional world we live in, we vibrate at an energy level that responds to tragedy. By collective karma, I'm referring to souls joining together for a common cause to transform a tragic experience into a positive change that makes the world better and stronger. You see many people who've experienced tragedy in their lives devote themselves to some related cause after going through their suffering. I worked with a client whose son committed suicide due to his serious mental health issue. His mother established an organization in his name that focused on research for a better understanding of depression. You both might have been on that plane to make some kind of positive change in the airline industry, or for some other reason—who knows?"

"I mean, what would the odds of that be? I'd have to play the lottery."

"What are the odds of any of us connecting again in this vast, huge world? I suggest the odds are good because we preplan it that way."

"I'm glad you said that, because I feel less crazy thinking this ..."

Their eyes met. "Tell me," Dr. Hobbs urged.

"Okay ... I have this strong feeling that I was previously Sammi's brother," Olivia said, her voice filled with emotion. "I think my name was Josh."

They both sat and stared at each other.

Then, Dr. Hobbs just nodded his head, very slowly, in agreement.

Chapter 21

Between Two Worlds

Nate

I'm going in and out of my soon-to-be baby body now. It's what we do before we're born, although souls choose to enter the body at varied times. I'm adjusting again to what it feels like to have bones, blood, flesh, organs. It's a whole different sensation than being vibrating light like I'm used to. A body feels dense and heavy, but I know I'll adjust—I always do. I'm looking forward to being born again and fulfilling my new missions and goals.

This is a period of transition for me; I need to adjust to being in the developing fetus and the world it's growing in. Sometimes the sounds of Aria's body are too much for me, and I need to leave again. But I'm feeling the connection and love for her, and I feel her returning that love to me as well. Those feelings of connectedness start really early.

Waves of happiness and comfort wash over me as Aria sits in her rocking chair, rubbing her belly, thinking warm and loving thoughts about me. She has no idea how helpful that is.

I've met once more with my spiritual mentors, and we've reviewed the things I need to work on to grow my soul and to help increase the consciousness of the planet once I incarnate. I'm going to try to hold on to my knowledge from the nonphysical world as long as I can as it will make things so much easier when I'm on Earth.

Sometimes I send telepathic messages to reassure Aria that everything's going to be okay. It's weird how sometimes I can sense her stress and her anxiety. I wish she wouldn't worry.

Pretty soon I'll be with Sammi in the flesh again. I felt bad about her nightmares, but it looks like she's released that trapped energy now, so I feel less guilt. I felt a sadness about my role for a long time even though it was an agreement we'd made together. I feel protective of Sammi, and I want to help her to be happy in any way I can.

I think I'll send her a telepathic message telling her that.

I'm going to help you, Sammi. I love you, and I'm going to help protect you.

Chapter 22

February 25

Aria was dreading the day. It was the fourth Friday of the month, and that meant a get-together of the LA *ladies who lunch*. Aria wished she felt a connection with the group of women, but she didn't find herself sharing the same interests. There was no point in ruminating over it: she had to go. Sometimes she had to play the networking game because of her job, but it was drudgery for her. The focus at the parties always seemed to come down to talking about what designer outfit someone was wearing or gossiping about a person who wasn't there— she found those conversations boring. *I really don't want to go*, she thought.

Aria stood behind Sammi as she sat on a white wicker stool at the dressing table in the master bedroom, brushing her hair into a ponytail. She's is just so precious. I'm glad she's going with me. Sammi was excited to be included in the invitation to the party, so Aria didn't want to burst her bubble of joy by telling her how she actually felt about going.

"There. You're perfectly adorable," Aria said as she finished placing two sparkly barrettes in Sammi's hair. "Sit on my bed, because I need you to help me decide what to wear." Aria stepped into her walk-in closet, pulling out two dresses on hangers. "We're having a Santa Ana, so it will be hot today."

Sammi climbed up on the bed and settled in against the decorative pillows. "What's that?"

"Winds that are really strong, dry, and hot. Which sundress do you like better? This one or this one?" She held out the dresses for Sammi to choose.

"Your skin is such a pretty tan, so I think the white one with the flowers would look the best."

"The white one it is. And which sandals? These?" She held up a pair, dangling them by the strap.

"Yes, those are pretty."

Aria looked lovingly at her daughter. "And you look very pretty in your dress. Are you sure you want to wear your pink boots, though? Because the sandals I bought you would look so pretty and you'd feel cooler."

"I'm not hot in them. They're just really comfortable. Can Maggie come along?"

"No, we can't bring our dog to their house, honey."

"Can I bring Dudley?"

"Well, since he's a stuffed dog, I think that will be okay."

They left for the party at 11:40 but arrived faster than expected; they were one of the first, if not the very first, to arrive. *So much for being fashionably late.* The party was a typical trunk show, with purses, scarves and jewelry, set up in a spacious home in Bel Air. Aria noted it was a stunning house, and the hostess was anxious to show it off with a tour: an ecoconscious residence that overlooked a canyon on a nearly two-acre lot landscaped with a beautiful pool hidden within lush native California flora and fauna. *I wonder what their water bill is in the midst of this severe drought.* The sweeping porch that spanned the front of the house gave it a homey appearance.

Aria thought the large gourmet kitchen was impressive, although the hostess said she never cooked. The natural grass and stone pools outside provided a special charm, and in true Bel Air style, the house had a few over-the-top amenities as well, such as a recording studio with a piano and full drum set. There was a bar set up poolside with pitchers of icy-cold sangria and frosty lemonade. The party was one of the trendy charity events—an "invite your girlfriends, shop, drink, and socialize" trunk show.

Aria looked at her watch. *Okay, we'll stay no more than an hour and a half.*

While the ladies chitchatted, Aria saw Sammi wandering around the perimeter of the yard, clutching Dudley close to her chest—finally finding a landing spot in the shade to sit and sip her frosty glass of lemonade.

Eventually, the hostess—a blonde wearing a lightweight red stretch-jersey dress—emerged from the house, strutting about on four-inch high heels, into the backyard, where the guests were milling around the pool with their drinks. She rapped a spoon on her sangria glass to gain the attention of the group.

"Ladies, we need to go indoors for our show. I've set it up inside since it's too hot and windy a day to spend much time out in the sun. We'll start with a delicious lunch. There's sangria, hummus with pita chips, lobster salad in lettuce cups, fruit salad, mini cheeseburgers, apricots with goat cheese, basil and Marcona almonds, and an assorted cheese tray. For dessert there are adorable cake pops, made by my friend Leslie, and mini lemon meringue tarts. Please enjoy and please buy! Remember, this is for charity. Let's make this event a success. Did I say there was sangria?"

Lunch was set up in a large room adjoining the kitchen. As the women moved the venue inside the house, they formed a line at the buffet table. Aria noticed how the women put food on their plates, but no one actually ate. *I wonder why people in California even bother to serve food at their events.* But the women were in a buying frenzy, busy modeling scarves and purses and trying on bracelets and necklaces. The room sounded like a hive of buzzing bees. Aria wasn't all that interested in the items for sale but did find a gold bracelet she liked that would be a nice gift for her mother, so she bought it and a few other necklaces, thinking she'd give them as holiday gifts for various friends. For some reason she just wanted to go home. She felt tired and out of place. She was glad she still wasn't showing a baby bump yet, so she didn't have to talk about her pregnancy with the ladies. She'd looked at her watch at least ten times already, wishing the minutes would fly faster. *Never mind staying an hour and a half. Thirty more minutes and we'll head home.* She could tell Sammi was getting a bit bored as well.

One of the women, an aspiring actress, cornered Aria to talk shop. She flashed her well-manicured nails as she talked with her hands—quizzing Aria about the latest movie she was working on, clearly seducing her for that special "in" she needed for an acting role.

Aria nodded and agreed, but she wasn't really listening: inconsequential conversation was not something she had the energy for. She escaped as soon as she could without appearing *too* rude—her mind was somewhere else. She wandered around the house and took a little lobster salad on her plate. She wasn't feeling hungry, still dealing with mild nausea from her pregnancy. Sammi seemed content with her mini cheeseburger and cake pop as she sat on the piano bench, swinging her legs as she ate.

*

Back at the house, Jonathan sat in the den at his desk working on his laptop, intent on editing the third draft of his script, when he looked up and jolted to his feet. His heart was beating wildly, and he had a prickly feeling in his head, followed by Nate's voice urgently speaking to him in his thoughts.

Jonny, dude. Call Aria immediately and have her get to Sammi. She's in danger. Call now. Do it! Tell her to get to the pool.

Jonathan knew better than to stop and think about it. He acted quickly. He called Aria, and she immediately answered. *Thank heaven!*

He tried not to scream but found himself yelling. "Aria, get to Sammi now and keep the phone on. She's at the pool. She's in danger. Move! Go!"

Aria instantly tensed and felt the sensation of panic flooding her body. Her head pounded like there were stampeding buffalo in her brain. She looked around and noticed Sammi wasn't sitting on the piano bench any longer. A sense of dread rushed her. *Where is she? She was just eating a cake pop there a few minutes ago!* Time slowed down and, like in one of her movies, Aria felt as though she were running in slow motion. She knew she'd die if anything happened to her baby girl. She should have been paying closer attention like a good mother would.

Aria saw it all unfold, but she didn't understand why she couldn't move faster: the slow-motion effect was infuriating. From inside the house, she saw Sammi in the backyard as she leaned over the pool and reached for Dudley, who had fallen into the water at the deep end. Aria could hear herself yelling, "No … no … don't do that!" She raced to her in a panic, although it still felt like a snail's pace. *I need to get to her now!*

She watched as Sammi reached out further than she should and quietly fell into the pool with hardly a splash. What a deceptively quiet event it was as she saw her daughter bob and then submerge under the water! Silently. No splashing. No sound.

Aria screamed, "She's in the water! Help me!" Her whole body trembled and shook as she kicked off her shoes and jumped into the pool, fully clothed. Other people gathered and stood poolside watching, ready to assist. Why couldn't she get her body to cooperate quickly enough? Sammi had only been in the water a few seconds. As she treaded water, Aria grabbed Sammi around her waist, holding her for dear life, and swam her to where she could stand. She lifted her up from under her arms and handed her to someone standing at the side of the pool. Sammi was completely drenched and looked shell-shocked, but she was breathing, not coughing.

Aria screamed, "Oh my God, my baby."

While the woman attended to Sammi, another helped extract Aria from the pool.

The woman with Sammi said, "She's okay, Aria. She's breathing fine. Just a bit scared."

Sammi looked at Aria with chagrin. "Mama, I'm sorry."

Aria grabbed her beloved daughter pulling her tightly to her chest, rocking her back and forth while she sobbed. "It's okay, baby. You're okay. Everything's okay. Your mama is here."

She could hear Jonathan yelling at her through the cell phone she'd laid on the side of the pool. "Someone please hear me. Aria! Aria, please! What's going on? Is she okay? Aria, talk to me!"

Aria was shaking so hard she thought her teeth might fall out. Tears streaked down her face in the aftershock of fear. She could feel her heart still pounding in her ears. Weak and unable to stand steadily on two feet yet, she stayed seated and held Sammi close to her breast as she grabbed the phone.

"Jonny, she's okay!" she said breathlessly. "Thank God she's okay. She was only in the pool for a few seconds. She reached for

Dudley and fell in. How did you know to call me? You saved her life! There was no one out here. She was all alone." She sobbed, deep and heaving. "My baby, my baby ..." She'd never felt so horrified and scared in her life. She could hardly breathe. What kind of mother was she to even be in this kind of situation? It was her role to protect her child at all times. What if Jonathan hadn't called her? How did he know?

"Nate saved her, Aria. Nate did. I'm in the car on my way to pick you guys up. I'm almost there. Stay where you are. Try to calm down, and I'll be there in a few minutes."

Jonathan was already en route to get them, sweating bullets as he drove. He had visions in his mind of what *could* have happened. He knew, without Nate's message, Sammi could have just slipped under the water into a silent oblivion, slowly sinking to the bottom of the pool. In seconds, one's whole world can change. It certainly was a wakeup call for him. Reality set in. Maybe he'd been too self-absorbed lately. Perhaps it was a message to him to tune in a bit more to what's truly important in life.

He was shaking so hard he pulled to the side of the road and sat back for a minute, collecting himself. His breathing slowed. What he felt was gratitude. Gratitude that he'd heard the message given to him.

"Thank you, Nate. Thanks, my friend."

That night, after tucking his tired girl into bed, Jonathan crawled into his own bed to read while Aria sat at her dressing table, looking in the mirror, removing her makeup. He could tell she still felt rattled.

"Babe, you doing okay?"

She pivoted on her stool to look at him. "I can't stop ruminating about this. Jonny, this has been one of the most frightening days of my life. How does anyone handle the death of a child? I would perish as their very soul left the Earth. I still feel sick about this. And beyond grateful you called. I just don't understand how you knew to call me."

"I've told you I get inspirations from the other dimensions in various ways. I try to keep myself clear to hear those messages that direct my life. I was just sitting there when my head began to pound, and I felt like it was splitting open. Energy was just flowing through the top of my head. Then I heard Nate. It was his voice, the way he spoke. Clear and direct like he was standing next to me. He warned me to call you to get to her. He saved her."

"I can't express how that makes me feel," she said as she grabbed her comb and started pulling it through her long black hair. "I've been kind of a curmudgeon about him being the soul to come to us, out of my own jealousies, yet he was there for her. Out of love, he saved her from leaving us. How do I go about thanking him, Jonny? I feel I owe him an apology, and I want to express my gratitude to him. It's not like I can bring a pie to his house or write him a note on pretty stationery. So how do I reach him?"

Jonathan fluffed his pillow so he'd sit up higher. "With telepathy. Think the thoughts you want him to hear and imagine sending them to him. Try it tonight while you're in bed. Nighttime is usually better. Ask to communicate from your highest self. Be relaxed. Visualize him in your mind. Send a light to him. Just have a heart-to-heart conversation."

"Should I expect to hear him speak to me?"

"More than likely not. He's in a different dimension than you are. Think of it like this—here on Earth, you're tuned in to a frequency, like a certain radio station. Nate is tuned in to a different frequency— a different radio station. He can lower his frequency to resonate with you and hear you, but in order for you to resonate and hear him, you have to vibrate at his frequency, which is much higher. You're not there yet. But he'll be able to hear you."

"Okay, I understand. I'll give it a try."

Jonathan grinned and patted the spot next to him. "Now, come join me in bed."

The cold night air blew through the open bedroom window, causing Aria to shudder as she lay in bed. Her mind was buzzing a mile a minute. After getting up and closing the window, she returned to bed, quieted her mind, and breathed deeply. She needed to talk to Nate—it was that important to her. She closed her eyes and visualized his face in her mind.

This is my first attempt at this, Nate. I'm trying to send you a thought wave here. I haven't been very welcoming to you. Not sure of all the reasons why. Just fear, I guess. But today, I feel your love and am so grateful to you for saving Sammi. I couldn't live if anything happened to her. I can never thank you enough, and I welcome you to our family. I look forward to being your mom. I'm feeling the love and am sending it to you. I hope you receive it.

Chapter 23

March 16

Olivia had taught a late-afternoon yoga class, so now she was running around her apartment, trying to get dinner ready for Jax before he arrived. It was 7:00. Jax was due at her house at 6:30. *He usually runs a half hour late, so he should be here any minute.* Sure enough, the bell rang.

Olivia almost jumped out of her skin when she opened the door. Always one for a joke, Jax surprised her by wearing a Venetian mask on his face.

"What the heck? You scared me to death," Olivia said. "Get in here."

He slapped his thigh, laughing hysterically. "God, that was so funny. I love scaring people. Wearing these masks is awesome. I'm totally into it."

He burst into the kitchen and set a pink cardboard box down on the counter. "Dessert. A surprise. I love, love, love these dinner get-togethers with you."

Olivia grabbed the bowl of onion dip from the refrigerator and stirred it. "I love 'em too. Where did you get that mask, and when are you going to take it off?"

Jax leaned against the counter. "Okay, are you ready?"

"For what?"

"For what's behind door number one?"

"Sure, where's door number one?"

"It's my face. One, two, three—reveal!" He pulled off the mask, unveiling his clean-shaven face.

"Oh my God. Put it back on!" she joked.

"You don't like?" He pouted. "If you don't like my new look, I can grow another beard right here during dinner. That's how fast it grows."

"I'm teasing. I totally love your clean-shaven face. You're too handsome. I can't bear it. It's blinding. You look ten years younger than your thirty years. You know ... you really do have a great chin."

"Hunter can't keep his hands off of me. I'm walking in dangerous territory without my beard to hide me."

She shook her head while laughing. "You need to take a few pounds of pressure off your ego. Just kidding, you really look great."

"Thanks. So what's cooking, good-lookin'? Do you realize it's been almost two months since our last dinner? I thought you were trying to get out of your obligation." He snuck a few potato chips from the bowl.

"Sorry about that. I've been teaching quite a few evening classes since Marilyn quit. At least you and I've been able to meet for coffee every week. Since it's mask-making time, I made finger food so we can eat and craft at the same time."

"Oh, the taste of papier-mâché mixed with a little wasabi horseradish sauce, or a little papier-mâché on my potato chips. So delicious!"

Olivia set the sandwiches, chips and dips, and a tray of fresh veggies on the kitchen table and filled the wineglasses. "Drink a little wine and you won't know the difference between the papier-mâché and the onion dip."

Jax picked up a bag he'd brought with him and removed a white object.

"What's that?" Olivia asked as she swirled a chip through the dip.

"Look at this! I created a cast of Hunter's face so I could make his mask."

She took the mask he extended to her and held it in her hand, rotating it, examining it. "That's cool, how did you do it?"

"I laid plastic wrap over his face, not his nostrils or mouth, and layered plaster paper over his eyes and nose and let it dry. Kind of an erotic process. Cool, huh?"

"Very."

"He was kind of a baby about the process, overly worried I'd let him suffocate."

"This gives me ideas. Was the process complicated?"

"Not really, just time-consuming. He wanted a traditional Pantalone mask."

"Love that nose."

"I know, it's ace, isn't it? I used modeling clay and foil to shape the nose. Now I have to paint it, and I need your artistic viewpoint."

They sat at the kitchen table, munching on appetizers and sandwiches while designing the masks, quiet for a few minutes while deep in their creative process.

Jax set his brush down and wiped his hands on a paper towel. "I've been thinking about this. I want you to come live with us for the time being. I'll come up with some excuse for it, like you're renovating your apartment or something, so I don't have to tell Hunter your secrets if you don't want. I worry about you being here by yourself.

We have two extra rooms, and you could use one for your past life work."

"Well, that comment came out of thin air. Just so you know, I'm feeling less afraid. Maybe it's all been my imagination, like I'm mixing my nightmares up with reality. I'm working with Dr. Hobbs on figuring out my karma with Curtis and the energies I need to balance it. I've been doing his karma-clearing program."

"Oh, honey, I don't give a damn about karma. Really. Why do you care so much about karma?"

Olivia grabbed a paper towel and wiped a blob of red paint she'd dropped on the table. "That's okay if you don't. But I do. I don't want to repeat any more patterns like this one going on with Curtis in future lives. And any remnants of the negative karma stops my ascension to higher frequencies, which affects my soul growth. As I keep saying, I'd like to stop creating bad karma that I have to balance and work out life after life."

"Well, darling, seems the world is one big banana peel—a setup for slips and falls."

"You have such an interesting view of life."

"As do you, my friend. I think my view is on the right track. At least from the parting words of my favorite patient. Let's drink a toast to him." He held his glass in the air.

"George?"

"Yes. He died in his hospital bed today. It was his eightieth birthday. I brought him a mini cake and candle to celebrate and was there with him holding his hand as his light went out, and he passed on."

Olivia raised her glass to his and clinked. "Oh, I'm so sorry. I know how special he was to you. You doing okay?"

"Yeah. He was in so much pain, and I didn't want him to have to endure it any longer. His son was trying to get there before he passed on, but he didn't make it in time. I tried to step in for his son so he wouldn't be alone in his final moments. He tried to hang on until his son got there, but he just couldn't, I guess. He was able to blow out the candle on his cake, and his final words to me were said with a big toothy grin on his face."

"Really? What were they?"

"'Jax,' he said, 'it's all about the love. My birthday wish is that the world recognizes that.' And then he died."

"Those are spectacular last words."

"Yeah, I like to think so."

Jax picked up his brush and resumed painting his mask. "I'm using a lot of gold paint. I guess it's my favorite of the colors. I like the mask you're doing."

"I've gotten quite a few ideas off the Internet."

Jax picked up a jar off the table, and Olivia quickly grabbed it from him, scolding, "Don't you dare open that bottle of red glitter in here. If you do, you'll have to die."

"Ah ... you killjoy, you party pooper, you're no fun."

"I'm fun, but when we do the glitter, we'll do it at your house. Then we'll see who the killjoy will be."

"It will be Hunter." Jax wiped his hands and grabbed a sandwich. "These sandwiches remind me of when I was a kid. My mom loved making us grilled cheese sandwiches, and she'd always cut them into four squares. It's so funny that Hunter used to make them for me for lunch and cut them into squares the same way. Oh, wait ... I shouldn't have said that. Now, you're going to think he was my mom in a past life. Seems kind of creepy."

"Never say never. He's in your soul group, and it's very possible. Not sure about making the grilled cheese from a past life, but you just don't know. I don't see the creepiness in it if he played another role in your life, though."

"So about this soul group stuff ... so as members of the same soul group, is it like we are all made out of the same stardust and each piece is magnetized so we are drawn to each other?"

"Ooh ... I like that description. Sounds kind of magical. I'm going to go with that explanation." She glanced at Jax's mask. "I'm loving the paint job you did on that mask. You have a hidden artistic talent."

"Yeah, mask painter extraordinaire. My second career. But it's pretty cool if I do say so myself."

"Really, it's so unique. It almost looks like a hawk. How did you create the ridge that runs from the point between the two eyes to two inches above the top of the mask?"

"I molded aluminum foil and then covered it with the papier-mâché."

"The nose is so cool! And I like the upward-slanted almond eyeholes. The colors you picked are outstanding. With a pinkish-red beak and then the pastels of yellow, green, blue and purple, with gold as the neutral color, well ... it just looks great."

"Thanks!"

Olivia wiped her hands on a towel. "I need a break. I'm going to make coffee to have with our secret dessert."

"Don't be ticked, but I'm going to grab a smoke while you do that. And no lectures please ..."

"I won't say a word, except open another window please. I don't like the smell."

While Jax stepped out for a smoke, Olivia opened the dessert box that had been sitting on the kitchen counter and discovered twelve mini cupcakes from Sophie's bakery. *Oh, she must have made flavor samples. How thoughtful.* She couldn't wait to try them. Each cupcake was topped with a purple sugar-molded mini mask. As she brought out plates, forks, and a knife to cut them, she began to sing at the top of her lungs.

"For the love of grilled cheese sandwiches, make it stop!" Jax yelled in to the kitchen.

Olivia looked up and saw Jax had opened the door to the balcony to avoid smoking in the house. *I wish he'd quit smoking. He knows how bad it is for him.* The breeze wafted through the room as soon as he opened the door. It was when she saw him shake a cigarette out of his pack—ready to light it—that she heard a cracking, creaking sound.

Instinctively, she screamed, "Get off the balcony, now!"

Jax leaped off the balcony and back into the living room as though he had been hit by a bullet.

He shook uncontrollably. "What the hell, Liv, are you trying to kill me? That balcony sounded like it was ready to go down. You need to tape it off and call to get it taken care of immediately. That could have gone down with me on it. What are all the tools out there for? Holy crap!" He patted his heart and spoke to it. "Calm down, ticker, I don't need you going off on me now."

Olivia raced to the door, glancing out at the structure. "The apartment manager recently had a handyman come to check out the balcony. Residents had complained about warping and the door sticking. He was out there working and didn't say it was at risk of falling off. I think it just makes cracking sounds. He was ready to come back and finish whatever he was doing, but his wife went into labor and he canceled. I'll call him to reschedule."

"Holy smoke—I'm shaking like a leaf." He sat at the table, hands trembling, while Olivia stood behind him massaging his shoulders.

"I'm so sorry, Jax. I never go out there myself. I didn't know you were going out there."

"It's far beyond just being warped and creaking. It feels loose like it's ready to go down. Damn, I could have died tonight and hurt other people along the way!"

"So sorry. It didn't even cross my mind you might go out there. It's that bad? I didn't realize that. I'll put a call in right away. I thought it was just warped."

"I don't want to make a big kerfuffle over it, but that cracking sound scared me to death. I think you owe me a big favor now."

"What is it?"

He looked over his shoulder at Olivia and grinned. "Another five nights of dinners. Well, maybe it should be a month depending on how close you came to killing me. I think I need another drink. Now I'm all worried it's my karma or something. I hope you're not destined to kill me." He flashed her a fake smile.

"Don't be ridiculous. I love you ever so much," she said, kissing him on the top of his head.

Since he couldn't seem to concentrate, Jax declared their crafting for the evening was over. He packed up his things as he prepared to leave.

"You okay, Jax?" she said, her voice racked with guilt. "Aren't you going to stay for dessert?"

"I'm fine, Livie. Just shaken, and I have an early shift tomorrow. I'm not in the mood for cupcakes right now. I'll bring them with me to yoga class tomorrow, and we can pig out in your office afterward, okay?"

"Okay, that's a plan. See you at class tomorrow." She felt guilty about scaring Jax so badly, but she had no idea the balcony was such a problem. She'd call the apartment manager in the morning.

Jax gave Olivia a big bear hug. "Love you, Livie. Sweet dreams."

"Right back at ya."

After he left, Olivia plunked down on the living room couch, still feeling revved up with emotion. *This is the most bizarre thing ever. Could Curtis have snuck in while I was at work and tampered with the balcony?* She wondered if he was indirectly trying to kill her, but she figured those were just paranoid thoughts. Or ... was he trying to kill Jax?

She just didn't understand what the heck was going on!

Chapter 24

April 12

In her bedroom, Margo sat at her dressing table, carefully peeling off her false eyelashes in front of the mirror. She caught herself daydreaming about her last visit with Thomas; she'd enjoyed it much more than she'd anticipated. They'd been seeing each other fairly regularly, with Thomas making frequent trips to San Diego—he'd even talked about moving! She found him easy to be with. Their conversation flowed in ways it didn't with other people, and she loved his sense of humor—a man who could make her laugh meant everything. A great sense of humor and a fun-loving nature, along with a great physical connection, was something she looked for in a relationship, never thinking she'd find it. That spark people yearn for. That urgent aching for another person. For her, it was actually more like a lightning bolt. When she'd discovered she felt it with Thomas, she was startled. The last thing she wanted to do, however, was get carried away with her feelings. She didn't want to set herself up for disappointment. *It's best to let go of any expectations.*

She pulled her hair back off her face, gently rubbing her crow's feet as though her fingertips were an eraser, wondering when she'd gotten so old. She decided from age fifty on, she'd started to unravel.

She placed the first two fingers of each hand on her cheekbones and pushed upward to see what her skin looked like less slack. *Oh, there I am, hidden under saggy skin. That old age thing slowly creeps up on you. In my thirties, my knees started aching from being a runner, then I developed presbyopia in my forties; next came the dreaded hot flashes of menopause, and then came the loss of muscle, saggy skin, and wrinkles.*

At least she didn't look like one of the apple dolls she'd made as a kid yet, but she felt droopy. If her self-esteem had been superglued to youthful beauty, like it was for so many women, she was sure the aging process would have sent her into an emotional tailspin.

How does time go so fast? It seemed like fifty years had sailed by while she was asleep one night. Maybe she hadn't been living in the present moment. She knew she did her best to avoid thinking about the past but recently found herself drifting back to favorite recollections. There could be another ten or even twenty or more years left of her life, so it was time to make some new, exciting memories. But what did she want? Even though it had been a short period of time in their developing relationship, she and Thomas had started to talk about a future together. She just wasn't sure. Was marriage necessary? Was it something she wanted? Was there even a point to it at her age? She'd done fine not being married all these years.

She didn't *need* a man, but she knew what she was missing in her life, and that something was sharing her love. When her family had died, and she didn't know what do to with all the love she'd had, she'd realized it needed to be shared, so she'd volunteered at the local pet adoption organization. All those dejected and rejected dogs and cats were desperate for a kind word, for a hug, for love. She'd worked diligently to give each one of them her surplus love and find them their forever homes. As if she had an innate sense of knowing which pet matched with its perfect human, she'd placed more animals in homes than any of the shelter workers. *When you feel sad, there's nothing like providing service to others to make you feel whole again.* It was probably what had helped her heal the most.

Although Margo now floundered back and forth with her thoughts, she was moving forward with the idea of getting married. Married! The word didn't easily roll off her tongue. It just kind of stuck there at the back of her throat. There was only one thing holding her back: she wanted to know her kids and father were okay. Some kind of reassurance. In her heart, she knew they were fine. But she wondered if Dr. Hobbs could make contact so she could directly communicate with them.

Monday morning was here, and Margo headed off to her early-morning yoga class. Now that her muscles were loosening up more, she could assume more of the positions; it felt good to see visible progress. First stop—coffee. Deja Brew was unusually crowded, but she stood in line to order a vanilla latte. Maybe she should have waited for her fix until she finished exercising, but she decided she needed the benefit of the caffeine to get her motivated. She handed the cashier a ten-dollar bill and told her to pay for the coffee for the woman behind her, then headed to yoga class. Sophie was there on Mondays, and being the good listener that she was, Margo wanted to talk to her about her thoughts on marriage.

After class, Margo saw Sophie rolling up her yoga mat, so she grabbed her attention by waving at her.

Sophie yanked off her sweatband and fluffed her hair, approaching Margo with a smile on her face. "You seem happy, Margo. What's happening in your life?"

"Hey, I like your new haircut. So, things are good. You know? I'm actually living more fully again. It took me a long time, but I'm getting there. So, I have kind of shocking news—Thomas and I are thinking of getting married! He proposed, and he's waiting for my decision. For some reason, I wanted to pass that by you."

"You want to get a coffee and talk?"

"I just had one before class, but I'm thinking another one would be perfect."

They walked over to the Deja Brew and found seats in the corner, where the music wasn't blaring so loudly. Sophie placed the order for their "usual" and brought the steaming cups to the table.

"So, what do you think?" Margo asked as she stirred her coffee.

"Well, I'm excited for you. You know ... when it's right, it's right. At our age, it's easy to recognize what you want and don't want, so snatch up what you want when it's there," Sophie said. "There are no timelines we have to adhere to."

"That's true," Margo said, nodding. "It's not like we have time to wait for a long engagement. We're good company for each other, but I'm not sure if marriage is necessary. Thomas is a bit more traditional and really wants to make it official. Still, I want to start with a clean slate and feel a bit reticent due to some unresolved feelings about my family tragedy, and I was thinking of making an appointment with your husband to see if he could make a psychic connection with them. Maybe contact with them would help me deal with the residual pain that lingers in me."

"You should try it. Why not see if it gives you any resolution? You'll love working with my husband. For me, it was a life-changing experience."

Margo paused for a moment and sipped her coffee. "You know what? I'm going to do it. Why not?"

"And for your wedding, I'll make the cake!" Sophie said, grinning. "Do you celebrate the holidays at all? I was thinking about that the other day—how your birthday is hard for you—and I wondered if other holidays were as well."

"Not so much anymore. One Christmas, about ten years after my family passed, I had a very intense dream, or I had an actual visitation from my kids. Not sure what it was, but they came to me to tell me to enjoy Christmas again. When I was a young mom, I just loved the holidays. From Halloween to New Year's, I loved everything about them: picking out unique gifts, baking, making holiday decorations. Later on, I worked at the animal shelter during the holidays, and I was always committed to finding every sweet animal a home. Lots of people would say don't get anyone a pet for Christmas, but I found people were much more open to getting a pet during the holidays. It worked, and I was able to place tons of cats and dogs into loving homes. It just warmed my heart. I took funny photos of each animal, usually in some festive outfit, made captions on their photos with a little story about them, and posted them online. I crocheted some cute pet sweaters—you know, the ugly Christmas sweaters, only for dogs—that really captured people's attention."

"Oh, I love that!"

"Every holiday season, I throw a party at the shelter, and it grows every year as more and more people become aware of it. I was thinking it would be cute if you made cupcakes or a big dog and cat cake for the party this year. For the humans to eat. I usually start making plans about a year in advance. Do you know someone reliable who could cater the food for the event? Animal-themed, of course."

"This is right up my alley, and I've done it before. I have tons of photos online of different cakes and things, and I do know several people who could do a great job—reasonably priced—on the food. I'll give you my website and password and you can look at it all. Let me know how I can assist."

"You're always so helpful."

"If it's a party with cake, I'm there. So which will come first, the wedding or the animal party?"

"I don't think we'll have an actual wedding. Just standing up in front of a judge or something, if we do it."

Sophie drummed her fingers on the table. "Okay, but we need to do something special. A dinner, some kind of celebration that includes one of my cakes. I insist."

"That sounds great, Sophie. Thanks. And thanks for treating me to a coffee. I have a client, so I have to get going."

Sophie pulled out her phone and sent her website link to Margo. "You know, Margo, you're a very strong woman. I really admire you," Sophie said.

"You do? Well, thank you. That means a great deal to me. I used to think you had to be a ball-busting woman to be strong, but I realized that wasn't necessary, and I could just be myself. Strength comes from the mind."

"I agree with that. Sometimes women are portrayed as either a tough bitch or else totally milk-toast. There are shades of gray between the two!" Sophie stood and jingled her keys in her hand as she prepared to leave.

"Thanks for the chat. You're a great support. I think I know what I'm going to do now," Margo said.

Sophie hugged Margo. "And I think I know what that's going to be. I wish you all the best!"

As Margo arrived home at the end of her work day, she heard the familiar Virtual-Time ding and answered it without the webcam turned on. It was Thomas.

"So, I was calling to see if you had thought anymore about my proposal? And your webcam isn't on," Thomas said as his face appeared larger than life on the computer screen.

"I don't want to turn it on tonight, if you don't mind. I just showered and don't feel presentable."

"You know that doesn't matter to me."

"I was going to call you up myself as I've given this great thought, Thomas, and ..."

She made a long pause.

"And ...?"

"The answer is yes. I do want to marry you."

His grin nearly stretched across the entire computer screen. "Wonderful! That's what I hoped I would hear. I was thinking ... how about honeymooning in Paris?"

"Paris it is!" Her heart was dancing. It wasn't fireworks she felt, but rather an inner glow of light inside of her, spreading through every square inch of her body. She broke a smile that threatened to crack her face if it got any broader.

Just what I wanted. Life isn't over until you come to the last page of the story.

Chapter 25

Nate

My birthday is getting closer, and I'm very excited. Overall, the planning of a new life for a spirit incarnating on Earth is a fascinating process. The whole point of incarnation is to evolve our soul as we learn from the human experiences we're offered. Before we come into a body, we choose our lessons. My plan is outlined, my soul contracts have been made, and I'm ready to begin this life.

Essentially, we write, direct, and act in our own play and may join some of our soul companions who have agreed to play out some of the various roles with us. They may be family or a friend. They may even be an enemy. We also plan our entry and potential exit points.

The planning part is enlightening and creative. You meet with your council and decide what you need to work on to grow your soul. We all go to Earth for a reason.

For the last few incarnations, I selected short lives where I served primarily in the role of teacher to those people in my life. I'm usually in the role of either teacher or student. When I come as a teacher, I'm conveying a valuable lesson, and I keep my life fairly short. My last two lives were that way. One recent life was with Sammi, and another was when I was best friends with Jonathan.

I usually pick a few exit points in my life plan and evaluate how things are going as I progress. But it's my soul that makes the choice of when to end my incarnation, not myself in human form.

Jonathan and I went to La Jolla High School together, and our connection was as instant as a reflex reaction. My favorite thing in that life was my love affair with the ocean. I couldn't have picked a better place to live because, God, how I loved the water. It's where I felt free and connected with nature. My passion was to surf and fish.

I enjoyed all of that for twenty-six years. In my world, twenty-six years is like one grain of sand in the Sahara Desert. But I had a task to do; I was specifically on Earth to teach. When I died, it significantly impacted all of my friends and family, and I had many friends. Many. It delighted me so much to see that most of them got the message I intended to convey with my death. They all seemed to know they would reconnect with me again someday. They recognized my message about living in the now, and that the purpose for living is all about love. If you read my Facebook pages, you'll see that almost everyone understood the lesson I intended, so I'm pleased. It makes that life more than worthwhile. Many of my family and friends were aware that we'll meet up again, knowing that the soul goes on. Each new generation awakens more. The world does evolve. It seems slowly at times, but it's always changing.

When I died, it caused a pause in everyone's daily routine. It was a jolt. A time-out. A reminder to everyone that life is short! We all will die. Live in the moment and enjoy the experiences it offers. And my loved ones did the best thing ever. They didn't just mourn. My community of surfers celebrated my life with a glorious paddle-out. I died in the best way ever, doing what I loved, and they all recognized that too. Some think people on Earth aren't awakening—indeed they are.

There's a plan, and my friends and family recognized mine. They still were talking to me on Facebook months after I transitioned and were aware of visitations with me in their dreams. I feel their eternal love, and that's what it's all about!

This time my major role won't be one of a teacher, even though we are *all* teachers and learners. Instead, I'm coming to help with the collective awakening that's happening right now. Earth has transformed to the fifth dimension, and now people are opening themselves to that concept. People are expressing compassion and feeling an urgent need to get rid of the dysfunctions of society on an impressively large scale. I'm being born at a time of big changes— something extraordinary is happening in the world.

People are noticing the acceleration of the planet, and it's sometimes hard to keep up with it. There are times it feels like things are falling apart, but in reality, the old ways have to be destroyed before the new can emerge. We're even reincarnating faster, with less of a waiting period between incarnations. The new generation is growing in consciousness so quickly. This is such a defining moment on Earth; I think of it as a turning point. Now that we understand karma better, we are able to absolve it so much faster than we were years and years ago. For the awakened souls, they can now liberate their karma during the life they created it. This is big! We will no longer have to wait for eons to work it out. The changes that are happening are amazing.

Intriguing times are ahead. I'm happy to do my part.

Not much longer now until I'm born …

Chapter 26

Nonphysical World

Pneuma: As I've pointed out, we don't have a lot of guidance to do with this soul group: most of them are pretty enlightened and on track. That's what happens when you're more spiritually evolved. People just do what they need to do, readily tuning in to their intuitions.

Neshamah: I imagine some of the souls who are newer to incarnation on Earth require quite a bit of intervention.

Pneuma: There does seem to be a lot of trial and error. The universe really wants an individual to try to stick to what they planned for themselves in a life. That's part of what they agree upon before they're born. When a person uses their free will to try to go against the life they planned for themselves, the universe will often toss some deterrents their way to try to discourage the person from going against their chosen path. In that circumstance, the person will feel like they're swimming against the current, and nothing seems to go right for them.

Neshamah: That's a definite message.

Pneuma: In the spirit dimension, we communicate with thoughts that influence the reality we live in. The moment we think of someone, we can be there with them. This is beginning to happen on the Earth plane too, for those people who have raised their vibratory levels.

Neshamah: The creation of the Internet has been an incredible tool for us. Right there alone, there's instantaneous connection. And years ago, who, on Earth, would have ever conceived of that as a possibility?

Pneuma: Yes. Our goal is to get humanity to the point where it can run its own affairs, but there's still some work for us today. I want to point out something on the monitoring device I'm not sure you noticed. Follow the lighted line on Olivia Buffet's life path. What do you see?

Neshamah: It appears this line was aborted. It's stopped in red. Now this green light is on a different path. But it looks like it intersects with another line here. What does it mean?

Pneuma: You will see. Very soon.

Chapter 27

June 15

Olivia was singing to a tune on her playlist and feeling lighthearted. In order to complete her five-meal obligation to Jax, she'd decided to shake things up a bit and make brunch instead of dinner. But she realized the shared meals with him were no obligation at all and something she planned to continue with her friend—spending time with him simply made her happy.

It had been almost two months again since their last dinner at her house, forcing her to finally take stock of her overbooked work schedule. One of the instructors who'd taught evening classes had moved out of state, and Olivia had taken over her schedule. Realizing her work life was getting too much play time, she'd decided to create a better balance for herself by hiring another instructor.

Feeling in a cooking kind of mood, Olivia had planned a feast for her ever-hungry friend: spinach-artichoke cheese quiche, roasted potatoes, yogurt parfaits, and cinnamon rolls. She thought maybe she'd overdone the menu, but she rarely had anyone to cook for and was enjoying it. Why not set the table with cloth napkins and put a big bouquet of flowers for the centerpiece? The champagne for her mimosas was chilling in the refrigerator.

Finding herself in the frame of mind to dress nicer than usual, she decided to forego her yoga pants for textured leggings, black booties, a jewel-toned jersey tunic, and some Cherry Bomb lip color.

With three short bursts of the doorbell, she knew Jax had arrived. After finger-combing her hair, she opened the door, greeting him with a buoyant smile. "Hi, handsome." Olivia immediately noticed he looked tired and his eyes were rimmed in red. "What's wrong? You look pale. You okay?"

"No, I'm not. My life as I knew it is over." He thrust a bouquet of flowers at her. "Here, for you."

Oh no … what awful thing happened? she thought. "Thanks, they're beautiful." She set them on the counter and gestured to him to sit at the kitchen table. "Sit down and tell me what's wrong. There's twenty more minutes until the quiche is done."

He plopped onto the kitchen chair, looking pitifully sad, his hand supporting his head. Olivia stood behind him with her hands on his shoulder, gently massaging the knots in his neck. "Spill, my friend. What's going on?"

"I need this like I need a boil on my ass."

"Tell me!"

He shook his head. "Hunter left me. Said it's over. Packed up his bags and moved out. He's not answering his cell. I don't even know where he went."

Olivia slid onto the chair next to him, slumping her shoulders. "Oh God, no … this can't be. When I was at your house for dinner a couple of weeks ago, everything was great. What happened between the two of you?"

"I was an idiot. You know, I gave him free rein on the wedding. I didn't really care. I was content just going to Vegas or something to tie the knot. For some reason, I started to feel like he was going over the top spending money. I didn't say anything about it as most of it's money he made anyway, and if that's how he wants to spend it, who am I to say no?"

"Right, go on ..."

Jax dragged his hand through his hair. "Well, he was getting ready for work, and I thought he was in the shower while I was talking to my mom on the phone. I'd just picked up a bill that he'd laid on the desk and my eyes bugged out at the cost for the entertainment. My mom asked how the plans were going, and I ran my mouth. I said my thing about how weddings are just an exercise in narcissism and how the money we were spending was obscene and how we could have given that to feed a ton of hungry families or given them warm jackets to wear, yada yada. I flowed at the mouth. Well, of course, like in the movies, he was standing in the doorway and heard every word I'd said. His feelings were so hurt. He said nothing. Wouldn't talk to me. Just said, 'We're over,' and left the house."

"Oh, Jax. Knowing Hunter, I imagine he felt so insulted. He's such a generous man, with his money and his time. You can make this right again with him. Don't worry. Give him some space to work it through."

Jax rolled his eyes. "What I love about him so much is his kind heart and generous nature. I don't even know what compelled me to say what I did. I just feel horrid. And I can't stand it when someone walks away, refusing to work things out with me. He wouldn't listen. Just up and left."

"Let him think things through. When he's feeling less hurt, you can sit down and talk to him."

"Planning this wedding was making him so happy. He was enjoying it so much and doing it for us. It wasn't ego involved in this. It wasn't self-satisfaction. Why did I say what I did? Why? Is this some kind of test of our love I have to pass? I don't know what to do," Jax said with a strained tone of voice.

"Well, let's see if we can figure it out."

He reached out and gave her a big hug. "Livie, you're always the bubbles in my champagne. The caffeine in my coffee. The air in my balloon. You always lift me up."

Olivia filled the two flutes with orange juice and champagne and handed him a glass. "Speaking of champagne—first, have a mimosa and take the edge off a bit. I need you to be a bit more mellow for what I'm going to suggest."

"Can we eat first? The smell of those cinnamon rolls is making me insane."

"Not unless you want to eat them raw. They're still baking. Okay, so when I have a problem or misunderstanding with a person, this is what I do. I call it *standing in their shoes*. You're going to have to role-play a bit here."

"Oh no, not the dreaded role-playing ..."

"Come on, get over it and just try this."

"I can't. I'm too amped up."

"Jax, work with me here. Let me unpack your baggage for you, okay?"

"Go ahead. Unpack."

"You need to chill. So stand up and take some deep breaths and blow them out slowly. Now, in your mind, I want you to go back to the scene where it happened with you and Hunter—only this time, I want you to *be* Hunter. I'm going to be you. I want you to imagine your essence merging into his body. When I do it, I imagine something that kind of looks like white smoke exuding from me and traveling to another person and entering through the crown of their head. Do whatever works for you. Stand in his shoes, hear what he hears. Feel what he feels. See what he sees. So first, I need you to continue to relax. Take deep breaths. Breathe in to the count of five, breathe out to the count of eight."

Jax stood with his eyes closed and performed the breathing routine.

Olivia stood opposite to him. "Good. Imagine you're back in the same location where this all took place. Now see the essence of you entering into his physical body. You're in his body looking out through his eyes. I'm going to play the role of you."

Jax continued the deep breathing.

Olivia held up her hand to her ear like she was talking on a phone. "'Yeah, Mom, the wedding plans are still going on. For me, I don't really need a wedding—they're just an exercise in narcissism. The amount of money we're spending is obscene, and I can't even imagine how many needy families we could help with that money, feeding them or giving them warm clothes to wear.' Now feel what you feel as if you're inside Hunter's body. What's your internal dialogue?"

Jax continued to stand with his eyes closed, apparently feeling and thinking, viewing the world through Hunter's eyes. Then he spoke. "I'm feeling shock at hearing those words. Like a bullet ripping through my heart. Really? Really? That's what you think of me? We say we're in love and getting married, and that's how you judge me? You don't think the money I contribute to people in need is valid or enough? You think I'm narcissistic? I'm shocked. How can you think that of me? That's so not how I see me! I feel an intense hurt and pain tearing through me like a speeding train. I'm so hurt right now. So incredibly hurt. I thought you, out of everyone in this world, accepted me as I am."

Olivia noticed tears pooling in his tear ducts. "When you're done, imagine your essence leaving his body and moving back into your own."

He opened his eyes. "Wow. That was really trippy. I felt like I was looking through his eyes! If those were anything close to the thoughts he was experiencing, I'd be amazingly hurt too. I don't even know why I said what I did. I was on call for work, and I had plans for things I had wanted to do, and I was in a bad mood. I sure don't think those things about *him*, and personally, I would have been insulted too. I'm not sure how to fix this one. He may never come back to me."

"You're underrating love in a big way. You can't dissolve love so easily. If you can, it wasn't love in the first place. He needs some time to sort through the feelings, and then you need to talk it out and resolve it. Sometimes some space is necessary. And remember, what we don't say is more powerful than what we do say. Try to view this as an opportunity for mutual growth. You're learning things about each other and how to resolve the inevitable issues that are going to surface in your marriage. If you use this opportunity to your advantage, it can put you on the path to a deep emotional healing that will only bond the two of you closer. You know what I mean— bringing out your insecurities in each other and addressing those issues is a way to achieve a deep healing. It's a gift that two people who deeply love each other are willing to give each other. Do you see that?"

"I hear what you're saying. Not sure I believe it, but I hear you."

"That's what people in our soul groups do for each other. We're catalysts to evoke growth and healing."

"I don't think I've ever experienced our relationship feeling so raw and vulnerable before."

"It's an incredible opportunity to advance. It's helpful to reframe how you look at things and try to find the gift in them. People we love the most have agreed to work with us to help us evolve. In your mind, thank him for this opportunity for helping you progress. As we trip down the path of life, we often find things that lead us off course. At those times in our life, we may have to contend with a personal crisis. When those difficult times come, and they always do, they serve as the catalysts for us to make changes. Face those ugly parts of yourself that you don't like, shine some light on them, and invite your transformation to begin. You'll both be fine. You're removing your masks with each other. You're allowing the vulnerable parts of yourself to be shared. Think of Hunter as giving you a great gift. Now it's your choice how to respond."

"I'm on overload at the moment. Can we eat now?" Jax went to the oven and opened the door, peeking in at the rolls.

The timer on the oven went off. "Perfect timing. I hope you're really hungry. Now sit at the table, please. Coffee?"

"I'd love a cup. Thanks."

She poured them each a cup and then cut two wedges of quiche and plated them with a scoop of the buttery roasted potatoes. The scent of cinnamon and sugar wafted through the room when she pulled the oozing rolls out of the oven and slathered them with cream cheese icing.

"I'm genuinely enjoying cooking for someone who actually likes to eat!"

"That would be me." Jax hungrily dove into his food. "This meal is to die for. Everything is fantastic. Hunter loves cinnamon rolls so much."

"Take a few home for him."

A dollop of frosting fell on his shirt. "If he comes home again ..."

"Trust me. He will. I know love when I see it."

Jax ate like a field hand who had been working the ranch all morning. "Okay, in justification for this, I haven't eaten anything since this all happened with Hunter."

"You certainly don't have to justify enjoying your meal to me. I love that you eat and enjoy your food."

She turned her lips upward into a maternal smile. "It's going to be okay, Jax. You'll mend and be stronger for it. Trust me. Don't waste your pain, learn from it."

"Speaking of mending and being stronger, how are your efforts going to absolve your karma with Curtis?"

"I guess we won't know until it's tested, but I've been working on it with the karma-clearing program Dr. Hobbs gave me. I'm striving to achieve agape love."

"What's that?"

"Genuine love. The highest form of love. To love without expecting any return. For me it's a process of letting go of the hurts, wounds, rejections and disappointments. Unconditional love and acceptance. It's hard to do. People often use love as a weapon—a means to control others by giving and taking the love. That's not authentic love. Once we have expectations of others, it's not unconditional love."

Jax helped himself to another small sliver of quiche. "I don't know if it's possible not to have some expectations."

Olivia pushed her potatoes around on her plate. "I'm just saying, if there are expectations, it hasn't yet reached unconditional love status. We often link our love to a person's behaviors."

"Even if you're able to do the work on your end, I'm sure Curtis isn't doing any work on his end. I still want to hire a private detective to see where he is and what he's up to. Let me, okay? Please? It's that or an attack dog ..."

"Can you even imagine me with an attack dog? I feel like I'm making progress. I feel good about this."

"Well, I'm ninety percent happy for you."

"Just ninety?"

"I'll be one hundred percent when I know he's not a danger to you in any way. I'm sitting here with a belly full of guilt right now."

"Why guilt?"

"I feel guilty about how I treated Hunter."

"And you let yourself feel the emotions of what happened, so now you can move on to healing it."

"I hope so ..." He nodded with his chin toward the balcony door. "Hey, you did get that balcony fixed, right? I still have nightmares about it."

"The manager left a note on my door that the handyman had been here. I never go out there, so I didn't check to see exactly what was done. I'll call the manager to find out what the problem was and to be sure it's properly fixed."

"Well, I'm sure as heck not going to check it out for you, but I do need to check on my work schedule. Can I look it up on your computer?"

"Sure, my laptop is right there on the island. I have the quiche recipe pulled up."

He tinkered around with the computer for a few minutes. "Dang. I knew it. I'm on call and have to work. Before I go, let me ask you— Livie, have you been Virtual-Timing today?"

"No, why?"

"Your webcam light is on. Have you noticed that?"

"No ..." She leaned over his shoulder to look.

"Okay, well, my concern is you're being watched through your webcam."

"Chills just went down my spine. How is that possible?"

"You may have inadvertently installed RAT software onto your laptop."

"How?"

"Disguised links. Email attachments, free music and stuff like that."

"What's RAT?"

"Random Access Tool. Your Wi-Fi is secured, right?"

"Yes, and I have a pretty complicated password."

"Do you work with it in public Wi-Fi spots?"

"No."

"For now, we'll block it with electrical tape. Close it when not using it and turn it off. I can take it to work with me and have my coworker check for malware on it. It would be good to check this out."

"Do you think it's Curtis?"

He scratched his head and frowned. "My intuition tells me yes ... but why would he draw out this process of watching you and spying on you for months on end? Why wouldn't he just confront you?"

"I don't know. Maybe he loves the challenge. I can't even guess his game plan."

"Hey, Livie, I'm sorry, but I need to get going." Jax stood in the doorway before leaving, taking her laptop and some cinnamon rolls with him. "Please come and stay with us. I'm just going to worry about you too much."

"I'm okay, Jax. I'm just going to go to the studio to teach a class. Thanks for coming over this morning."

He stood at the door and reached out to give her a one-arm bear hug, looking her squarely in the eyes. "Know that I love you. So no toe tag at the end, okay?"

"It's not in the plan. Love you too. And Jax ... everything is going to be okay with you and Hunter. Hang in there. He'll be back."

He gave her a squeeze and walked out the door.

Chapter 28

July 15

Jonathan waited in the kitchen, gulping down a cold cup of coffee, while Sammi packed her bag with her favorite panda bear towel. After her experience in the pool, Jonathan had decided he needed to sign Sammi up for swimming lessons. He'd found a Daddy and Me class, and they were attending their first lesson that afternoon. The terror he'd felt that day she'd almost drowned still stuck with him. He'd realized no matter how much he wanted to, he couldn't always protect Sammi from harm. He just didn't want any life lessons that forced him to deal with more loss—he'd had enough. Of course, swimming classes would not guarantee safety—after all, Nate had been an accomplished swimmer. *Things happen that you can't plan for.* Still, it gave him peace of mind to think of her learning to swim; he'd probably be pushing karate lessons someday too.

Wearing her pink-striped swimsuit and flip-flops, Sammi dragged her bag across the floor, heading toward the garage.

Jonathan glanced at the long hair framing her face. "Sammi, let me brush your hair into a ponytail before we go. They don't want you having loose long hair in the pool. Can you get me a brush and an elastic?"

She ran to her room to get the items and returned, sitting on the footstool next to the couch while Jonathan stood behind her brushing her hair.

"Daddy, we can be fishes together."

"How fun is that! You don't feel scared to go in the pool after what happened to you, do you?"

"Not too much. I didn't think about dying, but I'm glad Nate saved me. He knows what it's like to drown."

"I'm beyond grateful to him."

"I do remember some of the other ways I died when I've been here before, but I don't think about it much."

Jonathan stared at her, his eyebrows raised. "You do?"

"I've been so many people that I can't remember them all. But I drowned before, so I know what it might have been like for Nate."

"When was that?" he questioned as he brushed through her long, silky hair.

"I don't remember everything, but it was Easter. I was a young lady, and I lived with Father and Mother and my younger sister. I always wore my hair piled on my head in wavy curls. My name was Georgia. I wore long dresses with pretty hats with feathers, and I carried a fancy umbrella a lot."

"An umbrella. Perhaps a parasol?"

"I don't know what it was called. I remember we were drinking tea and eating square cookies called Laura Dunns or something like that. Father brought them home as a surprise for teatime, and they came in a package!"

"Laura Dunns? There's a cookie called Lorna Doones. They still make them, I think."

"I liked those cookies. Could we get some at the store?"

"Maybe ... we can look."

She talked matter-of-factly, gesturing with her hands. "We don't celebrate Easter in this life, but when I was Georgia, we did. We went to church one Easter, and it was a cold and rainy day."

"Do you remember where you lived?"

She shook her head no. "It rained all day long. And then it got windy. It just kept raining and raining and raining. The river near us grew really really big and the water went everywhere. Daddy, the land couldn't drink up all the water."

"Tell me more."

"It kept getting worse, and the next day everyone was so worried."

"Do you know how old you were?"

"Nineteen. I remember my sister, Gemma, was talking about a doctor who said if you eat pie every day you'll be healthy, and we were sitting at the dinner table laughing when we heard a roaring sound, and all of a sudden the water came. Lots and lots of water. Father said we had to get to high ground, but it was too late. Police were shouting at everyone."

"Go on ..."

"People were screaming for help. The water came, and it was freezing cold and then there was so much water it was up to my neck." She hugged herself and shuddered. "Father tried to save me, but the water took him first. It was swirling and moving too fast. I remember gulping water, and then I was sucked under the water and I drowned."

Jonathan grabbed her panda towel from her bag and wrapped it over her shoulders to warm her up. "Were you feeling scared?"

"Not so much. I didn't know what happened, and then I floated out of my body, and I was watching it get pulled away by the river. I didn't feel any pain."

"Wow, Sammi, that's an incredible story."

"I'd felt like something bad was going to happen, but I didn't know what. All of my family died with me."

He put his arms around her, hugging her tightly. "That's so sad." *And yet it seems so matter-of-fact to her.*

"Sometimes I get icky feelings when I think something bad is going to happen. I don't like that."

"I don't think I'd like that either. Especially if you don't know what it's about. Let's see if we can find anything about that on the Internet." After he finished adjusting Sammi's ponytail, he sat at his desk with his laptop. "Come sit next to me. I'm going to do a search. Do you think it was in the United States?"

"I don't know."

"Do you remember who was president?"

"No."

"So let's search for *Easter* and *flood*." He typed the words and reviewed the list that came up.

"The first thing that comes up in my search is a flood that happened in 1979, but there's also the Great Flood of 1913. From how you described your dress, it could have been back then. Maybe you'd been living in Ohio. This article says there was a superstorm in Ohio that began on Easter Sunday in 1913. It lasted for four days. First, the tornadoes came, followed by days of relentless, forceful rain beating down. Wow! The levees, which are like walls, couldn't hold back all that water from going places it wasn't meant to go. In some places in Daytona, the floodwaters were twenty feet deep. Yikes! That's a lot of deep, cold water. Over four hundred people ended up dying in that flood."

Jonathan brought up the images and clicked through the photos of the damage from the flooding, one by one.

Sammi pointed at the screen. "Those pictures look like where I lived. It makes me sad to see it."

"Then let's not search anymore." He closed his laptop.

"Daddy, I should tell you something. When I said I sometimes see bad things, I think I have a bad feeling about Olivia."

His brow furrowed as he tried to figure out what Sammi meant. "Olivia? The lady you played with? What kind of bad feeling? Like she's a bad person, or something bad is going to happen to her?"

Sammi shrugged. "I don't know. I just see her with a black cloud over her head. I don't know what it means. It makes my tummy hurt."

Oh no ... Jonathan thought. What now? He knew he should warn Olivia of impending doom, but what would he actually say to her? Sammi saw a black cloud over her head? Likely it wouldn't resolve anything and only alarm her. He'd have to think about it. *No, I have to call her.*

Sammi had already shifted gears and was on to singing songs. "Daddy, after swim class, can we go to the store and see if they have Lorna Doones? I'd like to have some."

"We can look, but I'm not sure if they still make them. Let me do one more search on the computer before we go."

He sat at his laptop again and plugged in the search data. "Sammi, you're in luck. You can still get them. I see they have them at Walmart, or we can order them online. Did the cookies you loved look like these?" He showed her the image of the cookies.

She jumped up and down. "That's them! Let's get some, Daddy, and have them with tea."

He marveled at her ability to shift. One minute she was talking about dying in a past life, and then the next she was excited to eat the cookies that had been her favorite. He wondered how many of the things he was fond of, or even felt disgust for, in his current life that stemmed from an experience in another life.

"Let's go or we'll be late," Jonathan said. "Let's go learn to swim!"

He decided to give Olivia a call before he left, but the call went to voice mail. Although he wasn't sure exactly what to say, he left a message for her to call him as soon as possible.

I hope she's okay...

Chapter 29

July 16

As the morning light slipped into the bedroom, past the tiny crack in her blackout curtains, Olivia woke, her eyes still in a hazy, dreamlike sleep. She'd been having nightmares about Curtis again. Thinking of him spying on her through her computer was a chilling image. *Of course he is*, she thought. *Maybe it's time to go to the police. But what can they do? Nothing, really.* She even thought she saw him towering over her with his crystalline blue eyes and his biceps, three times the size of hers. As her eyes focused, she wasn't so sure it was a dream. She'd imagined him entering her house stealthily in the night, worried that somehow he could sneak in and kill her. Maybe she hadn't been imagining it.

She turned over, pressing the pillow over her head, and snuggled down into the covers, feeling comforted by the soft sheets and blankets—ready to go into the dream world she loved to visit.

The imagined ghostly figure spoke. "Hello, wife. Surprised to see me, Leticia? You tried to get away from me, but I told you: It's. Never.

Going. To. Happen. You're mine until the day you die. Your death can be today or fifty years from now. Your choice."

What she hoped was a dream was a reality; she saw his six-foot-two, two-hundred-and-twenty-pound body towering over her. Oh God, it's really happening. It's him. He's here to kill me. This is probably my last day on Earth. She wondered how her family would find out what happened to her. She was mute. Nothing would come out of her mouth until she squeaked out an oh God.

"First time I've been called that, but Leticia—or should I call you Olivia now?—I am your God. The determiner of your fate. Whatever made you think I wouldn't eventually find you?"

She didn't know if she should speak. Sometimes when she talked, she just made him angrier. She decided to try to rationalize with him. "Curtis, let's just let bygones be bygones and let each other live our lives. We don't need to play out this game together. I hold nothing against you, as I hope you don't against me."

His bulky body loomed over her, his hands encircling her neck, his thumbs pressing deeply in the indentation of her throat. "Oh, Christ. Pass the bullshit repellent. Well, I do hold something against you. You ran out on me. And. That's. Not. Okay. Not a word. Just up and disappeared." She didn't react, so he released his death grip.

"You were in prison. What difference did it make?"

"You're my wife, and you will not leave me. No one leaves me. I've been watching you for quite a while. Who's the guy you see?"

"I don't see any guy."

"I seen you with him."

"Oh, you mean Jax. He isn't with me. He's getting married soon. He's just my friend."

"Good thing for him that's all he is."

Olivia spoke softly, pleadingly. "Curtis, please. Can we just sit together like human beings and talk this out?"

"Shut up with that stupid shit talk. I'm the boss and you're going to do what I say! Now get up out of that bed and take your pajamas off. I need you to prove you still love me. You're still my wife. Get up! I've been waiting for this moment for a long time."

She noticed him licking his lips like she was a grilled steak he was waiting to consume. She stood from the bed and stared at him. Breathe ... damn it, breathe! "Please, Curtis. I want to talk to you."

"No talking. Take them pajamas off now."

"Curtis, I—"

"Don't talk. Just strip yourself naked or I'll do it for you."

She felt so vulnerable. Should she fight? Or comply and buy herself more time? She took off her pajama bottoms and then her top, standing stark naked in front of him. Goose bumps appeared on her skin. She wished she could evaporate. Just disappear.

"Turn around and let me look at you."

She turned slowly around as he gazed at her. His attempt to humiliate her was working, as it always had. She was violently shaking inside, hoping her vulnerability did not show.

"My, you're still one fine woman. Just look at you! We're going to have us a drink together. It always got you in the mood before. Let's go in the other room, and you pour us a nice stiff drink."

"Can I please put a robe on?"

"How can I drool over those huge tits of yours if you put a robe on? Now get in the other room."

She plodded into the living room, not sure if she was going to be raped, beaten, killed, or all three. Trying to cooperate to buy herself some time, she poured him a drink and one for herself. I'm not sure what to do! Don't panic!

He took several deep gulps. "Now once you're feeling more in the mood, I want you to put on some music, and I want you to dance naked for me. Real seductively. Tease me. Woo me."

She couldn't think straight. I can't. I just can't. His eyes look crazed!

He picked up one of the masks she'd been making off the coffee table and threw it at her. "Here, put this mask on and seduce me. Now!"

"Please, Curtis—" She uttered something incomprehensible.

He slapped her across the face with the back of his hand. Blood dripped from her nose. "Don't make me mad! The last thing you want to do is make me mad. You know how I get when you disobey me." He leaned in and brought his face next to hers, touching nose to nose. "I don't like it at all. And when you disobey, I need to punish you. Now put on the mask and dance, and do it seductively," he sneered.

She wanted to rub the blood and tears off her face but didn't want to give him the satisfaction. Knowing how he loved to intimidate her, she refused to let him see what she was feeling. Where would this end? These were more than likely her final moments on Earth. She hoped this would end it with him. She didn't want to come back and play out some karmic thing with him again in another life.

"Put a mask on and start dancing."

She turned on the music and forced her mind to go somewhere more pleasant as she put on a mask and danced naked for him.

"Put more enthusiasm into it," he commanded.

She continued to dance when he shoved her against the wall and began to kiss her nipples.

She fought hard not to vomit. "Please don't. Stop! I need you to stop!"

His anger spiked to fury. "Need me to stop? What about what I need? You're going to satisfy me just like you used to, and then I'm going to let you pick what punishment you want me to give you for leaving me. And you're gonna beg me for it. Got it?" he said shaking his fist at her.

She forced herself to hold back from sobbing. "Stop! Don't!"

"Don't bother crying. It's so pointless and annoying. We'll begin with the punishment first if you cry." He put his hands around her neck again. "Do you want to be choked? Is that the punishment you want?"

She tried to back away from him, but couldn't. "I don't deserve a punishment. Let's forgive each other and move on. Let's do that."

"Forgive? I didn't do anything that needs forgiveness." He began to squeeze her throat.

Feeling panicked, she kicked him and dropped to the ground and screamed.

He returned the kick with his foot landing on her rib cage. "Don't you dare scream, you bitch. You'll be very sorry if anyone hears you and comes to your rescue. I'll just close this balcony door so no one hears, and looky looky—I see a nice roll of duct tape sitting by that mask."

Olivia didn't respond.

"If you scream, you die." He unrolled duct tape, tearing off pieces with his bare hands, placing it across her mouth. He tore off two more pieces and taped her wrists to the coffee table legs and chuckled. "That's how I like you the best. Naked, vulnerable, and quiet."

This will NOT be how my story ends, she thought. I won't let it. She could see him as he walked to the balcony door to shut it—last evening, as she was locking up the house for the night, it had gotten stuck on a warped plank and wouldn't close tightly. From inside the house, Curtis grabbed the door handle with two hands and jerked it. The door wouldn't budge. Infuriated, he walked out onto the balcony and firmly shoved the door from behind. It still didn't budge, so he bent his knee to his chest and, with full force, slammed his foot into the door.

It budged. He pushed it hard again.

Olivia heard the creaking sound.

She heard the crashing sound... and the scream.

Olivia couldn't move or make a sound, but she saw the scenario in her mind's eye. The precarious balcony had finally given way and crashed down. She hoped and prayed there was no one else who got caught in the fray.

The sounds of blaring sirens assaulted her ears, mixed together with the shouts and screams from below. She imagined the emergency crews racing to the scene. She visualized the balcony, completely detached and perched precariously on the balcony below. *I cannot believe what just happened!* She waited—there was nothing else she could do. She felt her too-rapid pulse and her heart thumping as loud as a bill collector banging on a door. She wondered if he was still alive. Was he on his way back inside to kill her? Then she felt a calm come over her and she heard a voice in her head. *It's all going to be okay. Everything's okay.* And so she waited.

Finally, after what seemed like hours, the rescue team pried opened the door to her apartment, saw her bound on the floor, removed the duct tape from her mouth and wrists, and wrapped her in a blanket. Strangely, she heard the sound of peaceful, gentle music playing in her head.

One of the uniformed men approached her and said, "Did you know this guy?"

"My husband," she said. "He's my husband."

"Sorry, ma'am. He didn't make it. Looks like the balcony went down. Maybe dry rot of the wood structure."

She didn't reply.

"We should get you to the hospital for an exam."

"No, I decline to go. I just want to stay here. I'm okay."

"Were you raped?"

"No... no, I wasn't. Was anyone else hurt out there?"

"Fortunately, no. Were you hit or harmed in any way?"

"No, just taped and a bit of a bloody nose. I'm okay."

She didn't hear what they were saying. She knew she'd have to give a report of what happened. But what did happen? She felt sad it had come to this. No one had to die. Or did they?

I forgive you, Curtis. I'm sorry it ended this way. Let this be the end. No more bad karma with us. I send you to wherever you're going with my love.

While the people went about their business in her apartment, she put on her yoga pants and T-shirt and picked up her phone.

She clenched her fists, then unclenched them. Speaking into the phone, she softly said, "Jax, it's over. He's dead. Please come get me."

Jax arrived within fifteen minutes and barged through the front door, grabbing Olivia and pulling her close. "You have no idea just how good it is to see your face." He wrung his hands and paced, then pulled her to the couch, with his arm lovingly placed around her. As they sat together, Olivia pushed her head against his chest and described what happened in great detail.

Jax shook his head, near tears. "This is truly the definition of a sphincter-clenching moment."

"That's one way of looking at it."

"I can't even grasp this. I'm not believing any of this. I mean, if it weren't for that balcony, you'd probably be dead right now. I could never have lived with myself. Seems like you absolved your karma, but he didn't." He got up and paced the living room.

"I don't know ... I don't know ..." She dragged her fingers through her hair, trying to self-soothe.

"What a completely horrifying experience. Sorry, but this time you aren't saying no. I want you to come to our house and stay in the guest room tonight. I want to be there to nurture you and be sure you're okay."

"Why don't you just stay here?"

"Since Hunter and I worked things out, we're doing better than ever. But as you know, he went back to be with his dad for a couple of weeks, and he's arriving home tonight. I just think I should be there, if you can understand. But I insist you come with me."

"I don't want to horn in on what I imagine will be a romantic night."

"Please, Livie, I insist. I need you to come with me."

She quickly conceded. "Okay, I'll pack a bag and come with you. I don't want to be here alone tonight."

Jax's voice was still shaking. "I finally feel like I can breathe again. I'm sorry he died, Livie, but things could have turned out another way. Thank God you're okay. Now let's grab your bag and go. I was starting to plan dinner. You can help me."

It's over, she thought. *The years of abuse and fear are finally over. I don't know what to think at the moment other than I'm free.*

I'm finally free.

Chapter 30

August 30

Nate

The process of being born is an exciting one, coming into a new body and personality with a new name and different experiences to look forward to. I always liked my name, Nate, but this time around I'll be Tyson.

It'll be an interesting experience having Jonathan as my father. Being best of friends in my last life leads me to believe we'll have a great relationship this time, and we didn't previously create any karma together that we need to resolve. As we all do, I had some troubled moments in that past life, but I felt I had gotten things together before I left the Earth. Believe it or not, all of us have preplanned not just one, but a few exit points in every lifetime. The ocean death was my second possible exit point, and I took it. I passed by my first exit point after I had a serious case of pneumonia as a kid. Now it's important to remember that it isn't our conscious selves that choose our exit points—it's up to our soul to make the choice. When you're on a long road trip and you see those green exit signs along the way, that's similar to what I'm talking about. Once we've gone past the exit, we can't go back. You see, the soul leaves when it's ready and has accomplished what it needed to—the exit is all part of the plan.

I'm looking forward to going to a world full of experiences with the opportunity to feel a wide range of emotions and simply to feel a physical body in motion. It's exhilarating.

Aria is having contractions, so I know it's time for me to leave this dimension. What a rush. The way I think of birth and death is like a coin. There are two sides to it, but they are both a part of the same coin. Birth and death are two parts of a whole called life.

Jonathan and Sammi are here with Aria in the hospital, and they have Virtual-Time set up to show the grandparents my first moments of life once I arrive. Aria's mom and dad plan to come and help take care of me for a few weeks once I'm home. Lizzie and Mark and Sophie and Matthew are pacing in the waiting room. My new grandparents and godparents!

Getting used to being in the confines of a body is going to take some time, as it always does. It feels really restrictive at first. But I'm sure I will quickly adjust again. My biggest frustration about being a baby is my inability to talk. In my opinion, communication by crying isn't the most effective way to make a point. Or maybe it is ...

So today's my birthday and the time has come. I'm being born. I'm sending lots of telepathic messages to Aria to relax. She's so uptight; I feel it in her body.

The moment is here. I'm moving through a dark tunnel now, and I feel a squeezing kind of action. It's happening faster than I thought. I remember going through this before. I feel my lungs expanding. I feel compressed and squeezed. Looking through my eyes feels a bit blurry, and I'm kind of twisting and turning. My head is going down first, and I'm trying to help get out of here as best I can. Aria is pushing down hard now, moving me along. I can feel how tired she is.

I see some bright light. My body is going to have to fend for itself now. My nervous system is reacting to the sudden change in temperature and environment. I have to breathe on my own. Okay, I'm emerging, and I take my first breath and open my eyes. The eagle has landed. Here I am on Earth again!

Boy, it's really noisy and bright. I recognize the familiarity of Aria's voice. I'm smelling things; I can smell Aria. My breathing is a little erratic. They're laying me on my mom now, skin to skin. This is what it's like to be physical. Feeling my warm flesh against hers is wonderful. Here I am with my new mom. I'm so excited. The beginning of an adventure.

Now Jonathan is holding me and staring into my eyes. "There you are, buddy, I see you in there. We're together again," he says. "Let the good times roll."

Sammi joins us while Jonathan is holding me and touches my fingers. "Hi, Nate, I mean, Tyson," she says. "I'm so glad to be with you again." She kisses me on the cheek.

Here we go.

Let the lifetime begin.

Chapter 31

September 13

Once she'd finally called and made the appointment with Dr. Hobbs, Margo had been anxious for the date to arrive. Her sense of urgency had grown, and she wanted some kind of message from her deceased family—something that would provide her with peace of mind.

Margo arrived twenty minutes early for her appointment, waiting patiently in her car for time to pass. She didn't want to arrive too early—she was an on-time person. She looked in the rearview mirror and touched up her face with some concealer and a fresh coat of lipstick. *It's ridiculous I'm this nervous!* Maybe she was afraid he wouldn't be able to contact them, and she didn't want to admit how important it was to her.

She rang the bell to his office, and his receptionist showed her to the waiting area. Before she even sat, Dr. Hobbs came out of his office with a big grin on his face and placed his hand in a comforting gesture on her shoulder.

"I'm so glad to finally meet you, Margo. I feel like I know you from my wife. She thinks so highly of you. Did I hear correctly that you're getting married?"

"Yes, you did. I'm almost embarrassed to tell people because they get this puzzled expression after they realize how short a time we've been together."

"Congratulations! The length of time isn't relevant. You probably have known his soul from before. Please come in and have a seat wherever you like. So what would you like to work on today?"

Margo selected a comfortable-looking chair next to the fireplace. "I want some peace of mind before I move forward and get married. Death, loss, is a powerful change. It's the biggest change there is. Let me know if this is too much to ask, but I was wondering if you'd go to the Plainsbrook Cemetery with me and see if you can pick up any messages from my family members that have died. I should've asked this of you ahead of time, but the desire just became overwhelming as I was driving here. I tend to feel more peaceful when I'm there even though I know their spirit isn't locked to that cemetery. I want to see if you can make contact with them. They died many years ago. I know it's quite the drive, but thought I'd ask. It could be whenever you want."

She observed Dr. Hobbs as he thought about her request and hoped it wasn't too outlandish. *It didn't hurt to ask—he could always say no.*

Dr. Hobbs sat in the chair across from her and stroked his chin, giving her question consideration. "Although I don't feel it's necessary to go to the cemetery to do this, if that's a place that provides you with comfort, I'm certainly willing to go with you. I think I could get my receptionist to change a few things around and open up a space later this morning since it's a fairly long drive. I'm pretty booked up next week, so if today works for you, I could do it.

I'd like to go. My dear friend is buried there, and sometimes I like to go there and visit. Gives me a sense of comfort and a moment in time to devote just to him. Let me finish up some things here. Could you go in two hours? I can pick you up at your house. Leave me your address."

Margo waited at the curb in front of her house for Dr. Hobbs to arrive, passing the time by picking lint off her top. She hoped this visit to the cemetery would work; she just wanted to hear from her family. Finally, he pulled up in front of her house in his metallic-silver Tesla. He parked at the curb, got out, and opened the door for her. After they were both buckled in, he took off, talking while he drove.

"So, Margo, tell me. Have you been having increased thoughts or dreams, or what is bringing this to the forefront now?" Dr. Hobbs asked.

Margo exhaled her pent-up emotions by blowing air out through her pursed lips. "I've recently been having a lot of memories and dreams about certain moments with my family. I was thinking about how I went to bed the night after they died, before falling asleep, and I saw my daughter and son standing in the doorway of my bedroom. I wasn't on any medications or anything. They were no longer physical beings; they were pure energy—a fluid, multicolored light like a halo around their bodies. I could hear them, and their voices sounded like they were on a soundstage.

"'We're okay. Don't worry, Mom. We're okay,' my son said. Then I saw a shimmering white light around them, and I knew they were gone from this dimension. I sensed the finality of it all. And in that second, my world both ended and began.

"My daughter told me that I must not be sad forever. She said, 'Be sad for a while, Mommy, and then go on and do the things you're supposed to do.' Then she said, 'Remember the ...' and I couldn't hear what she said. It frustrated me so much, and I always wondered what she wanted me to remember. I'd like to hear the end of what she said. For some reason it's important to me."

"Many people get those immediate visitations after their loved one transitions. They often come to soothe the person left behind."

"And in hindsight, I think my daughter had a premonition before she died. She said, 'Mommy, when I'm not here, what are you going to do with all of my toys?'"

"That's interesting. I was recently working with a woman whose husband had died on 9/11, and she said her husband had said similar things. Preparing her for him not being there after he died."

Margo could feel herself choking up. "I've heard about that. No one ever talks about this, but one of the hardest things is dealing with all the love you have for the people who leave you. Love is an energy, and energy can't be destroyed, so what do you do with all that love when they've up and gone?"

"That has to be one of the hardest things to bear. Loss brings us such profound lessons," Dr. Hobbs said sympathetically.

"That's the truth. Through the arduous task of self-introspection, I learned. My lessons came to me and I learned, because death did what death does best. It pushes you to places you don't want to be pushed. You have to confront and deal with all sorts of things you never thought you would."

"What I consistently see with people I work with is that it takes traumatic events to slow you down and put you directly in front of what you need to deal with."

Margo unscrewed the cover from her water bottle and took a deep gulp. "So true. Before the tragedy, I was very preoccupied all the time. You know ... consumed with the distractions life demands: making a living, establishing a home, keeping the kids safe, fed, and warm. Paying taxes. Daily routine chores. Tragic death shoves it all aside. It pushes and drives you to seek answers. It provokes us to pursue the question—what does it all mean? What is the purpose of life? Most of our life, we live in a world of 'being busy': work, taking kids to school, homework, job, holidays, other obligations. All of this is a distraction from dealing with the things we need to deal with in terms of our spiritual growth. We usually don't take the time to do our inner work when we have all the other things—called life—going on. Hardship and suffering force us to stop, and we are compelled to introspect. Most people don't grow from their everyday jobs or routines. It usually takes something to shake them up. A death is actually shocking, even if you know it's coming. The sudden shock causes you to change course."

Dr. Hobbs nodded. "That's the simultaneous agony and beauty of loss. It's so big and so powerful, we have no other choice but to slow down and deal with it. It makes way for us to focus on what's important and why we're here in the first place. We need to find the meaning in it all. And what loss or death does is it demands the search."

Up ahead, the traffic became congested, and Dr. Hobbs slowed down, removing his sunglasses and scanning the road ahead. "I wonder if there was an accident," he said, then continued. "The thing that comforts me is that we reunite again. Over and over. I've had a bit of loss in my life too, and it takes time to work through the anger and guilt."

Margo craned her neck to get a better view of the traffic situation. "No, I don't think it's an accident. It looks like there's a stray dog in the road, and someone is getting out to rescue him. Poor pup! Anyway, I was angry that my world as I knew it was coming to a halt, but it didn't stop for other people, and that made me mad. How could their world go on when mine was shattered? I literally felt like I was a mirror, reflecting visions of things that weren't real, and then the mirror shattered along with everything I knew and believed. People left the funeral and just went on with their lives. I didn't understand it."

"I remember feeling the same when my wife died. How is everyone continuing on, I wondered?"

"In the days and years that followed my crash course of living life without my family, I quickly learned that there were no books, no articles, nothing—nothing that could help me learn how to cope, know how to feel, or what to expect. After a while, people thought I should be over it. They determined it was time. It wasn't time for me."

"Right, there is no timetable. It's a different process for everyone."

Margo searched through her purse, looking for a tissue. "People said the service and funeral would provide closure. Perhaps it did for them. But for me, there's no such thing as closure. How do you close out the lives of your family?"

With the dog safely out of the road, Dr. Hobbs resumed his speed. "We hear people talking about *closure* as if there's a door that can be shut after experiencing a tragedy in our lives, losing a loved one, or being witness to a horrific event such as the terrorist attack on the World Trade Center. Well-meaning friends might ask, 'Haven't you reached closure yet?' There's no closure, but there's a point where people reach acceptance, even peace of mind, and are able to move on to a different frame of mind—a frame of mind that leaves them uplifted by the memories."

"Why would anyone really want closure?" Margo asked. "Why would anyone want to close the door on thoughts about a departed loved one? Grief will soften over the years after a loss, but the door to memories should always be open. I think we yearn to find a place of peace more than closure. We seek to complete what is incomplete."

"That's a significant conclusion, Margo."

"You wonder, 'How can I live through this?' and the truth is you just do. You just live through it." Margo dabbed at the stream of tears forming in her eyes.

"And they remain forever in your heart," said Dr. Hobbs.

"You know the play *Les Misérables*? The song 'Empty Chairs at Empty Tables'? The song is right that empty chairs can haunt you. Chairs are meant to be filled with people living life. My chairs were suddenly empty. The hardest thing for me to bear were all the empty chairs. They were always there. Always a reminder of what was gone."

"Empty beds too. But I don't think there's a song about that."

"I have learned so many things. Anything can happen. Anything happens all of the time. Never take anything or anyone for granted," Margo said wistfully.

"Life is short, life is scary, and life is awe-inspiring. Through loss, we are shown firsthand how short it truly is—how all of it can go away in a split second. Perhaps the greatest gift and struggle I've dealt with is knowing that and wanting to live every second. It's beautiful and paralyzing all at the same time. Sometimes this gift of knowing how delicate life is can start to feel too real. It makes you feel stuck, anxious, and scared of losing everyone you love. Grieving is not a movement through sequential stages, but rather circular."

Margo—at a loss for words—nodded her head in agreement.

It was midafternoon when they arrived at the cemetery, both deep in thought. Their silence was interrupted by a dog barking in the parking lot. Dr. Hobbs found a spot near the entrance and parked the car—surprisingly, the grounds still looked a lovely green in spite of the drought.

Margo led Dr. Hobbs to the area where her family members were honored. *It's such a peaceful place.* She pointed to three trees with plaques on them, as a feeling of comfort came over her, reminiscent of the sensation she felt when she listened to the rain as she fell asleep. She'd loved watching the trees grow and mature over the years. She took a deep breath and let the peace and serenity course through her.

She noticed that Dr. Hobbs looked surprised—maybe expecting gravestones, not trees—and then she remembered she hadn't told him about their deaths. She looked at his puzzled face and responded. "Ahh, I didn't mention the details, did I? They didn't recover any of the bodies, so the lovely people at this cemetery allowed me to plant these three trees and mark them with plaques. I like to come here and see how much they've grown in forty years. Three strong trees entwined together through eternity. I love them."

"What a fantastic idea, Margo. May I ask how your family members died?"

"Oh, sorry, I figured Sophie told you."

"No, she thought you might come talk to me sometime, and she didn't want to say anything that you might consider confidential."

"My twins and my father were killed in a plane crash."

Dr. Hobbs jerked his head, staring and waiting for her to go further.

Margo noticed his reaction. "You look like your hair is standing on end."

"It is. I got a rushing tingle down my spine, and it does feel like my hair is standing on end. Continue, please."

"The thing is I felt such guilt. I had this nagging feeling of not wanting to let them fly—that something wasn't right. However, I didn't want to hold them back from living because of my fears, so I said yes."

"That's a common remnant we are left with. Guilt we didn't save them or do enough, even survivor's guilt. 'Why was I the one that was saved?'"

Margo stood in front of the trees, rubbing her hands over the plaques, as though the energy of her loved ones was seeping from the branches of the trees directly into her heart. "My father was the first officer on the plane, and he kept assuring me my children would be okay. He wanted to take the kids to see their grandmother on her birthday. He said I always worried too much. But somehow I knew something was not right about it, and I didn't act on my own intuition. Somehow I didn't protect them."

"Every parent's worst fear is that they won't keep their child safe," said Dr. Hobbs.

"Exactly. So I ran this script in my head. 'Why, why did I let them go?'" Her shoulders slumped forward, and she bowed her head. "I need a minute, Dr. Hobbs. I'm feeling a profound sense of grief right now."

He placed his hand gently on her shoulder. "I'll give you a few minutes while I go to my friend's gravestone, and I'll be right back," he said.

Tears flowed down her cheeks as Margo stood in front of each tree, gently caressing the plaques as she spoke out loud. "I'm wondering if I'll hear from any of you and if you're okay. I know you are, but I'd like a sign to confirm. My darling daughter, I keep thinking of the message you tried to tell me the night you left. You started with 'remember.' What were you telling me? All I can say to you, your brother, and my father is I feel such love for you—every moment of every day."

And just like when she was in yoga class, she could feel an opening in her third eye chakra. Colors—brilliant ones—swirled before her eyes and suddenly there was no sound. There was total quiet, and her mind went empty. Then, clear as a bell, Margo could hear her daughter in her head, sending her thoughts.

"We're quite fine. What I said to you was, 'Mommy, remember we'll always be with you because we'll be in every beat of your heart. All this happens for a reason, and it's always about love.'"

Margo couldn't believe how distinctly she heard her daughter's voice and message. She was blown away. Her face—just moments ago feeling heavy and old—suddenly felt years younger, as though the lines on her face were magically melting away.

It was a short message, but a momentous one.

It's always about love.

When Dr. Hobbs arrived back to meet up with her, Margo smiled with satisfaction. In that moment, the sun set in her heart, and an overwhelming sense of peace flowed through her veins. It was just the connection she needed.

Margo dabbed at her eyes. "I actually did it without your help," she said. "I heard the message."

"You did? That's incredible. What was it?" he asked in amazement.

"'Mommy, remember we'll always be with you because we'll be in every beat of your heart. All this happens for a reason, and it's always about love.'"

"I'm thrilled for you, Margo. What a perfect message."

"Yes, how perfect is that?"

She rubbed her hand over one of the plaques. "Here's my father's tree. Jim Stockton.

"This is my son's tree, Josh Phillips." She gently kissed her finger and touched it to the plaque.

And as she was speaking, she noticed Matthew studying one of the plaques with a shocked, rattled expression on his face.

Margo placed her hand on his arm. "You okay?"

As he appeared to regain his composure, he replied, "Sure, yes."

"And this is the plaque for my daughter," Margo continued. "Christina Phillips."

Chapter 32

September 24

It was finally Saturday, and Jonathan decided to forego working on his script, wanting nothing more than to spend a day of fun with his daughter. With Tyson and Aria visiting her best friend in San Clemente, Sammi and Jonathan had the whole day to themselves. They both slept in, watched cartoons, and hung out in their pajamas until noon. Jonathan stood in the kitchen with Sammi, perched on a stool at the kitchen island, slathering peanut butter on a piece of oatmeal bread, no crusts, thinking about how much he loved spending time with her.

"Do you want anything on this other than peanut butter?" he asked as he wiped the knife clean on a paper towel.

"No, that's good. Are you going to have one?" she asked as she swiped her finger across the peanut butter and licked it.

"I don't think so." Jonathan eyed his daughter lovingly. "Have I told you today how much I love you?"

"I know you do, Daddy. Before we go to swim class today, can I talk to you about something?"

"Of course. Always. Anything." He sat on the stool next to her, giving her his undivided attention.

"You do know when I played dollhouse with Olivia, the little girl doll was me and the lady doll was my mommy from a different life, right?"

He nodded. "I thought that might be the case."

She swiveled side to side on her stool. "I know my other mommy is alive, and I need to find her. I feel like she's calling me in my head. She needs me. I try not to talk about it because I can see it hurts Mama's feelings, but it shouldn't, because I love her very much. I just want to see my other mommy so she feels free. Can you help me?" She gave him a look, imploring his assistance.

"How come you didn't say anything about this after it happened?"

She hesitated for a moment. "I didn't want to make Mama sad, and I thought you'd figure it out."

"How are you so sure she's alive now?"

She shrugged. "I just know it."

"So you need to free her?"

"Free her so she isn't sad."

Jonathan looked at the genuine love and innocence radiating from her sweet little face. "I'll help explain it to your mom when she and Tyson get home. I don't want you to feel you can't talk about these things."

She stopped swiveling and looked Jonathan directly in his eyes. "Okay. Thanks. But will you help me find her?"

"I'll do my best, Sammi. I'll look into it."

"Thanks."

Jonathan retrieved some carrots and celery sticks from the refrigerator and placed them on the plate next to her sandwich. "I was wondering. Do you think Tyson was your brother in that other life?" Jonathan asked.

"No, Tyson wasn't my brother then." She giggled. "You see why people have to forget their other lives when they're born. It's too confusing! Tyson was Grandpa Jimmy with me, then he was your friend Nate, and now he is your baby, Tyson."

Jonathan stopped midstream as he screwed the cover on the peanut butter jar—he was having a lightbulb moment.

"Tyson was your Grandpa Jimmy?"

"Yes. Before he was Nate. The little girl was me. The little boy was Olivia, and the grandpa was Tyson."

"Olivia ... the lady Olivia who you played dollhouse with? She was your brother?" he asked incredulously.

"Yes."

"Why didn't you tell me that? Did you know that then?"

"Yes. Sorry, Daddy. I don't know how much to tell about it."

"You can tell me *all* of it."

"It's Mama I worry about. I don't want to make her more sad."

Jonathan's phone trilled. "Hold on, Sammi. It's Matthew and I need to talk to him. Here's your sandwich. Why don't you start eating?"

Jonathan plunked himself down on a stool at the kitchen island. "Hi, Matthew. Interesting timing on your call."

"Hi. Well, you won't believe this. We have two pieces of the puzzle in the Sammi nightmare scenario. Sit down for this. I took a client, named Margo, to the cemetery, and she showed me her daughter's plaque commemorating her—you won't believe what it said—it said Christina Phillips. Christina! I'm inclined to think that Sammi was Margo's daughter, Christina Phillips."

"Wait ... wait ... let me go in the other room. Hold on a sec." He turned to Sammi and said, "Sammi, you eat your lunch while I go in my office and talk for a few minutes." He quickly went to his office and sat at his desk. "So, continue, Matthew. What are you talking about? Huh? You've actually met the mother? That easily? I don't know what to say. Sammi was *just* telling me she has to find her mother. This is all so surreal. So who is she? She's a client of yours? What ...?"

"And I think Olivia Buffet was Margo's son, Josh."

Jonathan slapped his thigh. "Get out of town. Sammi just said that. She knew and didn't tell me!"

Jonathan reflected back to Sammi's initial attraction to Olivia; this explained why she'd said, "You're pretty *this time.*"

"I haven't figured out who the grandfather was yet or if that soul is currently here on Earth. They all died in a plane crash."

"Freaking unreal. Well, I just found out who Grandpa was."

"No, you did not! Who?"

"Our son, Tyson. Sammi just confirmed it."

"What? I have seen lots of unusual things in my career, but this is blowing even my mind! I wonder if you or Aria have some connection with Margo from another time. So interesting two of her family members became two of yours, isn't it?"

"It sure is. Makes you wonder. Sammi wants to find her mommy *from before.* She said her mother is calling her. Oh, this is going to play out as one of the most interesting things in our lives. I see another movie script in my future based on real-life events. My two kids were previously Margo's family. Is that the strangest thing or what? I don't even know how to integrate this information. I wonder what the connection is." Even as multidimensional as he was, Jonathan was surprised at seeing the revelations actually play out.

"So, I was wondering. What do you think about introducing everyone to Margo?" Matthew asked. "I've been thinking about it, and honestly I'm just not sure. It could open a hornet's nest of emotions for people. However, having actually worked with Margo, the mother, I think this could be healing for her. She believes in past lives and actually wants to communicate with her family. She could be open to meeting in real life. Not sure how all the players would be with this, however, and it's something we need to consider. This could change your life in a big way. It might bring another person into your world."

"I agree. We need to think about the impact. Part of me does think it should be done. Sammi wants to bring peace to her other mother. I'm guessing Olivia would be interested, and, well, Tyson doesn't have much of a say at this point. I want to be sure it's okay with Aria, though. I don't want this to negatively impact her view of herself as Sammi's mother."

"Absolutely."

"She has come a long way in all of this since Nate saved Sammi. She changed that day in many ways. She's been reading and talking about past lives, ascension, karma and other stuff, and she just might be okay with it all."

"But we need more info before we do anything. Some investigation on the topic."

"We need to be sure Olivia is okay with it too. We have names and lots of info. Can't be that hard to search now that we know the mom is Margo. We'll just run a search on the names. We could also ask her the info, but I think it'll all come up right away with a computer search. It's also interesting how Olivia and Margo are my clients. The universe works in spectacular and fascinating ways," Matthew said.

"That's for sure. I was planning to research this right after Sammi met with Olivia, but I had an urgent project to finish, and she stopped having her nightmares after that, so I didn't pursue it." Jonathan glanced at his watch. "But, hey, Sammi and I have to run—swimming class. Let's touch base tomorrow. I'll research more tonight."

*

That evening, Jonathan sat down at the computer and tracked down airplane crashes, along with names of passengers. It took no time at all to pull up all the information he needed. He found there actually had been a plane crash in San Diego in 1979—Eros Airlines coming from Sacramento, crashing in San Diego. He checked the passenger manifest and found the names of two children and the pilots. *It's all a match. I'm actually stupefied over all of this*, he thought.

In the cast of characters of this remarkable story, Jonathan was now convinced that Margo Phillips had previously been his daughter's mother.

His son, Tyson, had played the role of James Stockton/first officer.

Olivia Buffet had been Josh Phillips.

And his daughter had been Christina Phillips.

Mind-blowing.

Miraculous.

Later that evening, Matthew and Jonathan connected on Virtual-Time, and after sharing what they found in their research, Jonathan deliberated with Matthew over the possibilities, carefully playing out different scenarios on how things *could* turn out. To have everyone meet was a monumental decision to make. Jonathan planned to have some conversations with Aria on potential outcomes; he wondered if it was a good idea to bring "another mother" into the picture at a time when Aria was trying so hard to work through her jealousy issues. If it was going to negatively impact her, Jonathan simply did not want to move forward with the plan. He also knew Sammi wouldn't want to proceed if Aria wasn't completely okay with it. Their agreement was for Matthew to talk with Olivia to confirm findings with her and to see if she had any desire to participate. If she agreed, they decided

Matthew and Jonathan would get together with Margo to discuss more concrete plans. Jonathan wasn't surprised when Matthew called him and told him Olivia was excited about pursuing the possibilities.

I wonder how all of this is going to play out!

Chapter 33

September 29

While she was in the midst of making taco salad for dinner, Margo answered a call from Dr. Hobbs, asking if he could stop by with a friend of his who was in town. She agreed but felt beads of sweat forming on her brow. *What could it be about?* It seemed out of character for Dr. Hobbs. He didn't give out any information, wanting to discuss it all in person. Just who was this mystery person he wanted her to meet, and why was he bringing him to her house? And why such a last-minute request? She didn't know if she should fix herself up first or straighten up the house a bit.

Vanity won out and Margo quickly changed into a nicer pair of slacks and a clean top, pulled her hair into a chignon, and refreshed her lipstick. She didn't feel like putting her contacts in so she just wore her Windsor-rim glasses. She only had a few minutes to declutter the coffee table and fluff the pillows on the couch before the doorbell rang. When she opened the door, Margo was surprised to hear her own voice was so shaky. "Come in. What's going on? You look like two popped bottles of champagne."

"Hi, Margo," Dr. Hobbs said. "You're a good sport to meet with us on such late notice, but Jonathan just arrived here from LA. You're probably going a bit crazy wondering what this is all about. I just thought it was better to talk in person."

"Yes, I've been a bit tense wondering." She eyed the young man he'd brought with him, thinking he looked familiar.

"This is a dear family friend, Jonathan Cohen. Jonathan, this is Margo Phillips."

Jonathan extended his hand to Margo. "It's my pleasure to meet you."

Margo firmly shook his hand. "My pleasure as well. Come in and get comfortable on the couch in the living room."

She sat down on the love seat across from the men. "So what's going on?" She resisted the urge to bite her nails.

"We have some exciting news, Margo. Good thing we're all sitting for this one," Dr. Hobbs said.

Feeling tremendous anxiety, Margo jumped up from the couch. "Okay, first let me get some coffee. Should I lace it with bourbon?" She laughed in an attempt to lessen her stress. In a few minutes, she emerged from the kitchen carrying a tray with cups, coffee, cream and sugar, and a plate of cookies, setting it on the coffee table in the living room. She returned to her original position on the love seat.

"Okay, I see you're shaking, so I'll cut right to the chase," Matthew began. "We think we've found your family, Margo."

"What family? I don't have any family alive anymore. Unless you're talking about …" Her eyes darted back and forth from Jonathan to Dr. Hobbs. "Don't … don't tease me with this."

"We believe we've found the reincarnated souls of your father and children," Jonathan said.

Margo turned visibly white. She thought it was a good thing she was sitting or she might have fainted. Shaking with a convulsive motion, Margo drew her hands to her face, placing one on each cheek. "How? Who? All three of them? Where? What do you mean you found them? Where are they? Are you sure? I don't understand. How is that possible?"

What are they saying? she thought. *What are they saying?* She was screaming inside. Or was she actually shouting out loud? She could hardly comprehend their words as they went over all the facts and figures of what they'd found as she sat staring back and forth between Matthew and Jonathan. They were talking and explaining, but Margo was hearing clocks ticking backwards in her head as she drifted into the past.

She sat on the love seat shaking her head. "I'm sorry. This just doesn't seem possible to me." She looked Jonathan directly in the eyes. "Let me play back what I *think* I heard. Your daughter and new baby were previously *my* daughter and father? There's a woman living in San Diego who was apparently *my* son? How is that possible? Do you realize how crazy this sounds? If this wasn't Dr. Hobbs telling me this, I'd think you were both looney tunes."

Jonathan poured some cream into his coffee and stirred it. "I know. It's fascinating how all of these pieces have fallen into place. It's hard to conceive of it all. I can't even imagine what you're thinking and feeling right now."

"My mind is just rejecting it. Nothing seems logical, and I can't believe it. And yet I do! Something is screaming at me inside telling me this is the real deal. I do try to listen to my gut, and my instincts say this is authentic. But why? Why is this happening?"

"The why question is difficult to answer. Maybe we just don't know that right now, although I suspect it is about a balancing of energies. The issue we want to discuss with you is there's the possibility you could meet them in person, if that's something that interests you, along with everyone else involved. But there are lots of considerations for you to think about," Dr. Hobbs said.

"On one hand I think, how could I not? On the other hand ... I guess my biggest concern would be the letdown I would feel if this turns out not to be real—if I found out somehow they weren't really the reincarnated souls of my family. And what if we didn't like each other? And what role would we play in each other's lives? Would this be a wise thing to do? Or should things just be left as they are? I'm not sure what this would stir up in me." She pressed her hand over her heart, letting her eyes water, but fighting the tears.

Dr. Hobbs nodded his head. "I understand completely. There are many considerations, and only you can decide what is right for you. I do think this is being presented to you as an opportunity for some greater reason."

"I've thought about this long and hard as well, Margo," Jonathan said as he cleared his throat. "The compelling thing for me, and the reason my wife, Aria, and I agreed to this, is my daughter Samantha feels an intense drive to find you to let you know she's okay. She's been in a state of unrest about this and wants to heal a pain she's aware of in your soul."

Margo could no longer stifle her flood of tears, instead letting the rawness of her emotions roll down her cheek one tear at a time. "How beautiful is that?"

"She's special girl, a unique soul. She said she wants to bring you peace and show you how the soul lives on," Jonathan said.

"How can I deny her that opportunity?" She pushed her index fingers against her tear ducts, hoping to stop the flow. "I can't imagine, though, what it would feel like to actually see them as different people than Christina and Josh, in different bodies. I'm not sure how my brain would even accept that. That would just be the weirdest feeling ever. Would I recognize them in their new bodies?"

"No way to know that. Their personalities and bodies are definitely different," Dr. Hobbs said.

"Let me share something with you from my own life," Jonathan said. "When my godmother first met me in my new body, as a baby, she said she immediately recognized my spirit through the energy vibration she felt. She said there was no doubt in her mind."

Dr. Hobbs moved to sit next to Margo on the love seat and placed his hand firmly on hers. "This is a great deal for you to take in, Margo. We want you to take your time and consider everything. If you choose to meet them, I'll facilitate a meeting. If you choose not to, that's fine too. It's strictly up to you at this point. We support you with whatever you decide. I'll be available to talk to you if you want to process this more, but we'll leave it up to you so you can plow through all of your considerations and figure out what's right for you. Usually, your gut instincts will drive you to the right decision. Just let us know what you decide."

"So the option is there for all of us to meet in person. But everyone has to be in agreement with this, and you need to look at all aspects of what it could mean for you," Jonathan said.

"Thank you so much for your understanding. I do need to think about this and how it would impact my life. And I'll need to talk this through with Thomas as well." She glanced at Jonathan's puzzled look. "Thomas is my fiancé."

He nodded. "Of course."

Hearing the words and feeling the buried emotions surface jolted her to a different place in time as she sorted through the thinly woven threads of her past memories. It was as vivid as when she'd lived the scene over forty years ago. The possibilities were screaming in her mind. She breathed in and out deeply, waiting for the fog in her brain to clear. *What the heck is happening?*

"Before you go, I'd like to tell you both my story. I'd like for you to have the background as I recall it," Margo said.

"Please do, Margo," Dr. Hobbs said.

"Yes, please share it with us," Jonathan agreed.

She propped the striped toss pillows behind her back as she sunk into the couch and talked and remembered, telling them her tragic story. The men said nothing but nodded now and again. But the memory didn't seem like a memory to her; it just seemed like a sad story she lived over and over again.

Chapter 34

Margo

It was a day forever etched in my mind. December 3, 1979. My twins went on a trip to visit their grandma in Sacramento. My dad, an experienced commercial pilot for many years, wanted to take the kids on their first plane flight to see their grandma for her birthday.

In hindsight, I can see how I'd always been an overly protective mom, but the bottom line was I didn't want them to go. Maybe it was because I knew something was going to happen to them, or it was just the kind of person I was—always anxious about my kids. I couldn't go with them as it was a busy time of year at the hair salon, and my main colorist was out on maternity leave. My dad, assuring me all would be fine, was going to be first officer on the flight—that felt comforting to me. I'd always been a bit fearful about flying, but the kids were so excited, and they weren't going to stay long. Dad's favorite flight attendant was going to look out for them, and, well ... I just thought it would be a good experience. I really did. I wanted my children to experience the opportunities life had to offer. I was always so hung up by my fears and didn't want them to feel that way. Still, a sensation in my gut haunted me.

It was a beautiful day—perfect flying weather—when they flew out. Seventy-six degrees, crystal-blue cloudless sky. But I couldn't shake my jitters. I didn't know if Christina was having some kind of premonitions herself, but she didn't seem afraid to go. She stood in the doorway of the kitchen before the trip and said, "Mommy, what are you going to do with my toys when I'm gone?"

"You're only going to be gone a few days. They'll just stay where they always are," I said.

"Don't throw them away when I'm not around. I want other children to be able to have them," she said.

The flight out was fine and the kids loved it. I felt so much better once they landed. Even my dad was excited. He enjoyed sharing his experience of flying, what he loved to do, with his grandkids.

I'd fed them their favorite pancake breakfast the morning they left, packed them some snacks to take on the airplane, and gave each of them an activity bag of things to do, like Silly Putty and crayons. I saw them off, kissing them and hugging them, and all went well. They called when they got to Grandma's, and it was such a fantastic surprise for her celebration. I relaxed, knowing how often I worry for no reason.

On the day they were returning home, I closed the shop early, watching the clock the entire day. Time moved so slowly. My mouth was dry all day, and I felt nauseous. I knew I'd feel better once they were home and in their own beds. My dad was going to bring them home once they landed.

I was outside watering the plants when my head started pounding so badly, and I looked up into the bright sunshine. Seeing those planes come at me was a sensation I hope I never have to relive again. When I looked up, I knew. I knew it was their plane coming right at me. It was surreal, and it all happened so fast. As they approached the San Diego airport, the aircraft was diving at a steep angle and one wing was on fire, flames shooting everywhere. A neon-orange fire erupted on the wing, and it grew in intensity as the aircraft plummeted. I remember hearing a loud, metallic crunching sound—a sickening sound—and the plane disappearing behind a group of tall trees. The ground shook like an earthquake, and the deafening roar of the impact followed the explosion. I just knew it was them. Why couldn't the plane have landed on me? Oh my God. My children were on that plane! My dad! The plane that was plummeting to earth, on fire. There are no words and there never will be the words to describe my feelings.

It was an absolute nightmare. It seemed like the entire neighborhood was on fire. I never knew panic like I felt at that moment, and my heart beat so hard I not only felt it but could hear it. I couldn't hear anything but its deep, incessant beat. People were running and screaming, and I stood there as though I was glued to the sidewalk. I couldn't lift my feet. Oh, how those screams cut through my sleep for many, many nights, haunting me obsessively.

I hoped some piece of flying debris would take me out too. I knew there would be no survivors, and I didn't want to be left. Oh my God, I just didn't want to be left behind. I knelt on the ground and beat my fists against my chest wailing and pleading with God not to take them, or to take me too.

Then something protective washed over me. I guess it was shock. Time disappeared. I just remember bits of flashbacks. I saw the wing of the plane burning as it fell to earth. I remember a mushroom-like cloud from the crash and the sound of that impact. The house shook, and the windows rattled. I heard that sound for years; it was the sound of death.

It seemed like immediately, the TV stations and news reporters were converging on the scene along with the first responders. I think I just knelt there for the longest time. It seemed as though people were mouthing things to me, but I was deaf to their words. I remember people were urging me to leave, but I don't recall anything they said. There were only distant sirens in my brain. I had shut down. I was on overdrive, overwhelmed, and my system went down like a computer losing Internet connection.

In a short period of time, the police and several residents had blocked off the streets to traffic, and I remember hearing people yelling for help. The screaming didn't stop. Everyone seemed to be screaming. Trees were on fire. I felt myself choking from the shroud of thick smoke and something in the air reeked: like burning fuel. My eyes were tearing and felt irritated. There just seemed to be people everywhere, and I don't know where they appeared from and who they were—so many people running around and shouting, trying to help the injured. But there were no injured; they were all dead.

Suddenly it was eerily quiet except for the distant chaos; I thought I'd been transported directly to hell. Finally I let loose of my body lock and darted out into the street. As I ran, I had to avoid the debris that was everywhere. That realization was shocking. I stepped on someone's glasses—someone who wouldn't be using them again. There were suitcases, shoes, articles of clothing, and mangled body parts. Then I tripped over a leg with a high heel on it on the sidewalk.

People were everywhere. Rescue people. Medical people. Police. They were evacuating the neighborhood and told me to get my things and get out as soon as I could. I didn't go.

The other smaller plane that crashed into the Eros jet landed about 3,500 feet from the 727. One of the wings lodged in a house as it nosedived to the ground.

Horrified—horrified is the best description of what I felt when I was told that the passengers and crew were ejected from the plane. Were my children sent flying through the air? Only two flight attendants, and one passenger, were found with intact bodies. Too much for any one brain to take in and comprehend.

It happened so quickly.

Walking the streets, I wandered around, hoping to find my family alive, but of course I knew that couldn't be possible. When I was trudging through the debris, I saw parts of arms and legs and a half of a torso. The bodies of my family were never found. Just as well. I couldn't have taken it.

Afterwards, the neighborhood was busy being "fixed"—put back together as much as possible—because that's what we do as human beings: we adapt, we fix, we recreate, we move on. Eventually everyone went back to their normal lives. But there was no normal left for me.

How does one even think of coping with such a tragedy? About five times, I went to see a psychologist, and she helped me sort out my feelings and made me understand that what I'd seen was very traumatic. She mentioned several times that I was doing well considering the circumstances. She said I would be forever changed— she had no idea. I have since had some recurring plane crash nightmares, but nothing unexpected according to the people that determine these things.

I was diagnosed with situation-specific amnesia. For a long time, I couldn't remember any of the event that happened. I don't even remember the funerals.

The crash happened at 2:22 p.m. on December 3, 1979, and the jet hit the ground right in our residential area. To this day, I don't really completely know what happened. I never wanted to read anything about it. I just didn't want to know. But I do know the Eros jet was on its final approach to the San Diego airport when a smaller plane struck its wing and damaged the hydraulics and flaps. It also caused the fire and then the crash. The small plane went down fairly close to the Eros jet. There were 170 people on the large jet, four in the small plane, and ten people on the ground killed in the accident.

They said it was a midair collision resulting from pilot and air traffic controller error. That devastated me: to think it was partially pilot error! My father would never rest in peace with that. Never. Not ever. The guilt would always be with him—through all eternity. I don't know if it was the captain's fault or the first officer's fault or both. I don't *want* to know. Fault didn't really matter.

Today, I just avoid the area completely. I can't imagine living there, knowing what had happened in 1979. I had to move away. I think a lot of those people have no idea what took place ... but maybe they do. When I drive past, I always say a little prayer.

That night, the kids came to me in a vision. They said they were okay. Christina told me not to live being sad. My son told me he loved me. I went to see a well-known medium in hopes of relieving my pain, and she told me we'd all made soul contracts. My kids planned short lives to pay karma to me—to teach me about loss, that the soul goes on. The three of them had agreed on a group karmic contract to make changes to the airline industry.

I did get stuck in depression and despair for a long time. Cognitively, I knew everyone has crap happen to them. Everyone. Everyone experiences loss. No one asks for it. So why does it happen? My way of thinking explains things to me in a way that makes some logical sense. It makes sense why we're here on this earth experiencing this stuff. My philosophy is what works for me. I don't care if others believe it or not. Life is birth, joyous moments, heartbreaking moments, celebration, mourning, love, hate, death, and a myriad of experiences and emotions.

I see the scenario play out as if I was an outsider, looking in and watching the players as each person participated in the story according to their life plan. As I remember it, it was like I was in another dimension, looking down at the actors playing their roles.

That moment in time was both an ending and a beginning. An ending to everything I knew or thought to be real. It changed me physically, emotionally, and spiritually. I did die that day along with them. Margo died, and I gradually became a new person. What can one say to even describe *why* it happened?

There was a detached hand with three fingers on it, with red nail polish ... in my yard.

It was a defining moment of my life.

Chapter 35

October 1

Life is full of strange happenings, Olivia thought as she stood in the bathroom, applying mascara to her lashes. She'd been surprised when Dr. Hobbs had called her and said Margo had agreed to meet all of them; she'd been convinced she'd say no. Maybe she was projecting what she thought *she'd* do, hesitant to open that door and invite in … invite in what? She had no idea. Maybe she didn't want to unsettle her comfortable life again. *I really want to believe this is all real, but it just seems so impossible.*

Only two days ago, she'd found out from Dr. Hobbs that the woman who was her previous mother had been the same Margo in her yoga class. How bizarre was that? *Truth really is stranger than fiction!* She'd realized that miracles are there if people are able to open their minds and realize them. All along, a person in her class had actually been a member of her soul group who'd once served in the role of her mother. It made her wonder about all the other people in her life: the mailman, her accountant … maybe they were part of her soul group as well. But how was it possible she'd been Sammi's—

Christina's—brother? How could her mother from another life still be alive? How was any of this possible? No one would ever believe it. Not that it mattered—she only had Jax to tell anyway. Yet somehow, she *knew* it was true. It was so interesting how all the players were coming together. It seemed impossible, yet it confirmed to her that everyone made soul contracts before incarnating. It was all meant to be—there *was* a greater plan. *That's rather a comforting thought.*

Olivia stood in front of her closet, planning what to wear. In preparation for their group meeting with Margo, Sammi and Olivia had decided to spend some past life sibling connection time together. A "girlie" outing—shopping, dinner, and the theater—sounded fun. They decided to pick out a gift to take to Margo, their previous mother—previous mother from a past life! Infatuated with the play *Alice in Wonderland*, Sammi had been thrilled to learn that Olivia was taking her to the theater at the Los Angeles Philharmonic to see it. Olivia settled on a cobalt-blue lace sheath dress that hugged her curves with neutral pumps and understated silver earrings and necklace. *I'm really looking forward to this.* Having lived alone for so long, essentially estranged from her family, she felt apprehensive about letting herself feel attached to anyone again. But she felt a draw, a connection, to both Sammi and Tyson—it was undeniable.

Allowing herself plenty of time, Olivia drove to LA to pick Sammi up, easily finding their house—a contemporary Mediterranean home situated at a high elevation with amazing views of the Hollywood Hills. Feeling a bit nervous, she rang the bell to the Cohens' house. She glanced around at the exterior of the house, admiring the original xeriscaping they'd put in, when Aria answered. *Wow, she's stunning.* Olivia wished she'd applied her own makeup with a heavier hand.

Aria, wearing a lovely red-and-white striped sleeveless dress, extended her hand to Olivia, her voice as smooth as an expensive

Scotch whiskey. "Hi, Olivia, come in. I'm Aria. It's so nice to meet you. How was the drive?"

"I'm excited to meet you, Aria. The drive wasn't bad. Thanks for letting me have some bonding time with Sammi. It's generous of you."

"Not at all. She's been looking forward to this so much. And I've heard so much about you! Please come in while Sammi finishes getting ready."

Olivia sat on the couch where Aria gestured. The living room was decorated as she imagined: laid-back, yet at the same time luxurious, in shades of white, gray, and peach. *How can she keep a perfectly white couch when she has a kid?* she thought. "So, Aria, how are you digesting all this new information? Pretty overwhelming, don't you think?"

Aria joined her on the couch. "Actually, pretty well. When I watch Sammi and hear her talk about it, it's so natural and she ... she just seems so serene—like this happens every day. I find that reassuring. I'm trying not to analyze or judge it. I'm just letting the experience flow."

"That's a great way to handle it, Aria. Perfect."

Jonathan, holding Tyson, came down the steps with Sammi, hand in hand. When Sammi saw Olivia, she ran and hugged her. "Hi, Olivia. I'm happy to see you again."

"Sounds like you've got some fun planned for our girl," Jonathan said.

"We're going to have a blast!" Olivia said as she eyed Sammi. Aria was right, she thought. Sammi *did* seem very serene—she could see it on her face.

Sammi grasped Aria's hand, looking up into her eyes. "Mama, you're okay with all of this, right? You know I love you so much."

"I do know how much you love me, sweetheart, and I love you. I'm very happy with this. It's hard for me to understand some of this past life stuff, but I'm trying, and I want you to have a wonderful time."

"If it makes you feel any better, Aria, it's a bit hard for me too, and I work with these issues for a living. I'll stay in touch and text you where we are and what we're doing. And although I only have two tickets for the play, you're welcome to join us for shopping and dinner."

"No, no … you two spend time getting to know each other," Aria said confidently.

Sammi, wearing a black-and-pink checkered dress with pink lace on the collar, twirled around in front of Olivia. "Look, Mama bought me a new dress for the theater. Do you like it?"

Olivia turned to Sammi. "I certainly do. You look so pretty."

"So do you in your blue dress."

"Thank you, sweetie." Olivia looked to Jonathan. "Mind if I hold Tyson a minute?"

"Of course not," he said as he placed his sleeping boy in her waiting arms.

"He certainly got Aria's head of dark hair, didn't he? What a cutie-pie! They're so adorable when they're sleeping. Welcome to this world, baby Tyson," Olivia said in a high-pitched tone, stretching out the vowels as she spoke.

"Yes, he did, and I think he has Sammi's eyes," Aria said, looking adoringly at her son.

"Oh, Sammi, I almost forgot! Before we go, I have a present for you. I saw it and just thought of you. Maybe not the typical gift for a six-year-old, but I hope you like it." She shifted Tyson to her left arm and handed Sammi her purse. "Open it. It's the wrapped box inside."

Sammi opened her purse and found a package wrapped with silver-and-gold striped paper, tied with a curly gold ribbon.

"Open it," Olivia encouraged.

Sammi threw herself on the couch, tossing the gray and white pillows to the side, and carefully opened the box. She peeled back the silver tissue paper, exposing an iridescent-looking heart. After removing it from the box, she held it up to the light. "Oh, this is pretty."

"It's a labradorite heart."

"It looks like it's glowing inside."

"It's sometimes called a magic stone. It has what they call a shimmering labradorescence, which is like the shield that protects starships. It'll help protect you and keep you safe."

Sammi hugged her. "I love it, Olivia. Thank you. That's what I want to buy for Margo—a heart for her collection."

"My friend Jax told me about a place we can go for that."

Aria pulled Olivia to the side, cupped her hand on one side of her mouth, and whispered, "I'm sorry she's wearing those darn pink cowboy boots. They're like her security blanket or something. I worry about the day she outgrows those. I tried to get her to wear a pretty pair of Mary Janes I'd bought her, but she said they hurt her feet. I do apologize."

Olivia grinned. "No need. I want her to feel comfortable and secure, and I think they're adorable. I have a few security items of my own."

Aria's eyes twinkled. "Well, when you see them every single day, they're not so adorable anymore."

While Jonathan transferred Sammi's booster seat from his car to Olivia's, Aria retrieved her sleeping baby. Once Sammi was buckled in, Jonathan and Aria waved goodbye as they drove away, heading toward a downtown gift store that specialized in tchotchkes.

"What do you think of all of this, Sammi? Does it excite you to think of seeing Margo again?" Olivia asked, speaking into the rearview mirror as she drove.

"I'm excited to see her. I think she needs to see all of us, so that's why it's important. What do you think?"

"I'm curious and nervous at the same time because I don't remember that life. I've had some dreams where I'm playing with you as your blonde-haired brother, but not much else."

"I told Mama that I didn't want Margo to be a mother to me again in this life. I just wanted her to see we're all okay and show her how we don't really die. She understood, and it made her happy. She isn't worried anymore."

"Oh, that's good, Sammi. I wondered about that."

They drove to a hidden area in Los Angeles with a narrow street of little indie boutiques and retail shops. The shop was quaint-bohemian in style, tiny, and filled with more heart-shaped objects than could be imagined. Olivia watched as Sammi roamed the aisles and searched the shop with eagle eyes—there was something particular she had in mind. *It's so cute how she picks up each object, puts it down, and shakes her head, indicating it isn't the right one.*

"Are you looking for something in particular?" the salesclerk asked Sammi.

"Yes, I am. I got my mommy a heart locket over forty years ago. I want to get her another one like it."

The woman looked at her oddly. "Over forty years ago? You look like you're about five."

Sammi just smiled. "Do you have any?"

"We do. We have some pretty ones. Let me get them for you."

The clerk gently laid them out on the counter on a piece of black velvet, one by one, so Olivia and Sammi could examine each locket.

Sammi immediately picked up the one in the center. "Olivia, look! This is the one. This looks like the one I gave her for Mother's Day. I put our pictures in it. We can take a picture of us and put it in the new locket."

"I'm actually capturing a memory in my mind of the one from the past. Oh, let's get that one. It's beautiful. I found some heart-shaped earrings. Do you like these?" She held up a pair of white crystal heart earrings for Sammi's approval.

"They're really pretty. I think we should pick out something from Tyson too. But I have an idea what it should be. Come closer so I can tell you."

Olivia bent down to Sammi's level, and she whispered in her ear.

"Hmm ... I don't know about that. Are you sure that'll be okay?" Olivia asked hesitantly.

Sammi nodded vehemently. "Oh, yes, I am."

"I think I'll let your mom and dad help you pick that gift out, okay?"

"Okay, but Daddy will say yes."

They waited while the clerk gift-wrapped the boxes. "I still can't believe we're buying something for a mother from another life," Olivia said. "There's so many things I wish I understood better. Sometimes I think it would be easier for all of us if we were born just knowing what our purpose is for being here on Earth. The way it is, we have to kind of figure it out and guess. Do you know what I mean?"

"I know that when I'm grown up I'm moving to London, and I'll be a digital anthropologist. I have something very important I have to do to help the world."

"Wow. That's incredible that you know that already. I don't even know what that is, much less how to pronounce it. Do you think it would help people to know what they are meant to do while they're here on Earth."

Sammi shrugged. "Maybe. My daddy told me something from his Native American life. He said they have a saying. 'The Great Spirit gave each of us a song. We're here simply to sing our song.'"

Olivia looked at Sammi with amazement. At times she was a little girl, and other times she talked like she was a sixty-year-old woman in a young girl's body.

"I love that saying, Sammi. Thank you so much for sharing that with me."

For Olivia, the theater was always an enjoyable experience, but seeing it through a little girl's point of view was absolutely fun—as well as a learning experience. She loved looking at the world through Sammi's innocent, nonjudgmental eyes. Right before intermission, Olivia had to stifle her laughter when Sammi stood on the theater chair and belted out one of the songs from *Alice in Wonderland,* singing along with the cast. No one sitting around them seemed to mind. *She's so authentic, so unrestrained. I love that.* After dropping Sammi off at home, driving away, she felt a tear roll down her cheek, realizing she already missed her.

At that moment, she knew she wanted that little girl to be a part of her life— always.

Chapter 36

October 19

Was all of this going to open a can of worms? Jonathan wondered. He felt excited and unnerved at the same time, hoping they were all making the wisest decision. He'd actually consulted his own spirit guides and received confirmation that meeting Margo would be a beneficial thing for all. A plan was needed. He didn't want to freak Margo out, he didn't want Aria to feel upset, he wanted Sammi to feel satisfied—he just wanted it to go as well as possible.

Sitting in the den with his laptop, he called Matthew on Virtual-Time. Matthew, working at his desk in his office, answered immediately. "Jonathan, I was just thinking about you."

"Hey, Matthew. I was calling to talk about our plans for the big meetup. Say hi to Tyson!" Jonathan lifted Tyson up in front of the laptop screen, bouncing him up and down.

"Hey, Tyson. You're already growing so fast, buddy. Can't wait to see him again. Well, I think we'll be able to contend with whatever happens spontaneously. My intuition tells me this is a good thing for everyone involved. What time are you planning on leaving LA tomorrow?"

Jonathan laid Tyson in a bassinet next to the couch. "I was thinking of leaving at ten, and then we're going to swing by and pick up Olivia and all go to Margo's together. Olivia had a good bonding get-together with Sammi, and I like the relationship they're establishing. Sammi wanted Olivia to ride with us."

"Great. Give me a call when you're about twenty minutes from her house, and I'll leave then."

Jonathan was a bundle of nervous energy, drumming his fingers on the desktop. "I was thinking about it and wondered if Tyson, on some level, will recognize the person that was once his beloved daughter. And of course I wonder if she'll recognize his essence. I still remember how Sophie described meeting me for the first time as Jonathan. She immediately recognized me as the soul who was her son in a previous life. What do you think?"

"Yes, that was an intense, life-changing moment for her. You know, I think he will on some level."

"I already started a script about this, but I'll have to see how this all plays out before I write more."

Sammi walked by and noticed Matthew on the computer screen. "Hi, Matthew, it's me, Sammi," she said as she leaned into the screen.

"Hi, sweetie. Are you all ready for our big day? Do you have any concerns or questions?"

"No, it's all going to be good. I'm not worried about Mama anymore. We had a nice talk and she understands. I feel happy about everything. Daddy and I got a special gift for Tyson to give to Margo."

"You did? Tell me."

"Nope, you're going to be surprised," Sammi said, giggling.

Jonathan laughed. "She has me wrapped around her little finger. Sometimes I do things she wants even if I'm not sure about it. Hope the surprise is okay."

"Okay, we'll see you tomorrow. Get plenty of rest tonight."

"Bye, Matthew, see you tomorrow," Sammi said.

Jonathan was pleased. It was great to see her so content. No more nightmares, and finally her soul would be able to rest ... if it all went as he hoped.

Chapter 37

October 20

Olivia was trembling so hard she had to sit or she might pass out. The day to meet Margo finally arrived. What would it be like to meet her now, knowing she was once this woman's son? Was she really her mother from another life?

She paced around her apartment, dressed and ready, not-so-patiently waiting as Aria, Jonathan, Sammi, and Tyson drove down from LA to pick her up. When they arrived, Sammi was talking a mile a minute on their way to Margo's house, where they were meeting Matthew.

They all stood at Margo's front door, staring at each other, waiting to ring the bell. Was it too late to back out? It was weird to think this was the final moment before their lives would change forever. Olivia noticed how Sammi seemed nonchalant, taking it all in stride like it was nothing out of the ordinary. Tyson, of course, wasn't old enough to have any clue what was going on. Jonathan and Matthew both seemed excited, and Olivia sensed that Aria was holding back a bit, probably wondering how her life would change after meeting the mother Sammi had talked about for so long.

Olivia's anticipation accelerated as obsessive thoughts filled her head. Her brain felt as though it was full of static, offering up a jumbled hodgepodge of possible scenarios she didn't want to contemplate. Her hands began to shake, and in an attempt to mask her nerves, she thrust them deep into the frayed pockets of her jeans. The strong desire to chew her nails was overwhelming. She felt like running,

Finally, Matthew rang the bell and Thomas opened the door and introduced himself.

"Hi, I'm Thomas, also known as moral support. Margo's just getting off the phone. Please come in."

They moved in unison, as though tethered together, from the front porch to the foyer. Olivia saw Margo standing in the living room, arms at her sides, trembling from her head to her toes as though the energy of each of them transported her back in time to the seventies. Matthew introduced everyone, but Margo didn't move. She just stood there, hanging on to the back of a chair for support as she visibly began to shudder, starting at her ankles and rising up to her shoulders and head. Olivia didn't know if she should reach out and hold her up.

Olivia studied Margo's face, seeking, looking, for anything that seemed familiar, anything that might trigger a deeply buried memory of this woman as her mother. Although she didn't recognize Margo as anyone other than the lady who attended her yoga lessons, she thought she saw something familiar in her eyes. This person who was once her mother might have been her father, her priest, her best friend, her master, her murderer in another time, another place. Whatever role she had played, that day, it resonated with Olivia that hers was a soul she was connected to.

Everyone stood staring at each other for what seemed like minutes on end, when Sammi broke free and ran to her. Margo knelt down on one knee and opened her arms, embracing Sammi as she rocked her back and forth, making moaning sounds.

She held Sammi at arm's length to look at her, searching deep in her eyes for the soul of Christina. Finally able to find words, she shouted, "Oh my God, it's really you. It's really you! My little girl! I'm beside myself." She slowly drew her fingers down Sammi's face, feeling the shape of her nose, the curve of her heart-shaped pink lips, the outline of her chin. She pulled her close, hugging her so tightly, Olivia wondered if Sammi could breathe. Olivia felt helpless to assist Margo as she watched her collapse to the floor on both knees, burying her head in her hands, weeping profusely. *I'm not sure what I should do right now.* Thomas leaned over, stroking Margo's hair as he let her cry it out. As she settled, Thomas pulled her to stand, and Sammi could no longer contain herself.

She wrapped her comforting arms around Margo's waist. "We found you. We're back! We're here! You don't have to worry or be sad now," Sammi said. She smiled so sweetly, it was as though honey oozed from her pores.

With the ice broken, Olivia came forward next and hugged her. Margo stood, hanging on to her chair just shaking her head. She looked as though she might burst into another river of tears that would never stop if she let go.

Olivia laughed to lighten the moment. "Hi, Margo. How shocking is this for you? Your yoga instructor was your child?"

"Probably as shocking as finding your yoga student was once your mother!"

More tears sprang forth. Tears of relief. Tears of joy. And tears that represented nothing other than tears. Margo looked toward the heavens, mouthing, "Thank you, thank you." Thomas kept his hands planted firmly on her shoulders to steady her.

"This can't be real," she said as she vigorously gestured with her arms. "How is this possible? I believe it and yet I don't. But I *feel* your energy that is uniquely each of you. And look, little Tyson has the same birthmark my father had on his right hand."

Olivia glanced around the room. No one knew what to say; it seemed like everyone had lost the knowledge of how to speak.

"Let's break the ice," Margo said. "It would make me happy if you all sat at the table, filling my chairs with your presence. I've had dreams of my chairs being full again. And I made Christina's— I mean, Sammi's and Josh's—favorite brownies."

They all sat at the table, filling the once-too-empty chairs. Sammi dug in and bit into the gooey warmth of the brownies. "These are just like the brownies you made us from before. You see we are all okay. Do you feel happy now?"

Margo just nodded as she stared at each of them one by one. Looking at Aria, she asked, "May I hold Tyson?"

"Of course," Aria said. She placed the bundled baby in her arms. Margo rocked him, then started to laugh uncontrollably. As she looked down at Tyson she said, "Dad ... Dad ... is that you in there, Dad? Imagine how ludicrous this seems. Rocking my father!"

While Margo cooed and chortled with Tyson, the girls winked at each other as they prepared to give Margo their precious gifts. First, Olivia presented the earrings, which Margo oohed and aahed over, immediately putting them on. Sammi gave her the locket with a picture of Olivia, Tyson, and her—and, not wanting to hurt her mother's feelings, she also gave the same pendant to Aria with a picture of her and Tyson. Olivia choked up when she saw the tears well up in both the mothers' eyes when they received their lockets.

"How did you know I like hearts?" Margo asked.

"Sammi just knew," Olivia answered.

Margo slapped her hand against her chest when she zeroed in on Sammi's pink boots. "Oh my! I just noticed—you're wearing pink boots!" Margo stood and said, "Wait a minute, everyone." She went down the hall toward her bedroom. When she returned, she was holding a small jewelry-sized box and a dusty old shoe box. She stood with her eyes closed, holding the boxes close to her chest, seeming as though she was sucking the memories from inside the box into her soul.

Returning to the present moment she said, "Look at this." She opened the small box and handed a piece of jewelry to Sammi.

Sammi jumped up and down. "That's it! That's the locket I gave you for Mother's Day."

"Open it," Margo said with excitement.

Sammi unfastened the locket and inside were photos of Christina and Josh— two photos, faded in color and grainy. She showed it to Olivia. "That's what you looked like last time," Sammi said.

Olivia held the locket, staring at the people she and her twin sister were in a past life. She gulped. It felt familiar. Just what was this that she was experiencing? *I never experienced sensations like this in my life!*

"Now this is fascinating ..." Margo picked up the box she'd brought from the hall closet and lifted the cover. She reached in and brought out a pair of old, worn pink boots.

It was then that Olivia noticed Sammi lost her composure. She reached to hold the boots, tears in her eyes. "My boots! Those are my boots!" She closed her eyes and hugged them to her chest like she had discovered rare treasure. Olivia noticed Aria staring at Jonathan with a look of total surprise on her face. *This is fascinating!*

Jonathan stood and said to Margo, "We have another gift for you. I hope this is okay, but Sammi absolutely insisted. Even though it was against our better judgment, she can be very persuasive. This is not something I would normally do."

"I'm very curious now. What is it?" Margo said.

They watched as Jonathan went out to the front porch and came back holding a cage with a black-and-white polka-dotted towel covering it. He opened the cage and pulled out a wiggling Boston Terrier puppy, wearing a collar decorated with tiny red hearts.

"From Tyson," he said. "You don't have to keep him if you don't want him."

Margo picked up his tiny body and hugged him to her chest. The puppy immediately licked Margo's face. "Not want him? How could I not keep this adorable little creature? I never learned to cry without looking ugly," Margo said. "I even practiced in front of a mirror so the corners of my mouth didn't turn down, with thick ridges forming between my brows and melting black eye makeup traveling down my cheeks. But you're just going to have to deal with the ugly cry today." More tears rolled down Margo's cheeks and once again turned into rivers of pent-up emotions finally being released. Thomas handed her another box of tissues.

"How appropriate that gift came from Tyson. Honestly, he looks just like Jimmy's dog, Brewster. Everything is now complete. Everything is whole again. I love him. Thank you."

"You can name him whatever you want, Margo," Sammi said. "We didn't name him so you could."

"I'm pretty speechless right now. I'm beyond overwhelmed with all of this. I think I believed all of this in theory, and then when something like this happens, I'm blown out of the water. Thank you all for everything, for arranging all of this. I feel at peace again. That incredible, wondrous feeling of contentment and peace."

"Me too, Margo. I feel at peace too," said Olivia.

"Me too," said Sammi, clapping enthusiastically.

From Olivia's point of view, it appeared as though the impact of the reunion on Margo was a knock-your-socks-off moment, and from the expression on her face, it seemed like she was unable to process the massive amounts of input pulsating in her brain, demanding recognition. Of course, the whole situation seemed overwhelming for everyone.

Piles of photo albums, some tattered and frayed with loose pages, were haphazardly arranged on the shelves next to the fireplace. Margo gathered up a stack, brought them to the table, and invited everyone to sit and pore over the memories of her life—they all looked through them with amazement, to the point where they all felt spent and overly emotional. Olivia studied them, one page at a time, mesmerized by the faded memories of Margo's life ... and hers. *Is that picture of Josh ... me?* She watched Margo, observing her facial expressions, as she lovingly ran her fingers over the photos, caught in a time warp of her past.

The group spent a couple of hours perusing the albums, until each of them appeared to be shutting down from overload. To Olivia, it seemed like that moment in the movies where there's that happy ending everyone wanted—like when the Tin Man finally gets his heart, the Death Star is destroyed, or ET takes his candy pieces and finds his way back home.

With everyone spent, the group said their goodbyes and headed over to Lizzie and Mark's house for dinner, while Matthew and Olivia stayed behind after the visit to ensure Margo was okay. Olivia noticed that Margo now seemed defenseless against the onslaught of emotions roaming around in her heart as she released a few more tears.

"You doing okay, love?" Thomas asked.

"Better than okay," Margo said, hugging him. "Just emotional."

Matthew bent down, holding a chew toy they'd brought with them to play tug-of-war with the puppy. "It was a fascinating day, Margo. Seeing all of this come to fruition, to actually see the healing that is going on—I can't describe what I'm feeling."

"I keep reliving my first glimpse of everyone over and over again. I'm like this new person. Cleansed. I feel twenty years younger. My energy is boundless. Like you, no words can describe it."

"So powerful!" Matthew said.

"I do admit I'm a bit overwhelmed," Olivia said, "but I also feel renewed."

Margo hung on to Thomas for support. "I just remembered that when I originally went to a psychic about this, he thought the plane crash was a karmic event that the souls on board had agreed upon ahead of time. He said that when tragic events happen that have more than a few people involved, it's frequently planned as a group to cause a ripple effect on consciousness, often felt around the world."

"Yes, yes. That makes perfect sense," said Matthew.

"He said he was able to channel Christina, who came across the strongest. He wasn't able to pick up the message she'd said to me, but he said Christina remembered the day she died. When she passed, she felt relieved to be floating, no longer in a solid body. Then suddenly she felt very peaceful, with no pain or discomfort, but she was confused, like many other people she met. She 'talked' to other people at the scene of the crash with her thoughts and saw them—their spirits—walking through things, like large debris, without even noticing it.

"She didn't know she was dead until people from her soul group came to greet her. Her soul had planned a very short life to experience childhood with a loving mother. My kids and dad had a soul contract with me to give me the experience of grief and loss, and to work through issues of abandonment. I'm going to need some quiet time to process all of this. It's a shock to my being."

"We'll leave you to your thoughts, Margo," Matthew said. "If you need to talk or process this with me, know that I'm always available. And you have great support with Thomas here. Call me day or night. I have some processing of my own to do as well. Let's get together soon and talk, okay?"

"Absolutely. Thank you for everything. This is a life-altering moment for me. Thank you both for the role you played."

"You're welcome, Margo. I hope your soul is now at peace," Matthew said as he gave her a warm, comforting hug.

Matthew took his keys out of his pocket. "I'll drop you off at your house, Olivia, or you're welcome to join us at Sammi's grandparents' house."

"Thanks, but I think I'll head home. I'm a bit bowled over and really tired."

As they were leaving, Olivia gave Margo a hug, then Thomas reached over and enveloped Olivia in a healing embrace. She knew when she got home, she'd wonder if the whole thing was nothing but a dream.

The next morning, as Olivia sat at her kitchen table drinking coffee in her pajamas, she decided to call Jonathan. *I need to know how Sammi is reacting. And I need to confirm this wasn't a dream!* "I'm just curious what your take is on how Sammi is doing after this," she said to him. "I had a hard time sleeping last night—kept replaying the whole thing in my mind over and over."

"It's really amazing," Jonathan responded. "She took it all in stride, didn't she? But I can actually feel a difference in her. Aria noticed it too. She slept peacefully last night. No nightmares. She wasn't even tired after it all. She relayed the whole story to her grandparents with a sense of joy and happiness. Before she went to bed, do you know what she said?"

"No, what?"

She said, "Daddy, my heart was like a puzzle that was missing a piece. Now, it's like a brand-new puzzle again because the missing piece is back in it!"

"Wow, that's powerful isn't it?" She laughed.

"The heart wants what the heart wants, doesn't it?" Jonathan said.

"I'm thrilled she was able to find peace."

"Me too, me too."

They chatted a bit more, and when she hung up with Jonathan, she had only one thing she wanted to do. She punched in the numbers on her phone.

"Jax ... you won't believe the story I have to tell you."

Chapter 38

NONPHYSICAL WORLD

Pneuma: Margo had soul contracts with Christina, Josh, and her dad. Margo had agreed, for purposes of growing her consciousness, to learn lessons as a result of the losses she experienced. Pain is a powerful teacher.

Neshamah: I see how that works.

Pneuma: We have an advantage of seeing this play out by viewing it from a different realm of existence. Each dimension has characteristics that define it, and all dimensions are learning opportunities. You see, from our vantage point we know we are all interconnected. What I do affects you and what you do affects me. We know that, but many people don't because they see themselves as separate individuals with separate bodies. Your death is not just about you and your experiences. It's just as much about your contracts with other people who are learning things with or through you right up to the end. Even in the death process, you're cocreating with others.

Neshamah: So souls choose relationships and family ties based on the lessons they wish to learn while they're in human form. You said that soul growth can advance more quickly through human incarnations than in spirit form because in the third-dimension duality exists. And on Earth, people learn best from contrast.

Pneuma: The Earth was previously only three-dimensional, but it has made a big shift through the fourth to the fifth dimension—it's a collective process. Earth still is the place to provide people with a vast array of experiences. These experiences come in various ways to advance the growth of the soul. In that dimension, there's day and night, light and dark, up and down. Experiencing the full gamut of the opposites teaches valuable lessons. You learn certain things coming from the perspective of being a male versus a female. Same with experiencing being different races, living in different environments, or being rich versus poor. Human beings tend to judge everything in terms of this duality. *He's bad. He's good.* Humans are evolving to a new paradigm, no longer needing to judge. As the world moves out of 3-D and the world of duality, and people awaken to see the new dimensions, they'll see they no longer require polarity to learn. They'll be comfortable with a merging of the two—seeing not just black *or* white, but black *and* white. When you recognize that the polarities exist, then you can seek to integrate them and achieve balance. There's opposition everywhere you look. Experiencing it is an opportunity to grow spiritually.

Neshamah: There are certainly an unlimited number of experiences, as I see it.

Pneuma: The souls on Eros flight 190 were teachers and cocreators. The accident caused changes that helped others in the future. It provoked a needed change in some of the air traffic rules at large, busy airports.

Neshamah: It all makes sense when you're able to see the big picture.

Pneuma: Always.

Chapter 39

October 28

Olivia had been feeling strong and empowered, as though she could lasso the moon. Her view of the world and her purpose had solidified; everything in her life was suddenly fitting together like a jigsaw puzzle. The meeting with Margo was confirmation of things she'd thought and felt but couldn't personally validate—until now. Something about the whole situation of meeting souls from her past life, and the understanding that went with it, elevated her consciousness and her vibration. A sensation of love and connectedness seemed to gush out of her pores to everyone and everything around her. The world actually looked different. More friendly. More colorful. *She* was more friendly and colorful.

Finally forcing herself to take a day off from work, she sat in the kitchen, basking in her joyful thoughts, drinking a cup of coffee. Jax was on his way over to pick up a box of masks she'd made for the wedding to decorate the tables at the reception. She'd already made omelets, keeping them warm in the oven until Jax arrived.

When she opened the door, Jax handed her a fat, happy jack-o'-lantern and eyed her up and down.

"Livie, I think you swallowed the sun this morning. You're all full of some kind of glitter, cotton candy, energy, and light. You're actually glowing!"

"Am I? I feel so cleansed and free. Hey, thanks for the Halloween pumpkin—he's so cute!" She set it on the kitchen table, next to her vanilla-scented votives. "Love your leather jacket. Is it that cold outside?"

"Yeah, it's pretty nippy out there. Something sure smells good."

"I made us omelets. Sit down, have some coffee, and let's talk."

"So, really—you look like someone took a yellow highlighter and colored it all over your body. What's causing it?"

She *was* glowing—she could feel light pouring out of her skin, diffusing into the air around her. She was high on life, and there was nothing more exciting to her than the thought of celebrating the love of her best friend at his wedding. Jax had even asked her to invite her newfound family to the event: Jonathan, Aria, Sammi, Tyson, Margo, Thomas, Matthew, Sophie, and Lizzie and Mark. The sensation of freedom she was experiencing also allowed her to feel her bond with her biological family—now that she didn't have to worry about Curtis—so she had plans for a family reunion with her mother, brothers, and sisters. *I'm happier than I've ever been.*

While Jax removed his jacket, arranging it on the back of a kitchen chair, Olivia poured a splash of almond milk into a mug, topped it off with coffee, and handed it to Jax. "I'm glowing because you're going to get a special treat this morning."

"Waffles?"

"No, better!"

"Okay, give it up."

Olivia flitted around the kitchen, finding it difficult to contain her energy. "Sit down and get ready to hear this ... I've reached it. I've reached a place I was hoping I could go. I'm filled with an overwhelming sense of unconditional love. I've searched my heart, my soul, and it's pure. There are no hidden expectations. It's a joyous feeling for me; I'm at peace with my decision."

Jax scrunched his eyebrows. "This is over my head. I must be daft."

"You're not daft. I haven't delivered the punch line yet, Jax. You're so impatient! Let the suspense build for a minute."

"Okay ..." He drummed his fingers on the table.

She bent down so she was eye to eye with him. "I've decided ... to be the surrogate for your baby!" She bit her lower lip with her upper teeth, raised her eyebrows, and waited.

Jax pressed both hands over his mouth and gently closed his eyes; he was speechless. He stood and pulled Olivia out of her chair so that she was standing, wrapping his arms around her while facing her, nose to nose, staring into her eyes, hugging her with a deep embrace. The strength of his arms and his masculine smell of clean sheets and musk were comforting to her.

He took a step back to look at her, gazing directly at her face as he drank in her large brown eyes, so comforting and warm, her full lips, her high cheekbones, but mostly the radiating beauty of her inner glow. "I've never met a soul like you, Olivia Buffet. Your act of love is the greatest gift of my life. There will never be words to express what I feel."

She grabbed his hand and held it in hers. "There are no words that are powerful enough to describe love. We're all waiting for love, but we don't have to, it's always there. It comes in all sorts of packages. And I have one suggestion for everyone in the world that can make a huge difference."

"And that would be ... ?"

"Simple. Set the default setting of your heart to love."

"I'm making a mental note—I like that!"

"You know, I'm beyond happy for you two. For what it represents to me, your wedding is a glorious thing to celebrate. To give you such a phenomenal gift of a child fills me with a deep love I haven't experienced before. It makes me feel so pure, so full."

"I know that. Thank you for being my friend. For being there for me. I love you, Livie."

"Love you too."

"What do you think opened your heart like this?"

"All the things that have happened. I feel these experiences have increased my vibrational level. In spite of Curtis dying, which I believe was a part of our soul plan, I feel a love for him, and a thankfulness to him for teaching me things I needed to learn. I'm sure that would sound so strange to someone else, but it's *my* reality. And this whole thing with Margo, Sammi, and Tyson ... well, it was just validation for the things I've thought were universal truths. I feel a bond with Sammi and Tyson that I can't describe. There just aren't words for something so powerful, so profound. It *is* life-changing. My heart is exploding with love."

"It's funny—I didn't go through what you did, but I feel something similar. I'm lighter and more expansive, and I understand that feeling of genuine love, not just romantic love. Thanks to you, my friend."

"Sit. Let's eat." Olivia served him an omelet. "Do you need any more help for the big day? Is everything set and ready to go?"

Jax took a bite of his eggs. "Even this omelet tastes extra special to me today. Thanks for that. I think the wedding organizer has everything under control. We just needed to finalize some steps to the song we're going to dance to. Let me pull it up on YouTube so you can take a listen: 'Dance Me To The End of Love.'"

They sipped their coffee while Olivia listened, head swaying to the music, with soft tears forming in her eyes. "That's so beautiful. The music moves me deeply. Great choice."

"Yeah, we both like it."

Olivia looked him up and down. "This is the last time I'm seeing you as a single man. I'm not sure why I feel so emotional about this. Not sure I can stand up for you without blubbering my eyes out."

He patted her hand. "I was thinking, Livie. You and me ... we've lived lives together before."

Olivia responded by unconsciously slapping her hand over her heart. "What makes you think that?"

He shrugged. "Just something I know. I feel it."

Olivia pressed her index fingers to her tear ducts, fighting back the flood that wanted to break through the dam.

As they finished their coffee and omelets, Jax continued. "Thanks for taking the time to make all of these masks. I guess this is it. I'll see you for the big day tomorrow." He stood to leave, plucking his jacket from the back of his chair and grabbing the box of masks.

"You're welcome. It was my pleasure to make them. I'll see you tomorrow, my friend."

They gave each other a prolonged hug.

Olivia felt her soul smiling.

There were simply no words.

Chapter 40

October 29

It was a glorious day for a wedding. The descending sun appeared as if it were a spotlight on a huge marquee announcing an extraordinarily unique day. As she drove to the wedding venue, Olivia realized how stunning the Temecula wine country was—the perfect location for a grand celebration. She arrived way earlier than she'd expected, parked, and stood in front of the house in awe, thinking that the photos Jax had showed her didn't do justice to what it looked like in real life.

She toured the house on her own as everyone was still busy setting up. The house was sitting on a six-acre landscaped garden. The dining room could easily seat forty people, and there was even a home theater, game room, bowling alley, indoor aquarium, one-hundred-and-fifty-square-foot art gallery, indoor spa, waterfall and pool. In the back area, there was a long trellis graced with winding young grapevines. Of course. It was wine country! The large luxury gourmet kitchen was impressive, and Olivia was surprised to find there were enough bedrooms to host fourteen guests. The courtyard, where the ceremony and reception were to be held, was already decorated with cascading florals and unusual masks hanging from the beams of the ceiling.

Olivia and Jax had spent hours crafting papier-mâché masks, painting them, and decorating them with feathers, beads, and costume jewelry. One mask had been carefully placed—along with a flower arrangement—as a centerpiece at each table. The look was spectacular; their dream wedding was the epitome of whimsy and enchantment.

Olivia pressed her hand over her mouth and allowed her eyes to water when Jonathan and Aria arrived with Sammi and Tyson.

Sammi ran to hug her. "Olivia, do you notice anything different about me?"

"Hmm, you're carrying a garment bag?"

"That's my costume. I'm going to be a fairy."

"Of course you are."

"But something else ..."

"Your lovely long hair is wavy and curly?"

"No ..."

"I'm not sure. Wait!" She scanned Sammi, looking up and down, when her eyes lit up. *She's not wearing her pink boots!* "Where are your pink boots?" Olivia glanced over at Aria and saw her nod with twinkling eyes.

Sammi smiled confidently. "My mama and I think I've outgrown them now. Do you like these?" She stuck her right leg out, pointing her toes.

Olivia looked down at Sammi's feet, noticing a pair of glittery Mary Janes. *How fascinating that once Sammi made the connection between the pink boots and her past life, she could let them go!*

She nodded with a knowing grin. "I do. I'll miss your special pink boots, but sometimes we have to let things go."

"Where's your costume?" Sammi asked as she twirled around in a circle with her garment bag. "I'm going to go put my fairy costume on now. This is so much fun."

"I'll be putting on my costume too. See you soon."

Olivia spoke to Aria and Jonathan for a few minutes, expressing how grateful she was to them for helping Jax and Hunter out. With their expertise in films, they'd given special advice on how to stage the room for the event and had come early to see that everything was in place. Olivia found the ambiance breathtaking and enchanting. Every detail was perfect with glamorous décor that included candles, blue, black and silver balloons on the floor and ceiling, and the soft lighting of fairy lights, strategically placed.

Jax and Hunter had hired some actors from their Renaissance Faire group to roam the room and make merry with the guests. Olivia was sure the court jester, a colorful character, would be a favorite with the children. Or would it be the mysterious storyteller or energetic juggler? She was anxious to see all the guests masked, sequined, glittered, draped, jeweled, bedazzled, and feathered.

But where were Jax and Hunter? She glanced around but didn't see either of them. Probably in some sequestered spot, getting ready. As she self-toured the upstairs area of the magnificent house, she found a dressing area where she could transform herself—Olivia Buffet, the mysterious moongoddess.

Thirty minutes later, she emerged from the dressing area wearing a long, full blue tulle skirt with a black sash and a bow on the waist with a leotard top. An antique moon necklace made of rhinestones on a crescent moon graced her décolleté. The crescent moon mask had turned out perfect—just as she'd hoped. She scanned the main room looking for Jax, figuring she'd find him busy directing the setup. She still didn't see him, so she searched the back bedrooms of the house, where she found him putting the final touches on his outfit.

She stared at him before he noticed her. *Oh, he is beyond handsome.* She felt a happiness and joy flow through her, making her tear up again. *Stop it. I don't want to mess my makeup.* He stood in front of a large floor-to-ceiling mirror, adjusting his costume. He wore a bright red velvet doublet with black and white vertical stripes and matching puffed sleeves and breeches. His cape was a one-shouldered style, bright red with gold satin lining. Beneath his breeches, he wore black leather pants. The black hat with gold cord and knee-high boots, along with the Pantalone mask he'd worked so hard to make, were the perfect finishing touches.

Jax noticed Olivia standing in the doorway and rushed to hug her. "I feel like I'm trying to bite my own teeth whenever I try to dress myself in these costumes. I need a valet to dress me. Doing it by myself seems an impossible task."

Olivia reached out to help him fasten the cape. "I'm here to help you."

"So, Miss Moongoddess, you are absolutely celestial and splendid. Gloriously stunning. How's my right-hand woman doing today?" He kissed her cheek.

"Why, thank you, kind sir. As do you. A fine day for a wedding, it is. That costume is positively royal. As for me? I'm in a state of grace and peace. This day is going to be so perfect. I've never seen you look so studly before."

Jax adjusted his cape and gave her an impish grin. "Thank you."

"Are you nervous? Doing okay?"

"No, not nervous. I'm just into the celebration of it all."

"Are you ready? Can you follow me for a minute? I want you to meet a very special fairy. My former sister."

After telling Jax the details of the Margo meeting, she knew Jax was most anxious to meet Sammi, soul extraordinaire. Jax followed Olivia as she headed toward the court jester, who was entertaining her. Olivia could hear Sammi's giggles and laughter as they approached.

Moongoddess Olivia curtsied to Sammi the Fairy. "Excuse me, Miss Fairy, I'd like you to meet my best friend. Best Friend, this is Sammi."

Jax, fully masked, bowed and tipped his hat. "How do you do, Miss Samantha? I'm so glad you could attend our celebration today. My mask doesn't scare you, does it?"

Sammi stared at him for a minute, then threw her arms around his waist.

"Bertrand, it's you!"

Jax looked confused.

"This is Jax, honey. Who's Bertrand?" Olivia said.

He squatted down and took off his mask. "Hi, sweetie, I'm Jax. What a charming fairy outfit you're wearing!"

"You're Jax *now*," she said emphatically. "You don't remember me?"

Jax looked confused. "I don't think I've met you before, but I've heard a lot about you."

"You're very handsome this time."

"Thank you."

"Ugh, don't tell him that," Olivia said, "it goes straight to his head. Do you think you know him from somewhere, Sammi?"

"I do."

"Do you want to tell us from where?"

"Not if he doesn't remember. As my daddy says, 'that's a story for another day.'"

They both laughed.

Jax shook his index finger at her. "So you're the one ..."

"The one?"

"Yes, I hear you're a mixture of a unicorn and Yoda in little girl human form."

Sammi grinned. "My body is young, but the rest of me is really old."

"I'm delighted to meet you, O ancient one ... come with me. I'm going to give you, and only you, a sneak peek at the magnificent cake." They left together, walking hand in hand.

Guests continued to arrive, costumed and masked, excited to be attending the unusual event. Once everyone settled in, the ceremony began. Olivia stood up for Jax and Hunter's brother, Roland, stood up for him. Hunter, tall and slender, wore a long-sleeved black shirt with lace cuffs under a black leather doublet. His one-shoulder cape, with gold trim, breeches, black tights and black knee-high boots, completed the look. On his face, he wore the Pantalone mask lovingly handcrafted by Jax.

Hunter's pastor, also masked and costumed, welcomed the guests and began his speech. As a surprise for Hunter, Jax's sister played the piano while his Josh Groban–lookalike brother sang a powerful rendition of "You Raise Me Up," one of Hunter's favorite songs. There wasn't a dry eye in the house.

The vows were a part of the unmasking ceremony. Jax stood facing Hunter, removed his mask, handing it to Olivia, and began to speak.

"Hunter, I remove this mask now to reveal to you my true self with the promise that I will attempt never to wear a mask of false pretenses to you. When you love, you're not afraid to take off your mask and show who you really are.

"I, Jax Radcliffe, take you as my spouse in the name of love." He turned to Olivia and reached for and grasped her hand. "I have learned so much from my dear friend about authentic love ...

"Love is much grander in scope than romance. Love is more than that thing that makes us swoon and weak in the knees and makes us feel vibrant and buoyant, swept up in a churning passionate sea. It's an intangible energy that withstands the pressures of life and the test of time. It's easier for me to describe what love isn't than what it is. How can anyone describe an energy so vast and powerful? I do know that love is the releasing of the ego. Yes, imagine me releasing my ego ..." The audience laughed.

"Authentic love is walking in that moment and feeling love without the expectation of receiving back—it's not attached to outcomes. It's compassionate and self-giving. It isn't exclusive and limited; love is expansive, contributive and unadulterated. It uplifts and elevates all that it touches. It awakens, penetrates, transforms and heals. It's truly magical. It always forgives. You can't dilute it; you can't erase it. I've learned that love is a state of acceptance—a spiritual vibration that always first begins with self-love. It doesn't seek gratification; it doesn't expect tit for tat; it doesn't expect compensation. It's egoless. Without strings. Learning to love with wholeness is a life lesson for many of us. My task in this union is to keep the open heart I feel today. Life's struggles will challenge it, but I'm up for the challenge with you by my side. Love is not just the final destination, it's the whole journey.

"I give myself to you, Hunter, without prior attachments. I give myself to you in the name of love. You can vow to love another person for a lifetime, to the end of love, but for me, I know that there's no end to love. I've learned that it's an energy that cannot be destroyed."

As they continued on with their vows, Olivia savored the moment; it was a delicious moment in time for Olivia to watch and listen to her friend. He was demonstrating a brilliant awakening—one that moved her deeply and profoundly.

Their vows evoked laughter and tears from their family and friends. After Hunter removed his mask and said his vows, it was time to dance. The strings began and Jax and Hunter waltzed to "Dance Me To The End of Love." Everyone joined in on the dance floor. A group of friends made merry to the Renaissance dance, Pavane, that they'd practiced for weeks. The hint of mystery and mystic filled the room—who was behind all the masks?

Olivia couldn't believe the bounty of food—fulfilling for both the eyes and the stomach. Wine flowed. The buffet table groaned under the feast of roasted beef, the favorite—large turkey legs—platters of pâtés and cheeses, roasted potatoes and vegetables. There were whole fish, handheld meat pies, artisan breads, and platters of fruits.

A sensation of joy and an incredible feeling of lightness overpowered Olivia. It was such a release no longer to feel she had to isolate herself and protect her identity. Her recent life experiences had opened up a place of freedom for her. She glanced over at the table where her new friends sat: Aria, Jonathan, Tyson, and Sammi, Margo, Thomas, and all the Hobbses. She realized she'd never felt so full, so happy.

After Jax and Hunter cut the magnificent cake, personally made by Sophie, Olivia joined them at their table as they enjoyed the dessert. She watched as Margo's eyes rested on Sammi.

"Sammi, you make a beautiful fairy," Margo said.

"Thank you, Margo," she responded. "I love your dress and fancy hair, and I like your mask, Thomas."

Olivia couldn't help but notice how changed Sammi seemed: unfettered and unencumbered.

"Thank you, my dear. And you're the perfect fairy, although I thought for sure you would be an angel," Thomas said.

As everyone stuffed themselves with cake, Margo stood and rapped on her champagne glass with a spoon to gain everyone's attention.

"Hello, everyone," Margo said. "I'd like to say a few words. Isn't this the most beautiful and touching wedding you've ever been to? I know I'm overwhelmed with emotion."

With mouths full of cake, they nodded in agreement. Olivia couldn't help but also notice how serene and at peace Margo seemed. She felt so happy for her—even more than Margo, she was happy for Sammi—Sammi's soul was at peace.

"We have an announcement to make," Margo said. Thomas stood next to her with his arm around her waist. "I guess all this love is catching, because Thomas and I got married! When we leave today, we're headed off to the airport on our way to Paris for our honeymoon—a lifelong dream of mine."

Everyone at the table clapped. In unison, the group responded. "Congratulations!"

"That's so special. I'm feeling a really happy heart," Sammi said to Margo.

"Thank you, dear Sammi. I'll send you a postcard and bring you back a special heart object from France."

"That would be great."

Margo returned to her seat and turned to Sammi. "Are you having fun?"

"Of course. Are you?"

"Of course!"

"What do you think about everything that's happened to us, Sammi? What do you feel?" Margo asked.

"I feel happy, but mostly I hope you do too. It's what I said to you before—isn't it, Margo?"

"What's that, my dear?"

Olivia marveled as she observed how Sammi shifted her consciousness from one dimension to the next. *She does it so seamlessly!* She watched as her little soul friend lifted her fluffy meringue dress above her knees and climbed up on one of the chairs to stand on it as though she were an angel on a cloud, with her sparkle shoes twinkling in the candlelight. As though they were wings, she raised her arms slowly from her sides until her hands touched over her head and slowly she drew them down to her sides in an arc.

"What I think is, love lets us sing the song that's inside our heart. It's always about the love."

What a succinct summary of life, Olivia thought.

It's always about the love.

Chapter 41

NONPHYSICAL WORLD

Pneuma: Neshamah, I'm sorry to see that you're moving on now. You did well, thank you for your help. I hope you enjoy your next venture and that you gained some insight from working with me. I'll miss working with you. I hope you received a beneficial lesson about love.

Neshamah: I learned so much. The important thing is when situations come from a place of love, life is so much easier. It's how it's supposed to be. The soul's connection to the source is so much stronger than the human ego. No matter what the experience brings, the soul is always hoping for one thing—that the individual chooses love above all else.

That's the soul's hope.

About The Author

Beverly Knauer lives in sunny San Diego, California. She's the retired Chief of Rehabilitation Services for the County of San Diego. She received her bachelor's degree from the University of Wisconsin–Madison and her master's degree from San Diego State University. When not writing, she enjoys wine tasting in the quaint city of Temecula, going barefoot whenever she can, spending too many hours on Pinterest, and indulging in chips, guacamole, and margaritas while catching up with friends. Her newest passion is crocheting dog sweaters for lonely, abandoned dogs at the animal shelter.

Because of her love of exploring esoteric wisdom, she chose to become a writer to communicate transformative life experiences in the form of visionary fiction, resulting in her first novel, *The Line Between*.

She can be contacted at:

Website: www.authorbeverlyknauer.com
Email: beverlyknauerauthor@gmail.com
Facebook: https://facebook.com/beverlyknauerauthor/
Twitter: https://twitter.com/authorbevknauer

Also by Beverly Knauer

The Line Between

Acknowledgements

To me, gratitude is the heart's way of saying thank you. For those people who have supported and helped me give birth to my novels, words cannot express how grateful I am.

Janet, thanks for your ongoing encouragement and belief in me. I'm eternally thankful for your support, input, insights, and lengthy discussions that have helped me hone my greater understanding of the meaning of life.

Carol, Amy, and Marjorie, a special recognition to you for your generous enthusiasm and belief in me as a writer.

To Betty and Jana, my gratitude for your tenacity in providing me with your sustained, uplifting encouragement and support.

To my friends, Larry and Bill, thanks for the role you've played in my life for many years where you've opened my heart and mind to embrace a fuller understanding of what love is.

Thanks to those of you who read this book and find something meaningful to take away from it—that's my hope and dream: that the messages within speak to you and help to unify the people of this universe, thereby raising our collective consciousness by utilizing compassion, tolerance, gratitude, and love as our tools to face the challenging situations that lie ahead.